Jill Kennedy & DCI Max Trentham
mystery # 1

Into the Shadows

INTO THE SHADOWS

Shirley Wells

CARROLL & GRAF PUBLISHERS
NEW YORK

Carroll & Graf Publishers
An imprint of Avalon Publishing Group, Inc.
245 W. 17th Street, 11th Floor
New York, NY 10011-5300
www.carrollandgraf.com

First published in the UK by Constable,
an imprint of Constable & Robinson Ltd 2007

First Carroll & Graf edition 2007

ISBN-13: 978-0-78671-963-1
ISBN-10: 0-7867-1963-X

Printed and bound in the EU

For Nick,
may our steps always rhyme . . .

and with grateful thanks to all those who have helped along the way

Chapter One

The stupid bitch thought she was God, all knowing and all seeing. Conceited cow.

He assumed she had driven to Burnley, as she had the last two Friday mornings. He'd followed her then, and he guessed he had at least a couple of hours before she returned.

Her bedroom was soft and frilly, all pastel blues and yellows, and a vase of flowers, huge yellow daisies, sat on the windowsill. He hated to see flowers in bedrooms. It reminded him of hospitals where dozens of sick bodies competed for air with garish blooms.

He peered around blue and yellow curtains and gazed at the brooding Pennines. It was easy to picture her standing here and admiring her view, so different to the one of office blocks and houses she'd had in Preston. She would admire it as it changed with the seasons – the hills lush and green in the summer months, wearing their snowy mantle in winter, or hazy in the mist of a November morning, as they were now.

A cat ambled into the room, saw him, spat at him and raced out again.

He liked cats; he'd had one once, a tabby kitten that he'd called Tiger. He'd been six years old at the time.

Very slowly and carefully, he inched open a drawer, the top drawer of a set of four in what pretended to be antique pine. Inside were scraps of material that made his breath catch. A silk bra in black – no, it was dark blue – caught his attention, then a tiny thong in the same soft silk.

He pulled off a glove, and allowed his fingers the luxury of running over the scanty silk.

Deciding to keep a souvenir, he shoved the thong into the pocket of his trousers, put on his glove again and slid the drawer back into place.

Her bed had been neatly made and he pulled back the quilt, inhaling deeply. Her scent was on the pillow.

Tonight, he'd smell her in the flesh, God willing. They would be at the same bonfire party, in the same house, talking to the same people, and although they probably wouldn't speak, he would make sure he got close enough to smell her.

It was tempting to leave the photograph on the pillow where, later, her pretty head would rest, but it was too soon for that. He would put it in an envelope and drop it through her letterbox.

After one last look at her bedroom, he left as quietly as he'd entered.

Chapter Two

Jill walked up the drive to Kelton Manor and wished with all her heart that she didn't have to be here. At the best of times, she wasn't a party person and today, despite the fact that Manor Girl had seen off the favourite and romped home at 22–1, wasn't the best of times.

There had been three brown envelopes on her doormat when she'd returned from Burnley that morning – a reminder that her TV licence was due, a reminder that the cats' inoculations were due and a photograph complete with newspaper clipping.

Nothing had been written on the photograph. Even the envelope, plain manila and self-seal, hadn't seen a printer or a pen. The piece cut from the newspaper was simply a large headline that read: *Serial killer arrested.*

She knew the photograph well. It had been taken a year ago when, flushed with success, she'd been snapped by the local press. Due in part to the profile she'd prepared, a serial killer who had been terrorizing the north-west for four years had finally been arrested. Oh yes, she'd been smiling for the cameras that day.

That was before Rodney Hill committed suicide. Before they realized they'd got the wrong man.

A rocket exploded into thousands of silver and gold stars that lit the overhead sky. Very pretty, but it did nothing to improve her mood. She hoped her three cats would be all right. They should be. There was unlikely to be much activity along her lane, and she'd locked the cat flap so they couldn't get out.

It was the dressing up she hated most about parties. Happier in jeans and jumpers, she resented occasions that required effort. She wasn't in the mood for being polite to complete strangers, either. Not tonight.

She pushed a heavy finger at the doorbell, a round brass affair set in the stonework, and pinned in place the brightest smile she could manage.

The door swung open and a babble of conversation and polite laughter drifted out.

'Jill!' Mary Lee-Smith, her hostess, air-kissed Jill's cheeks. 'Thank you so much for coming, my dear.'

'Thank you for inviting me.' The sound of talk and laughter from within cheered Jill slightly. It was a month since she'd moved into the Lancashire village of Kelton Bridge, and it was high time she met some of her new neighbours. This way, she'd meet a lot in one go. 'It's very kind of you,' she added.

From what she'd heard, Gordon Lee-Smith's family had lived at Kelton Manor, a gorgeous square building set in immaculate grounds that sat in the middle of Kelton Bridge, for generations. Although Mary's heart was in the right place, it was said she thought this gave them – well, her really, as Gordon worked in London during the week – the right to organize the other residents.

That, of course, was simply hearsay, something Olive Prendergast from the post office had told her. Olive, who struggled to find a kind word for anyone, was coming up to retirement and her heart was no longer in the job. Apparently, since losing her husband a couple of years ago, Olive's main purpose in life was to spread local gossip.

For all that, Jill could believe that Mary was a natural organizer, despite her small stature.

Jill's coat was taken from her and she was ushered through an impressive hallway into an even more impressive drawing room. It was already crowded.

'Let's get you a drink,' Mary said. 'Gordon!'

Her husband was across the room, out of earshot and

unable to see his wife's flapping arms, and then the doorbell rang again.

'Don't worry,' Jill said, 'I'll get myself one and hunt down someone I recognize.'

'Are you sure, dear?' Another fruitless gaze in Gordon's direction. 'I hate the thought of abandoning you.'

'I'm sure.' Jill was more than happy to be abandoned.

Ever since moving to Kelton Bridge, she'd been itching to see inside the manor, and would rather be nosy on her own. From the outside, it was an imposing building with a paddock and stable block to the side. Huge chestnut trees marked the property's boundary.

It reminded her of the large house she'd seen from her bedroom window as a child. Only a field had separated the council estate from Shelton House and Jill had spent hours watching the comings and goings. A girl, Penelope, the same age as Jill, had lived there. She'd attended a boarding school in Hereford but, during the holidays, Jill had watched her trotting off on her elegant silver pony. Jill had even fantasized about befriending the girl simply to have a ride on the magnificent animal. It came to nothing, of course. Their paths never crossed. The field separating the River View estate and Shelton House might have been a million miles.

The interior of Kelton Manor didn't disappoint. Everything was lavish – huge oil paintings, long and heavy velvet curtains, antique furniture and old wood that had been polished to within an inch of its life. With a glass of very acceptable white wine in her hand, Jill was on her way to inspect the Victorian conservatory when she bumped, almost literally, into Andy Collins. At least there was one person here she knew.

'Jill, I've been looking for you.' This time, her cheeks were kissed properly.

Tall, slim and blond, he wore rimless glasses, and his eyes were the palest blue, speckled with silver streaks.

'Hi, Andy, how's my favourite estate agent? Hey, I bet you'd like this place on your books.'

'Wouldn't I just,' he agreed, sounding wistful as he looked around. 'No hope of that, though. So how are you settling in?'

'Wonderfully well. I owe you.'

It was thanks to Andy that she had the cottage. Due in part to the little sod who'd burned her flat to the ground, she'd decided the time was right to head out of Preston and find a place in the country. She'd had several areas in mind. One day, she'd wandered into Andy's office and, from that moment on, he'd been tireless in his search for the perfect property for her. He'd certainly earned his commission.

While house hunting, Jill had begun to despair of estate agents in general. Despite giving them precise details of what she was looking for, they either sent brochures for properties that would only be feasible when she'd won the lottery, or they omitted to send anything until any possible properties were already under offer. Andy, however, had been a gem. He'd called her from his car phone after an appointment with Mrs Blackman to say Lilac Cottage was about to go on the market.

'I think it will be perfect for you,' he'd said. 'It's a bit on the small side, but there's plenty of room to extend. It needs a fair amount of work, hence the sensible asking price. It's well within your budget.'

She'd met him there that same day, fallen in love with the cottage, and immediately made Mrs Blackman an offer.

Andy had been right; it was perfect for her. On the edge of Kelton Bridge, midway between Burnley and Rochdale, and nestling in the shadow of the Pennines, she was less than an hour's drive north of Manchester. The location couldn't have been better.

All thanks to Andy.

He'd invited her to dinner twice, and twice Jill had declined. Perhaps she should have accepted, if only out of gratitude. Her excuses had involved pressure of work, but the truth was, she didn't want a relationship.

'Good grief, Jill,' Prue, her young and bossy sister had

scoffed. 'The bloke's offered to feed you. How can that translate as wanting his socks washed for the rest of his days?'

Prue was probably right, but all the same . . .

Jill slipped her arm through Andy's.

'Come and show me the conservatory. I walk past here most days, but the walls around the grounds are so high that I haven't been able to get a decent look at it. I've been tempted to bring a stepladder with me . . .'

'You're just plain nosy.'

'Merely interested in people,' she corrected him.

They wove their way around a small crowd and stepped through double doors into the conservatory.

'Oh, wow! It's massive. And no UPVC in sight. Are these real?' A finger on one of the tall, exotic ferns told her that they were indeed real. 'My entire cottage would fit in here,' she added.

'Not quite,' Andy replied with amusement, 'but it's a nice size.'

Jill spluttered with laughter. 'Oh, yes, I can picture your sales brochure – a nice-sized conservatory at the rear.' She nudged him and said in a whisper, 'The lights are a bit tacky though.'

Small white fairy lights had been hung from the ceiling for the party and a few of the ferns were adorned with lights.

'Behave yourself,' he grinned.

'Andy!' a voice boomed out.

They both turned, Jill hoping her disparaging whisper hadn't been heard, to see a couple who were strangers to her.

'Ah, Tony, Liz, lovely to see you,' Andy greeted them. 'Have you met Jill? No? Jill, this is Tony Hutchinson, headmaster of the local primary school, and his wife, the lovely Liz.'

Jill shook hands and went through the pleased-to-meet-you routine. Tony was in his mid-fifties, Jill supposed, a tall, handsome man with grey hair, and the lovely Liz looked a good ten years younger. She was also American.

'I've been over here for twenty years,' she explained, 'but I can't seem to shake off this accent.'

From the way she swayed on her feet, she'd also found the wine to be acceptable.

She was short and slim, one of those women with an inbuilt sense of style, and was wearing an exquisite pale mauve linen trouser suit. Jill guessed she only bought the best quality clothes. Her wardrobe would be full of cashmere and, unlike Jill, she wouldn't have spent a frantic hour searching for a pair of black trousers that were relatively cat-hair free.

'I'm surprised Kelton still has a school,' Jill said, 'when so many village schools are closing.'

'Fortunately, it's thriving,' Tony told her. 'Pupil numbers have increased each year for the last five years.'

'Thanks mainly to the two new estates,' Andy put in lightly, 'which, if I recall, Tony, you were against.'

'I wasn't against the estates, I was against the location,' he replied, chuckling. Turning to Jill, he said, 'How are you finding Kelton Bridge?'

'I love it. I've been very busy, work-wise, which is why I haven't met many people, so it's lovely to be here tonight.'

'The pleasure's all ours,' he murmured. 'Everyone's queuing up to meet our local celebrity.'

'Sorry?'

'Tony started a psychology course many years ago,' Liz explained. 'It was one of the Open University things. He's been fascinated ever since. Not fascinated enough to finish the course, you understand.'

Jill was startled by the animosity she sensed between husband and wife.

'But I'm not a celebrity,' she pointed out, confused.

'Your face was in our local paper for days on end,' Tony told her, 'when that serial killer was caught.'

The coincidence sent a shiver the length of Jill's spine.

No one had mentioned the case to her for months and now that photograph had been brought to mind twice on the same day.

'But as you'll be aware,' she said, knowing her voice sounded tight, 'it wasn't the killer.'

'I never know the difference between a psychologist and a psychiatrist,' Liz said, clearly trying to lighten the atmosphere.

'A psychologist deals with normal mental states,' Tony told her, 'and a psychiatrist deals with abnormal. A psychiatrist will have more medical training. Isn't that right, Jill?'

'Close enough,' she replied, eager for a change of subject.

'But the job, it must be fascinating,' Tony persisted.

'It's OK,' she told him with a tight little smile. 'Although not as glamorous as the TV dramas make out. As a forensic psychologist working with the police, I mainly advised on selection and training of officers, prepared behavioural information to support cases in court, and did a variety of counselling roles.' She shrugged. 'But that's in the past. I resigned as I wanted to concentrate on my writing.'

Liar, she scoffed.

'Yes, we heard you were writing. What sort of stuff are you doing?'

'At the moment, I'm writing a book to help sufferers of anxiety attacks,' she said.

From the expression on his face, she gathered Mr Hutchinson wasn't impressed.

'Panic attacks, you mean?' his wife put in. 'My sister has those. She's getting better, slowly, but it's a terrible thing. Her doctor has given her Valium and told her to do relaxation exercises.'

'I could have done that,' Tony scoffed. 'Don't you think,' he said, addressing Jill, 'that people could help themselves if only they put their minds to it? Is there any need for books?'

'I don't think we can help ourselves,' Jill argued. 'We can

often help other people, but we get so wrapped up in our own worries and anxieties that we often can't see the wood for the trees.'

'I suppose so,' he said, grudgingly. 'And do you enjoy it? Writing, I mean?'

'I love it.'

That was true. All Jill wanted was to forget Valentine, as the serial killer had quickly been dubbed, forget her work with the police, and concentrate on her life. She wanted to get the work done on her cottage so it was warm and comfortable, then sit back and enjoy life with her cats. A simple life appealed to her.

'It can't be as interesting as criminal profiling, though,' Tony persisted. 'But is there anything in it? I mean, really. Come on, Jill, you can be honest with us.'

'Of course there's something in it,' she replied, wondering what sort of moron he thought she was. 'We're all unique. We all have our different ways of doing things. Criminals leave tangible clues like fingerprints, footprints, saliva, blood and all the rest of it, but by the way they do things, they leave clues that are just as obvious.'

'What do you think of this conservatory?' Liz butted in. 'Isn't it grand? I am so jealous.'

Jill, grateful for the change of subject, warmed to her immediately.

'Me, too. It's gorgeous. I couldn't believe these ferns are real . . .'

Another man soon joined them. Jill didn't know him but she'd seen him about the village. She was ashamed that she hadn't made more effort to get to know these people.

'Hi, Bob,' Andy greeted him warmly.

'Bob's our local builder,' Liz explained and to prove that she really had had too much wine, she burst into song, 'Bob the Builder . . .'

The group laughed, as was expected, but Jill could see that Bob had tired of the joke long ago. Fortunately, he was too well mannered to say so.

The lovely Liz was struggling to keep her eyes off him. With good reason, Jill allowed. It was difficult to give him an age, probably late thirties or early forties. He was fit and strong-looking, with the sort of tanned skin that comes from working outside rather than spending a fortnight beneath a foreign sun. His hair was strawberry-blond, a young Robert Redford, and he had huge work-roughened hands. All in all, a very attractive man.

'So you haven't met our local celebrity either, Bob?' Tony remarked, and Jill groaned inwardly.

Bob looked blank.

'Jill, here, was in the papers when that serial killer was caught. Or, at least, the police thought they'd caught the serial killer.'

'I remember that, of course,' Bob said, frowning, 'but I don't recall the details.'

'Jill was the psychologist who worked out the profile for the police,' Tony explained.

'Ah, right.' Bob tried to look impressed and failed.

Jill had to smile. 'Don't worry, Bob, Tony's having you on. I'm no celebrity. I am in need of a good builder, though. Andy will vouch for that.'

'Oh?'

'I'm at Lilac Cottage,' she told him, 'Mrs Blackman's old place.'

'Ah.'

A man of few words was Bob.

'My roof needs checking over and making good as soon as possible,' she explained, 'and every door and window in the place needs replacing. In the future, I'm thinking of a loft conversion and a ground-floor extension.'

Bob wasn't surprised. Anyone who drove past could see the state of her roof and windows.

'Give me a ring then,' he said. 'I'm in the book.'

They chatted about other things – the way Kelton Bridge had woken to eight inches of snow on New Year's Day last year, how Tony, a keep fit fanatic, was determined to walk the Pennine Way next year . . .

'Jill, there you are.' Mary Lee-Smith appeared at Jill's elbow. 'You must come and meet our vicar and his wife. They say they haven't met you yet.' She sounded appalled at the latter.

'Not yet,' Jill admitted as she was whisked away.

Reverend Trueman was a tall, imposing man. He looked quite stern and, for a moment, Jill remembered her late grandmother saying 'And what shall I say when the vicar asks where you've been? I can't lie to a vicar.' Jill, eight years old at the time, hadn't cared what her gran said. No way was she sitting in church for hours while her friends enjoyed themselves outside and that was that. She felt much the same about church twenty-six years later.

During the customary 'lovely to meet you' and 'how are you settling in?' conversation that followed, his wife, Alice, appeared warm, friendly and down-to-earth, so Jill gave Reverend Trueman the benefit of the doubt.

Alice was also stunningly attractive which was strange, Jill thought, given that (a) she wasn't exactly a spring chicken and (b) she seemed to have made no effort whatsoever. Her hair could have done with a good cut, she wore no make-up, and her simple grey dress would have suited a Quaker. Despite this, her finely boned face with those stunning cheekbones, her height, her slim figure and long, shapely legs gave her a style and elegance of her own so that she couldn't fail to turn heads.

'I take it you're not a churchgoer,' Jonathan Trueman remarked.

'I'm afraid not, no.'

'Why afraid?'

'Silly choice of words. Although I do feel I need to make excuses for myself.' Blame my gran, she added silently. 'But you're right, I'm not. I love the buildings, and I love the whole idea of it all, but I'm not a fan of religion. It causes too many problems and creates too many fanatics for my liking.'

'For a psychologist –'

'Jon,' his wife scolded, 'this isn't the time or the place

for one of your theology discussions.' Alice gave Jill an apologetic smile. 'Once he gets started, there's no stopping him.'

'Nonsense,' he argued, slipping a fond arm around his wife's slender waist. 'We'll save it for another time,' he promised with a wink for Jill.

'Here's Michael.' Alice waved to a young lad across the room. 'Our son,' she added for Jill's benefit. 'Michael, come and meet Jill Kennedy.'

He came over to them, all smiles. 'You haven't run out of petrol lately?'

'I haven't,' Jill told him, laughing. 'We've already met,' she explained to his parents. 'Michael helped me unlock my petrol cap at the filling station.'

'His Saturday job,' Jonathan put in. 'He's in his last year at school and then it'll be off to university.'

Clearly Reverend Trueman wanted the world to know about his clever son, not the friendly lad who sat in the kiosk at the filling station. An intellectual snob, Jill decided.

They were discussing the universities they'd each attended when Mary appeared at Jill's elbow.

'Sorry to intrude, but Ella Gardner's dying to meet you, Jill. Ella's our resident historian . . .'

Jill knew she'd never remember anyone's name by morning, but she set off to be introduced to the resident historian.

'Spend too long in a place like Kelton,' Ella warned, 'and you'll be the one needing a psychologist. I swear all the misfits are born with an inbuilt route planner to get them here.' She frowned. 'I haven't seen you at church. I wouldn't go myself as I'm a confirmed atheist, but it's easier to go than put up with Jon's lectures. Besides, he enjoys the challenge.'

'I managed to avoid his lecture,' Jill told her.

'Ah, yes, he lulls you into a false sense of security and then goes in for the kill,' Ella warned her.

'I gather you're our resident historian,' Jill remarked.

'Ha! I seem to have earned that dubious title since passing the age of sixty.' Ella grinned. 'Before that, I was just another dull civil servant. Hmm. Exciting to have a resident psychologist though. Are you married?'

Ella, Jill suspected, excelled at the frank question.

'Widowed.'

Jill was accustomed to the shock on Ella's face. She'd seen it on dozens of faces before. She could understand it, too. Widows were grey-haired old ladies who knitted scratchy jumpers for their grandchildren while looking back on a lifetime's memories. They weren't smiling thirty-four-year-olds.

'What about you, Ella? Are you married?'

'Me? For my sins, yes. Tom doesn't get out much. Blames his arthritis but, basically, he's a boring old fart. As he'd tell me though, it takes one to know one. I love him really, and given tonight's crowd, I can't say I blame him. God, what a dull lot. In the next breath, they'll all be complaining that the youngsters leave the village at the first opportunity. Can you blame them? There's more life in the graveyard.'

'I'm enjoying myself,' Jill said, amused by Ella's scathing comments.

'Ah, but as the new resident, you're obliged to say kind things about us all.'

Mary soon put an end to their conversation.

'Come along, everyone,' she called, clapping her hands to round up her guests. 'Time for the fireworks.'

They trooped out into the garden to watch the display. It was, as might be expected, Jill supposed, spectacular. Mary wouldn't do anything by half measures. They oohed and aahed dutifully, although Jill had never been a fan of fireworks. She was pleased when they were ushered inside again, and she could warm her hands.

She was wondering if it was too early to make her excuses when Tony Hutchinson sought her out.

'I've been sent to apologize,' he said sheepishly. 'Liz thinks I was rude to you.'

'Not at all.' Jill was surprised.

'I really was fascinated by the case,' he explained, 'and I didn't stop to think how you must have felt when you realized it was the wrong man.'

'It goes with the territory,' she told him. 'You can't win 'em all.'

'Anyway,' he said, 'I'm sorry. Me and my big mouth, eh?'

'Don't worry about it.'

'So,' he said, 'are you really looking for a builder?'

'I certainly am, yes.'

'Then you won't go far wrong with Bob. He's fair and reliable, an excellent chap. Mind you, he has to be. Living in the village, we'd soon be up in arms if our houses started falling down.'

'Tony, there you are.' The lovely Liz appeared at his side, swaying even more noticeably now. 'I might have guessed.'

'I think it's time we got you home,' he said tightly and, again, Jill was struck by the animosity.

'Time I left too,' Jill said. 'Do you mind if I walk with you?'

She'd done enough socializing for one evening and her feet were objecting strongly to being forced into shoes that boasted a small heel. Besides, she didn't relish walking home in the dark with only exploding rockets for company.

'We'd be honoured,' Tony said, adding a scathing, 'When Liz falls over, it'll be easier to put her back on her feet if there are two of us.'

Chapter Three

'You bloody superior shit!' Liz's first job was to pour herself a large vodka. 'God almighty, you're pathetic. You have to bloody fawn, don't you?'

Her husband, the fine upstanding headmaster, said nothing. No surprise there. While he was more than happy to creep and grovel round everyone in the village, he knew his silent, superior air pissed her off. She was convinced he had perfected it deliberately. Every time they went out together, which wasn't often, he made a complete prat of himself, embarrassed her, and made a mockery of their marriage. Not that making a mockery of their marriage took much effort; everyone in the village must know how shaky that was by now.

'As soon as Mary said the new woman had been invited, I knew you'd be falling all over her.'

'I was merely being polite, Liz, and now I'm going to bed. Are you coming? Or are you going to keep your bottle company?'

'It's better bloody company than you are.'

'Suit yourself.'

He walked off, loosening his tie as he went. Sanctimonious pig.

Liz would have followed, if only to give vent to her anger, but she knew it was a waste of time. What would he do? Apologize for ignoring her all night, sweep her off her feet and make mad passionate love to her? Some hope of that.

She kicked off her shoes, stretched her toes, and threw herself down on the sofa.

There was a time when he'd swept her off her feet, figuratively speaking of course. She'd come over from the States to work in England, met Tony, been completely dazzled by him, and forgotten about returning to America. They'd been married less than four months after that initial meeting.

What had appealed to him? That she was American? That she was ten years his junior?

Sadly, twenty years later, she no longer looked ten years his junior. While he was terrified of growing old and took every precaution known to man, she was drinking herself into an early grave. Perhaps it was this fear of growing old that made him such an incorrigible flirt. Or perhaps he was simply bored with her.

She refilled her glass, then carried that and the bottle back to the sofa.

'The drink will numb the pain,' she promised herself. 'It always does.'

'Good party?' Tom asked.

Ella bent to kiss her husband's head, took off her coat, and made straight for the kitchen.

'Interesting. I'll bore you with the details as soon as I've made a brew. Do you want one?'

Silly question, Ella thought, smiling to herself. In the forty years they'd been married, had Tom ever refused a cuppa? She couldn't recall an occasion.

Her hands were cold and she warmed them on the kitchen radiator as she waited for the kettle to boil. Moving from a large three-storey house to a small bungalow had come as a bit of a shock but, three years on, Ella was glad they'd done it. The bungalow was easy to keep clean and, more importantly on nights like this, easy to keep warm.

When she carried the tea through, she was pleased to see he'd switched off the television and folded his newspaper.

He might not be interested in local gossip, but he was a good listener. A good husband.

'Was I missed?' he asked.

'Of course not. I excused your absence by telling people you're a boring old fart. Actually, I did,' she recalled, laughing. 'I met Jill Kennedy, the new woman at Lilac Cottage. I liked her immediately. She's one of those people you instantly warm to, you know? Anyway, I told her you were too boring to meet people. I don't think she believed me, though.'

'I think I've seen her about,' Tom said. 'Slim? Short blonde hair? Drives a blue Seat Leon?'

'That sounds like her, although I've no idea what car she drives. Andy Collins has his eye on her, I know that. He was quite peeved when Mary insisted on dragging her off to meet people. I was one of those she had to meet. I'm the resident historian. It's official.'

Tom laughed at that.

'Tony and Liz were looking daggers at each other all evening,' she confided, clucking her teeth. 'Liz had had too much to drink, as usual, and Tony was busy flirting with Jill Kennedy, Alice Trueman . . .' She paused, then laughed. 'I think I'm the only woman he didn't flirt with.'

'He knows the competition's too stiff.'

Ella reached out and gave his hand a squeeze. 'Perhaps he does at that.'

Tears welled up in her eyes and she had to blink them back. What was she going to do without her Tom?

When she'd stood in the church all those years ago and vowed to love him till death parted them, she hadn't realized that death would come long before she was ready to face it. Tom was only sixty-seven. He'd been by her side, putting up with her funny ways for forty years. She couldn't imagine, didn't want to imagine the day when he wasn't there. Yet that day was rapidly approaching.

Today was one of his good days, one of those days when she could pretend the word cancer didn't exist. Tomorrow could be a different story altogether.

'Six months,' the doctor had said. 'Maybe more . . .'

It was no use getting maudlin. That helped no one.

'Jill Kennedy's a widow,' she went on, forcing her mind to other matters. 'I had such a shock when she told me. It doesn't seem right, someone so young. I don't know what happened. I was still getting over the shock when we started talking about something else. Bob Murphy was there, and you know how all the young ladies lust after that finely toned body of his. Liz's eyes were out on stalks, but Jill barely spared him a second glance. Still mourning her husband, I suppose. Lord, Bob's a handsome chap, though. If I were forty years younger –'

'If you were forty years younger, my love, you wouldn't be allowed to go gallivanting on your own.'

Alice was exhausted when she climbed into bed. It had been a long evening; she'd found it difficult to pretend that everything was as it should be. She'd imagined people must know her secret.

It couldn't go on, the strain would kill her.

Jonathan came out of the bathroom and climbed into bed beside her.

'I'll invite Jill Kennedy to lunch one day,' she said, 'so long as you promise not to talk religion.'

'Alice,' he scolded, smiling indulgently, 'how am I supposed to do my job when I'm not allowed to talk religion?'

'By example,' she retorted, dragging a smile from God only knew where. She rolled over, feigning a yawn. 'I don't know about you, but I'm shattered.'

'It's been a tiring day,' he agreed.

Every day was tiring. It was so hard to live a lie. In the last seven days, there had been twenty minutes of joy in her life. Life was so empty that she was reduced to counting the minutes. Was it so terribly wrong to want more? She had Michael, of course, and she should be grateful for that. Next September, though, Michael would be away at university and then her days would seem endless. Pointless and endless.

'It was a good party, though,' Jonathan was saying.

'Yes, Mary always throws good parties. I sometimes feel sorry for Gordon. After working in London all week, you'd think he would want the house to himself.'

'Perhaps he does. Mary rules at the manor, though, and she can't seem to go a month without having a party for something or other. Tonight's fireworks must have cost a small fortune, too.'

'Hateful things,' Alice said.

Jonathan switched out the light. 'I enjoy Mary's sense of fun, though, don't you?'

'I do,' Alice murmured.

People did have fun – unless they lived at the vicarage. Life should be lived to the full, and that's what most people did. They grabbed it with both hands.

How long was it since she'd done something impulsive, something purely for the fun of it? A long, long time ago. It was a time she tried not to remember.

In the morning, she promised herself, she would sort out her life. On that optimistic but frightening thought, she drifted into a restless sleep.

Chapter Four

Jill held the phone away from her ear as her mother coughed and spluttered on the other end of the line.

'Still not given up the fags then, Mum?' she said when normality returned.

'I need some pleasure. And if your dad can throw his money at the bookie, I can spend mine on fags. In any case – God, I meant to tell you. You know the Kelly family? Moved into number 14?'

'No.' Her mother forgot that Jill hadn't lived on the estate for sixteen years.

'Moved in last year. A mother – as rough as a badger, she is – one son and a daughter. Well, the lad's been arrested for stealing a car and dangerous driving. I always knew they were a bad lot. Like the Westons. He's been done for aggravated burglary. Did I tell you? They should lock 'em up and throw away the bloody key. And then – you what?'

Jill rolled her eyes at the conversation, bickering more like, that was taking place at number 27, River View.

'Your dad wants a word,' her mum said, coming back on the line.

'OK, Mum, I'll speak to you soon. And I'll try and make it for your birthday.'

'That would be smashing, love. If you're not too busy, of course.'

The guilt was like a kick in the stomach. Jill really would have to visit. It wouldn't hurt her.

'And how's my favourite brainbox?' her dad bellowed down the phone.

'In Lancashire, not on Mars,' she replied fondly. 'There's no need to shout, Dad. And I'm good, thanks. How are you? Hey, I won a few quid on Manor Girl on Friday.'

'What on earth made you back that old thing?'

'Just a hunch. And that old thing, as you call it, came in at 22–1.'

'Huh. Give me a bell if you get any more hunches. I haven't had a decent win in ages. Not that I'd have backed Manor Girl –'

Again, Jill had to hold the phone away from her ear as her dad broke off to have a slanging match with her mother. Even with the phone six inches away, she caught the gist of it. Her dad, a man who fished as a means of escaping the house more than anything else, had committed the ultimate crime. He'd left his maggots in the fridge – again.

'They're in a bloody box, woman,' he was shouting. 'How the 'ell can they do any harm?'

Jill wondered, not for the first time, how she and her sister had survived life at number 27. Fights between their parents were a regular occurrence and the bickering was constant. To an outsider, it must look like hell on earth. The most amazing thing, however, was that they were devoted to each other. If her dad won on the horses, he'd walk through the door hidden behind an extravagant bouquet of flowers and his wife would melt in his arms. There would be kisses and cuddles for, oh, at least five minutes. Then the bickering would start all over again.

'Your mum's in an evil temper today,' he chuckled, coming back on the line. 'I'd better go and sort her out.'

Mum, Jill knew, would take some sorting out. She was a strong woman. Strong, opinionated, pushy – and Jill thanked her lucky stars that she was. If it hadn't been for her mum, pushing her to do schoolwork and get into university, Jill might be raising half a dozen kids at River View.

'OK, Dad. You take care and I'll be down to visit soon.'

She replaced the receiver and immediately picked up her diary. Perhaps this Saturday would be a good time to visit . . .

'It's open!' The shrill ring of her doorbell had her sliding her feet into her shoes but she didn't get a chance to grab the cash she'd put ready.

'Then it bloody well shouldn't be! Jesus Christ, Jill!' Max slammed the door shut and strode into the sitting room. 'Why in hell's name can't you use the bloody lock? God, if you saw a tenth of what I see –'

'I've ordered a takeaway and thought you were the delivery man.' Jill's heart raced uncomfortably at the shock of having Max filling her air space.

'That's a bloody good epitaph for half the people who end up with a tag round their big toe.' He shook his head in the cynical way he had. 'I suppose you reckon nothing happens in sleepy old Kelton Bridge?'

Jill took a deep breath and silently counted to ten. Doing this to keep calm was an art she'd mastered while she and Max had lived together.

'What brings you here, Max?'

'Detective Chief Inspector to you,' he said, and the slightly self-conscious smile touched her.

That was the problem with Max. She loved him, she hated him, she despaired of him, but she couldn't be unmoved by him.

'I heard.' She'd seen his photo in the local paper with a small write-up of his promotion. It had been cut out and put in her 'special box'. 'Congratulations.'

'Thanks.'

'So how's it going?' Badly if the smell of whisky on his breath was anything to go by. Nothing to do with her, she reminded herself. If he wanted to lose his job, fine.

'Ups and downs. Downs at the moment.' He took off his jacket, black suede, and threw it over the back of a chair. 'I need a slash.'

As he raced up the stairs, Jill picked up his jacket and

hung it on the peg in the hall. Then, remembering her days of tidying up after him were long gone, she took it off the peg and threw it back on the chair. He wouldn't be staying long enough for it to bother her.

She could hear him moving around upstairs. What the devil was he doing up there? She was about to go and find out when she heard him coming back.

'It's Day of the Bloody Triffids up there,' he said, shaking his head with amusement.

'I like plants in my bathroom.' *Her* bathroom. 'So what are you doing here, Max?'

'This afternoon –'

The ringing of her doorbell interrupted him.

'It's open,' Jill called out, smiling sweetly at Max.

He was never more than six inches from her right shoulder while she thanked the man and paid him, opened the cartons, took out a plate and cutlery.

'That smells good. I don't really have time, but I haven't eaten all day.'

Suppressing a sigh, she took another plate from the cupboard.

Samuel, too, had appeared from nowhere. All human food was high on that cat's list, but chicken was his favourite. Chefs at Indian and Chinese restaurants could do with it as they pleased; it was still Sam's favourite.

She had hoped Max wouldn't be staying long, but there was too much food for one, although probably not enough for two, not when one of the two was Max. But his need would be greater than hers; he seldom remembered to eat without being prompted.

He forgot to eat because he never found time, and he drank because – well, Jill reckoned life in general stressed him to hell and he reckoned he simply enjoyed a drink. They'd agreed to differ on that long ago. Not her problem, she reminded herself. They'd parted almost a year ago now. So long as they could be civilized on the rare occasions they saw each other, that was fine. It wasn't easy, but it was OK.

'Is there any wine in this place?' Max began searching, first the fridge, then the cupboards.

'There's a bottle of red in the cupboard above the microwave.'

He found the bottle and soon had it open. It was only the second time Max had visited her here, yet he managed to make himself comfortable as if he'd known no other home. The knowledge irritated.

Having eased her conscience by phoning her parents, Jill had planned to curl up in the sitting room with her food. Deciding the kitchen was less intimate, however, she put their food on the table and sat down. Max sat opposite. At least with two of them eating, it would be easier to keep Sam off the table.

It was ironic, she thought, but she and Max had probably sat down to eat together more times in the last year than they had during the time they'd been together.

She wondered if there was anyone else in his life. She never asked, of course, but she would dearly love to know. Half of her was jealous at the idea, but the other half, the sensible half, knew the poor woman was welcome to him.

'So?' she prompted, spearing a hot chunk of pineapple. 'You were about to tell me why you're here.'

'This afternoon,' he said, 'a woman was killed in Kelton Bridge.'

'Killed?' She thought he was referring to an accident, but Max wouldn't be involved in that. 'You mean murdered? Here? In Kelton?'

'In sleepy old Kelton Bridge, yes.' His smile was mocking. 'Must have been expecting a takeaway.'

She ignored his sarcasm. 'Who?'

'Alice Trueman. The vicar's wife.'

'No! Alice Trueman? But I only saw her on Friday night. I was talking to her.' It simply wasn't possible. Yet she knew it had to be true. 'Are you sure she was murdered? It couldn't have been an accident?'

'Difficult to accidentally slit your throat from ear to ear.'

'Good God. Who on earth would want her dead?'
'That's what I'd like to know. How well did you know her?'
'I don't really know her. I met her at a party on Friday night.'
'What was she like?'
Was.
Jill pushed her plate aside, her appetite gone, and leaned back in her chair.
'Very attractive,' she said, causing an impatient raising of dark eyebrows. 'Sorry. Um – down-to-earth, homely type, proud of her son, embarrassed by her husband. The vicar – what's his name? – oh, yes, Jonathan Trueman is a bit of snob. As soon as I said I'd already met Michael, the son, he had to make sure I knew that Michael was soon off to uni and that his job at the filling station was only a Saturday job. Alice wouldn't have liked that. She stopped him talking religion at me, too.'
And now she was dead.
'She was incredibly attractive, though,' she went on. 'No make-up, no expensive haircut, no showy clothes and yet she was stunning. An incredible figure, and long, shapely legs.'
Dead.
'What happened?'
'The vicar arrived home shortly after two o'clock this afternoon to find his son holding her. She was naked, his clothes were covered in blood, and he was holding the knife.'
'Michael?'
'Yes, we're questioning him at the moment.'
'You think Michael killed his mother? Never in a month of Sundays.' Something else occurred to her. 'How old is he?'
'Eighteen. He had his birthday six weeks ago.'
He'd looked younger, but Jill knew that was merely a sign of her own age. When you hit thirty, and she'd done that four years ago, everyone else started looking younger.

'I thought I'd have a chat with you,' he said, 'and see what you knew about the family.'

She wasn't convinced. With a murder inquiry only seven hours old, it would be action stations. There would be no time to waste. By now they would have spoken to dozens of people who knew Alice better than she had, people who had known her for years.

'You're wasting your time then, Max.'

'Hm. There's something else,' he said, and Jill wasn't surprised. 'I thought I ought to warn you that Meredith's planning to coax you back.'

'Ha! He'll be wasting his time, too.' Although she was grateful for the warning. 'I've given all that up, Max. I write. It's what I enjoy.'

'He's not asking you to give that up. He's simply asking –'

'No.'

'Why not, for God's sake?'

She stared back at him, heart pounding with a mixture of emotions, uppermost of which was anger. They were no closer to catching Valentine, the serial killer, and every two months or so, despite being off the case, Max tried to persuade her to return to her job. Now, it seemed, he had the backing of his boss. It was easier for them; having Rodney Hill's blood on their hands didn't seem to bother them as much.

She'd enjoyed her work, but offender profiling was still met with a huge degree of scepticism. It was often a last resort, something to try in desperation. It was over, though. She was happier writing. So long as the public was crying out for self-help books, she was guaranteed an income.

'Why not? How long have you got? Firstly, I'm no longer employed – I gave it up, my choice. Secondly, I don't know how Meredith has the cheek. What does he call my work? Psychology bollocks!'

Max was still eating, still looking infuriatingly calm.

'OK, so if you don't want to get involved with Valentine again, how about helping me with Michael Trueman?'

'No.'

'Just like that?'

'Just like that. I couldn't work with you, Max.'

'You used to enjoy spending time with me,' he pointed out mildly.

'You used to enjoy spending time with me,' she snapped back, 'until something better, something younger and more attractive, came along.'

'Oh, for –'

'Ah, I forgot. We brush the past under the carpet. You screw around, you come crawling back to me, you expect me to congratulate you on your pulling power, and then forget it ever happened.' She could feel her voice rising hysterically, but she felt hysterical. It hurt like hell. Even now.

'My head was fucked at the time,' he reminded her. 'What with pressure at work, you threatening to leave me every fortnight because of your stupid guilt trip –' He took a calming breath. 'We've done this to death and I refuse to go over the same old ground. It happened, I've apologized till I'm blue in the face, and I wish to God I'd never met the bloody woman. But that's it. Case closed.'

Forget it, he was saying. Your problem, Jill, you deal with it.

But she couldn't forget it. She still had moments of frightening fury at his betrayal. Just as she still had sudden painful visions of him and that woman together. Forget it, she instructed herself. He's not worth it. Be civil, be civilized, pretend it doesn't matter and get him the hell out of here.

A taut silence stretched between them.

When Max had come crawling back to her, his expression not hers, she'd been so angry that she'd hit him hard enough to draw blood. Then, as he'd held her close, told her it meant nothing, and asked her to marry him, she'd cried and cried. She'd clung to him, even agreeing to marry him.

They were together for nine weeks after that. Jill hadn't been able to stand it. Emotions had been too raw. Yet she'd never quite known if she was more angry or hurt . . .

'Everything we did together, we did well,' Max said at last, his voice level and calm once more. 'And I mean everything.'

Jill's head was filled with the scent of him, his masculine warmth as he made love to her –

'We worked well together, too, Jill. We care about the same things, and we think in the same way.'

She couldn't deny that. It was another reason she loved him – used to love him.

'Michael Trueman,' he went on, forcing her mind back to the reason for his visit. 'We're interviewing him now, but he's not talking. Ask him if he smokes, if he wants a drink – nothing. Zilch.'

'Shock probably,' Jill said.

'Will you come and see him? Talk to him?'

'Nope.'

'What harm will it do?'

Jill gave a short, mirthless laugh. 'Ask Rodney Hill.'

'Jill.' His voice was softer now, gentle. He could coax bees from honey if he put his mind to it. 'We arrested Hill because we thought he was guilty. The fact that he matched your profile was neither here nor there. You're not responsible.'

She'd heard all that before. It didn't help.

'Please, Jill. As a favour to me?'

'No. I'm sorry, but I can't.'

'I'm senior investigating officer on this one. I want it sorted, and fast.'

'No.'

'You can't keep living in the past, you know.'

The intensity of those blue eyes shocked her momentarily. It shouldn't have. Max had been using that piercing gaze to his own advantage for years. Now, though, she almost felt as if he could read her every thought.

She hoped not. In the midst of her thoughts, mostly bad, was that she still found Max very attractive. In anyone else, the drinking, the long working days, the lack of regular meals and the way he constantly drove himself would have taken their toll. Nothing had though. He wasn't handsome in the accepted sense of the word; his nose was a little crooked, he had a tiny scar beneath his right eye, and his mouth had a cynical twist to it. Dark hair, swept back from a face that could look arrogant and aloof one moment and as gentle as a playful puppy the next, was greying rapidly, she noticed.

'You're not prepared to spare a couple of hours?'

'No.' If it were only a couple of hours of her time, she might consider it. It wouldn't be, though. She would get involved, not through choice but through necessity. She always had.

His plate empty, Max looked at his watch, refilled his glass and topped up Jill's.

'OK.' He was thoughtful. 'So why do you reckon he's not saying anything?'

'I can't answer that, Max. Shock perhaps. Who knows? Has he asked for a lawyer?'

'He hasn't even bloody coughed.'

'What's his father said?'

'Precious little. About as much as anyone would say if they'd come home to find that their son had slit their wife's throat.'

Jill swallowed hard.

'He seems torn between weeping at the injustice of it all,' Max told her, 'and praying for all our souls. Other than that, he's just said over and over that he can't believe it. Jill, you know how things are. We need to get Michael talking – and quick.'

'And I'm sure you will.' She smiled. 'You find me an eighteen-year-old who can't talk the balls off a buffalo.'

Max returned the smile. 'I just have.'

'No.'

With a heavy sigh, Max drained his glass and got to his feet.

'Lock that bloody door,' he said as he kissed her cheek.

'I will.'

She almost had the door closed behind him when his phone rang and he stepped back inside to answer it.

'How come you horrors are still up?' he asked the caller, his voice warm and loving enough for tears to spring to Jill's eyes. She glanced across at the mantelpiece where a framed photograph showed Max's sons, Harry and Ben, smiling into the camera. God, she missed them.

'Yes, yes,' Max was saying, 'I'll get the tickets tomorrow. Promise. Now, go to sleep and I'll see you later . . . well, no, probably not tonight . . . er, no, probably not in the morning either . . . yes, OK . . . love you, too.'

He ended the call and looked at Jill, his expression saying more than words ever could.

'How are they?' she asked, her voice hoarse.

'Missing you.'

'Missing you more like,' she replied briskly, 'and missing their mum.'

'If that's what you want to believe.' He stared at her. 'One of these days, you've got to offload all this guilt, Jill. Yes, we fell in love while I was still married. It happens. And yes, Rodney Hill committed suicide. Sadly, that happens, too. It's a tough world, kiddo.'

She refused to discuss it. 'You smell like a distillery, Max. I trust you're not driving.'

'Jesus, you've got a nose like a bloodhound. I've had the smallest Scotch you've ever seen, just enough to make the glass damp, and a glass, two glasses, of that stuff you call wine. And as it happens, I'm not driving.'

Was he drinking less these days? She had to admit he looked relaxed and very much in control. He was good at his job, and it wasn't an easy role. As senior investigating officer, he needed to be the strategist and the tactician, responsible for every aspect of the inquiry. Also, because of the emotive nature of this crime, he would be working in the full glare of publicity.

'Jill, you can blame everything that went wrong between us on what you like – the fact I was drinking heavily, Rodney Hill committing suicide, me shagging that –' He broke off. 'There's only one thing that screwed us up, screwed both of us up, and that's Valentine.'

She shuddered at the mention of the animal's name.

'We'll get Valentine,' he went on.

'You were pulled off the case,' she reminded him, but he simply shrugged that off as a mere technicality.

'Dead or alive, and preferably the former, we'll get him,' he vowed. 'Off the case or not, with me it's personal.'

She knew that, had known it for a long time. Never mind that hundreds of officers from three police forces were after Valentine, to Max it was personal. Which was exactly why they'd pulled him off the case.

'Meanwhile,' he added, 'we have to put Alice Trueman's killer behind bars. It's budgets, resources, and all the rest of the crap. I don't have time to piss about with Michael Trueman and I need all the help I can get.'

He touched her chin in the lightest of gestures.

'Meredith will be giving you a call, Jill, and I'd think long and hard about it if I were you. You want Valentine off the streets as much as anyone. He's taken everything away from you – your work, your confidence, even the man you love.'

'Loved. Past tense,' she snapped back.

'If you say so.' Whistling tunelessly, he walked down her drive and headed back to the vicarage.

Chapter Five

Just after midnight, Jill padded downstairs and poured herself a large Scotch. She wasn't a great lover of whisky, but it sometimes helped her sleep. That was something else she'd learned from Max.

The wind had increased and it was rattling her bedroom window. She must get that fixed. Listening to it, and waiting for the loose roof tiles to crash to the ground was merely adding to her sense of unease.

It wasn't only the wind and wondering who might have wanted Alice Trueman dead that was keeping her awake. There was that photograph, too. She should have spoken to someone about it. Not Max necessarily, he'd be far too busy right now, but someone on the force. It was on the coffee table, wrapped in a plastic cover. There was probably no point in that as it was unlikely to have fingerprints on it. Nor was there any point in ignoring it and hoping it would go away.

Perhaps she should have mentioned it to Max.

What had he said? That she must stop living in the past? How was she supposed to do that when the past wouldn't let go?

He'd also said she must unload all her guilt and yes, she would admit to a fair amount of guilt. Who wouldn't?

There was her relationship with Max for a start. She could still remember meeting him for the first time, could remember his boss introducing them. There had been a stomach-clenching pull of attraction that had had her eyes darting to the third finger of his left hand to see if he wore a wedding ring. He did.

Yet, later that day, they'd gone out for a drink. Three days later, Max had been in her bed. It was convenient to blame Max for that. In reality though, it had just happened. They'd both been powerless to stop it. And that, she thought as she took a swallow of whisky, sounded like something from the romance paperbacks her sister devoured.

What she hadn't known, what Max hadn't told her, was that Linda was ill. To be fair, even Max hadn't known just how ill.

They'd been at Jill's flat, sharing a bottle of wine, their arms wrapped tightly around each other, when the phone call came telling Max that Linda had been admitted to hospital.

As far as Jill was concerned, that should have been the end of their relationship. Linda was his wife; she was the one who needed him. Max, however, could be very persuasive. He also lived by the premise that life was too short for hang-ups.

A little over a year after Linda's death, Jill moved in with him and the boys. It was the happiest time of her life. If she'd given birth to the boys herself, she couldn't have loved them more.

Max had been working on the Valentine case, and the long hours had taken their toll. Jill had been working on the same case, but she'd been able to work more sociable hours. Max had worked through the night many times and the strain soon began to tell on their relationship.

'We've got the bastard!' Max had come home late one night and danced her around the kitchen. 'We've got Valentine, Jill. It's all over, sweetheart.'

The relief was so great it was like finding a cure for cancer. Life was wonderful again. The sky was a deeper blue, the grass a lusher green. Birds sang again.

Four weeks after his arrest, however, Rodney Hill was

found hanging in his prison cell. Less than a month after that, Valentine struck again.

The cancer was back and the birds were silent. Max started drinking heavily: Jill was plagued by nightmares.

Valentine! Jill wished she'd never heard of him. Over the years, there had been seven murders. The attacks took place at intervals of anything from three months to a year apart, and the killer had struck in Blackburn, Manchester, Leeds, Blackpool, Preston, Nelson and Southport.

Each of the victims, all small-time prostitutes working the streets, had been strangled. When they were dead, the killer – with a skill that was frighteningly impressive – carefully removed a dozen heart-shaped pieces of skin from their breasts and abdomens. The hearts were uniform in size, about two inches at their widest point. They were neat, almost a work of art.

Hundreds of men fitting Jill's profile had been questioned, and then there was a breakthrough when traces of Hill's semen were found on a murdered prostitute. Nothing had been discovered on any of the other bodies, and they had assumed he was getting careless. Hill admitted to having been with the prostitute, but he strongly denied murdering her or any of the others.

For Rodney Hill, suicide was the only answer.

Jill had dreaded going to sleep, terrified by the nightmares in which she would be running for miles, all exits barred by Rodney Hill's body swinging wildly from a rope. She would wake in the middle of the night, drenched in sweat, her heart racing, to see Max sitting in the chair by the bedroom window, a bottle in one hand and a glass in the other.

Between them, for their own different reasons, they had been unable to handle it and their relationship had started to disintegrate.

One day in June, Max came home and told her he'd spent the previous night in a 'sordid little hotel' with someone else. For Jill, it had signalled the end.

There was no point, she decided as she refilled her glass, going over and over it. It happened. It was over.

Shortly after midnight, her phone rang. After the usual panic thought – one of her parents or her sister had been involved in an accident – she knew it was Max. A terrier with a bone had nothing on Max.

'Michael Trueman,' he greeted her, 'who was he with at the party?'

'Don't mention it, Max. I love being woken at this time of the morning.'

'Oh, hell. Sorry. I'd forgotten it was – hell, is it midnight?'

'It is.' She sighed. 'And as far as I know, he wasn't with anyone. Well, his parents, I suppose. I don't really know anything about him, I told you that. The first time I met him, I was struggling to get my fuel cap unlocked at the filling station. A couple of lads work inside on the tills and he came outside to see if he could help. I wasn't holding anyone up – there were only two of us getting, or trying to get, petrol – so I put that down to him being helpful. The sort of lad who'd instinctively help out. He'll give up his seat on a bus or train for women or the elderly. Anyway, he sprayed something on the lock – WD40?'

'Uh-uh.'

'The next time I saw him was a couple of weeks later, the same place. I handed him my credit card, thanked him for his help, told him I'd had no problems with the lock since, cursed the weather and left.'

She thought back to her third meeting with him, just three days ago.

'At the party, I was chatting to his parents. It was all the usual inane stuff people say at these things. Alice spotted him across the room and waved him over to meet me. When I said we'd already met, his father quickly – too quickly, I thought – pointed out that it was only a Saturday job.'

'Impressions?' Max asked.

'A normal eighteen-year-old – except I thought he looked closer to sixteen or seventeen. Polite. Friendly.

Helpful. Very well mannered. Relaxed. Happy. There weren't many young people at the party so he was stuck chatting to older people. I assume they were his parents' friends. Either way, it didn't seem to bother him.' She thought for a moment, but there was nothing else she could tell Max. Had she seen the future, she might have paid more attention, but she hadn't. 'Sorry, but there's nothing else.'

'How did he seem with his mother?'

'Relaxed. At ease. As if they had a close mother–son relationship. He seemed the same with his father, too.'

'He's not very relaxed at the moment.'

'Has he said anything yet?'

'Not a word. Right,' he went on briskly, 'put that bottle of Scotch away and get to bed. Take it from me, kiddo, the drugs don't work.'

Before she could even deny having a bottle of Scotch in the house, he'd cut the connection.

Why was Michael refusing to talk? Either he was guilty, and she'd already dismissed that, or suffering from shock, or protecting someone. So who could that someone be?

Chapter Six

Max didn't know what he expected to find at the vicarage. If he hadn't found anything yesterday, he was unlikely to find anything today. He knew something about this case didn't add up, but he doubted he'd find the answer in this large, gloomy house. Perhaps he was passing time until Michael Trueman talked.

He'd overheard Phil Meredith on the phone to Jill earlier.

'You know how things are, Jill,' Meredith had said in the coaxing way he had. He was a hard-bitten individual, without an ounce of sentimentality, yet Max wouldn't be surprised if she'd fallen for it. 'I've got all my available officers on this case and I still don't have enough. The last thing we need is a murder when we've still got Valentine on the loose.'

Max had no idea what her response to that was, but Meredith was quick to argue.

'Total bollocks. You're a forensic psychologist with qualifications up to your neck and a lot of experience behind you.'

Max couldn't decide if Meredith was a great believer in offender profiling, or if it was a case of clutching at straws. It was difficult to get a straight answer from him, although it was true they needed all the help they could get. The public was growing impatient and edgy, comparing Valentine to the Yorkshire Ripper – or, more accurately, comparing the force's lack of success with the well-documented mistakes in that case . . .

After a few words with a forensic chap, Max stood in the

hallway, gazing down at the bloodstains on the carpet, walls and even the ceiling. These forensic bods went into too much detail for his liking but, according to the preliminary report, Michael Trueman – or someone else – had grabbed Alice Trueman from behind and slit her throat. The trachea and carotid arteries had been severed and death would have been almost immediate.

It was a cold house. The heating was switched off now, but it had been working when he'd arrived yesterday and the old radiators hadn't had much effect on such large rooms. It certainly wasn't the sort of house where you ambled around naked on November afternoons. So why had Alice Trueman been in the hallway naked?

He walked upstairs to the bathroom, a big, white room, functional rather than tasteful or cosy, but tidy.

Max knew he was a slob, but this was too neat for comfort. In his own bathroom, shelves were covered in dust, shampoo drips were visible, toothpaste lingered on the wash basin, and white spots marked the wood beneath the toothbrush holder. Here, there was no dust, and no soap marks or toothpaste dregs.

So Alice Trueman had climbed out of the bath, presumably in so much of a hurry that she'd thrown her towel on the floor, then run downstairs to her killer.

What would make a vicar's wife run downstairs naked? Fear? Panic?

Or had Michael, or someone else, entered the bathroom, threatened her, and chased her down the stairs?

Alice Trueman had been a neat, organized person, that much was obvious. Also obvious was the fact that she didn't go in for creams, potions and lots of make-up. There wasn't even a mirror in the bathroom. A crucifix hung above a wooden cabinet, but there was no mirror. Surely everyone needed a mirror in the bathroom. How did Jonathan Trueman shave without a mirror?

Max had no answers, only questions, and he walked into the master bedroom where again there wasn't a speck of dust to be seen or a single item out of place. It was a vicarage, where perhaps a simpler existence was led, but surely there ought to be some signs of life. There should be opened books, a radio, or shoes lying on the floor.

The Truemans employed a cleaner, Molly Turnbull, but she'd been on holiday for the last four days, visiting her sister in the Lake District. Understandably, she'd been too shocked to help. She said she hardly ever saw Michael, or the vicar, but had been fond of Mrs Trueman.

'A saint, she was,' she'd sobbed.

One would need to be a saint, Max decided, to live in this mausoleum.

He moved on to Michael's bedroom and was struck by the sadness of the room. At the same age, Max's bedroom had been festooned with posters of semi-naked women. Old sporting trophies, busy gathering dust for years, had sat on shelves. Loose records, the sleeves lost long ago, had vied for space with half-empty bags of crisps, Mars bar wrappers and rotting apple cores. Admittedly, Max's mother hadn't employed a cleaner and, even if she had, she would never have lived with the shame of allowing her into her sons' bedrooms. All the same, Michael's room looked sad. Apart from a few books, all stored neatly in order of size on the bookcase, a brush, a comb and a can of deodorant on a set of drawers, there was nothing to say anyone used the room. There was no hi-fi, no CDs, no posters, and no mirror, either. Nothing. How did an eighteen-year-old practise his air guitar without a mirror?

Michael Trueman didn't come across as a fun sort of character. But it wasn't a fun sort of home. It was all furniture polish and crucifixes. Cleanliness and godliness.

No clues leapt out at him so he went downstairs.

In the sitting room, a couple of professionally taken framed photographs sat on the mantelpiece. There were no informal snaps; this wasn't an informal home. The long curtains were of velvet, presumably to keep out the cold, and were a little threadbare. The furniture, too, had a shabbiness to it. The carpet was dull and well worn. There was an upright piano that to Max's untrained ear seemed to be working well, and a fairly new television and VCR. It was a dreary room, though.

It was the same in the kitchen. Everything was drab and cold. Even the food in the cupboards, all stored neatly, was dull and unappetizing. There was a massive old freezer, a fridge, a washing machine and an old Rayburn. Crockery was functional.

The vicar's study was lined with books and the only bright spot in the room was a state-of-the-art laptop computer that sat on his heavy, mahogany desk. That hadn't come cheap. The books, Max noted, were mostly concerned with theology. Others were on local history.

Max reckoned that if he'd lived there, he would have had to kill someone, too. It was a house that sucked the life from you.

It was a depressing pastel green colour. Other than the bathroom, every wall in the house was painted in the same pale green. Kitchen, study, sitting room, bedrooms, hallway – all green. Who had said green was a relaxing colour? It was as depressing as hell.

He wandered over to the window and gazed at gardens that, even in November, boasted lots of colour in the foliage. He'd hoped that someone in the house had had a passion for colour and warmth but no. They employed a gardener, which wasn't surprising given the size of the garden. Jim Brody's statement had told them nothing. When Alice Trueman had been murdered, Brody had been at the accident and emergency department having a gash in his arm stitched. Understandably, perhaps, he'd been more concerned with his own problems than giving them a character study of Alice Trueman.

As Max walked back to his car, his mind chattered away to itself.

The vicar appeared to be a dull man wrapped up in his religion, a man who was too busy thinking of God to think of anything else. Did he have time for anything else? Was there time in his life for his wife and son? Did this family know the meaning of laughter and fun?

What about his late wife, Alice? If she was as warm and kind-hearted as everyone thought, a woman who enjoyed the simple pleasures in life, perhaps the vicarage had suited her.

Had Michael brought his young friends back to this house? Max couldn't imagine wild parties here, or young people listening to music at an ear-splitting volume.

He stood for a few moments, watching officers search the garden. Given that a car boot sale had been held in the adjoining car park on Saturday and that refreshments had been available in the vicarage garden, most of Kelton Bridge's residents would have tramped across those lawns . . .

As he drove away, none the wiser, Max mentally went over the details he would feed to the media.

Chapter Seven

'That'll learn me,' Jill muttered to herself.

Meredith, walking by her side, looked up. 'Sorry?'

'Nothing.'

He'd phoned early that morning, offering to buy her lunch. Deciding that forewarned was forearmed, Jill had accepted. Bad decision. How many times had her dad told her there was no such thing as a free lunch?

Before lunch, when she'd walked into his office, he'd asked, very casually, how she felt about coming back to work on Valentine's case. Jill had soon put him straight on that.

'I never had you down as a coward,' he'd murmured, shrugging it off.

Jill wasn't falling for that old ploy!

So they'd had a pleasant lunch, and then he'd brought her back here. 'You may as well say hello to everyone,' he'd told her.

And here she was, in the thick of it.

It was as if she'd been away a lifetime. She had forgotten how many people were packed into such a small building, and how they still managed to work, and she'd forgotten how hectic everything seemed. The reality was that everyone knew exactly what they were doing, but to an outsider, and Jill considered herself an outsider now, it looked chaotic.

She had soon lost count of the number of people to greet her with a 'Great to have you back.' In the end, she'd given up trying to explain that she wasn't back.

'The new interview room,' Meredith announced, pushing open a door. 'State-of-the-art stuff,' he added proudly.

'Very nice,' Jill murmured. And it was but –

On the other side of the glass, two officers were interviewing young Michael Trueman.

'You know Grace, of course,' Meredith said, 'and the other chap's Fletch.'

Jill didn't know Fletch, but she knew Max thought highly of him and was glad to have him on the team. He was a short, plump man who, judging by the way that he constantly pulled his trousers back up to his waistline, had lost a little weight recently.

Grace, on the other hand, was tall and reed-thin, and possessed a sartorial elegance to which Fletch could never aspire. Her voice was gentle as she spoke to Michael, but Jill had worked with her enough to know that her strong Geordie accent and no-nonsense approach to life could put the fear of God into the most hardened of criminals.

'We have trained counsellors who can help you, Michael,' she was saying. 'You're in a lot of trouble at the moment, but if you'll only talk to us, tell us your side of the story, I'm sure we can help you. That's what we're here for.'

Michael looked exhausted, which wasn't surprising. He'd been here almost twenty-four hours and the Lord only knew what was going through his head.

Another officer entered the interview room and announced the arrival of Michael's father. Jill caught the look of – what? fear? – on Michael's face. Why was he more frightened of his father than he was of the officers questioning him? If she were awaiting retribution, Jill would take her chances with Jonathan Trueman rather than Grace or Fletch.

Jonathan Trueman sat opposite his son, and Grace left the room. Seconds later, she was standing alongside Jill and Meredith.

'Hello, stranger!' she greeted Jill. 'I heard you were coming back.'

'I'm not,' Jill told her, scowling at Meredith.

Grace looked confused, but didn't comment. She was more interested in Michael.

'He's terrified of his father,' Jill murmured.

'Then let's hope he can get the little bastard to talk. Trentham's in a bitch of a mood as it is.'

'Oh? What's wrong with him?'

'The usual unexplained male stuff.'

Jill had to smile. At twenty-seven, Grace was the youngest of seven. She had six brothers, and often unwound with a session of male-bashing.

'Bullying is the last thing Michael needs right now,' Jill said.

Grace made no comment on that; she was of the opinion that police officers should be allowed to extract the truth by force if necessary.

They stood to watch the proceedings, breath suspended as they waited for a word from Michael Trueman.

'I don't know what to say to you, I really don't,' his father was saying. 'When the police told me you were refusing to cooperate, I couldn't believe it. Your mother and I have brought you up better than this, surely? These people are only doing their jobs, you know.'

No response from Michael.

'I can say this,' Jonathan Trueman went on. 'I forgive you.'

No reaction whatsoever. Not a flicker.

'You're my son, and I love you. No matter why you did this terrible thing, I can forgive you. More importantly, God will forgive you.'

Jonathan Trueman took a handkerchief from his pocket and blew his nose.

'You have to tell us why you did this, Michael. Above all, honesty is the thing.'

Michael stared at his feet.

'This is helping no one, son.' Jonathan Trueman's voice was steely now. Was he an impatient man, Jill wondered, a man with a quick temper?

'If there was an argument, if your mother did something to hurt you – well, you must tell them. You know that, don't you?'

Michael continued to stare at his feet.

Meredith wandered off, but Jill stayed put. Just a few more minutes, she promised herself, and then she'd head home.

Jonathan Trueman spent over an hour with his son. He talked, he scolded, he coaxed, he offered support, and he shed a few tears, but nothing brought a reaction from Michael. He tried to hug his son, but Michael pulled away. Eventually, with a shake of his head to the officers present, Jonathan left the room.

Grace returned to question Michael, but Jill sought out Jonathan Trueman. She caught up with him in the corridor looking lost and dazed as he gazed out of the window down at the car park below them.

'Are you all right?' she asked gently.

He turned round quickly, and it took him a moment to place her.

'Oh, Jill. So sorry, for a minute I didn't recognize you. I didn't know you were here.' He took a deep breath. 'Yes, I'm all right, thank you.' His eyes filled. 'Alice had written you a note, inviting you to the vicarage for lunch.'

'I'm so sorry.' He had looked an imposing figure at the party; now he seemed to have shrunk inside himself. He was terribly close to tears too, and Jill wasn't used to coping with hysterical vicars. 'Can I get you a coffee?' she asked. 'It'll be out of the machine, I'm afraid, but it should be warm and sweet.'

'Thank you.' He looked as if he was glad of the suggestion, and Jill felt an urge to take him by the hand and lead him away from this dismal place.

Jill not only managed to get two reasonable-looking cups of coffee from the machine, a miracle in itself, but she also found an empty office. Judging by the dust on the filing cabinets and the boxes stacked in all corners, it hadn't been used for a while. Meredith couldn't complain that she was trespassing. Nor could he fire her.

Oblivious to the dust, Jonathan Trueman perched on the edge of the desk and clutched the hot plastic cup in his hands as if he were clutching at life itself. Jill ran a quick hand over the windowsill and sat on the edge of that.

'How are you coping?' she asked, but she knew the answer to that. Badly. And who wouldn't?

'I have my faith,' he said.

At any other time, she would have involved him in a theological argument but she could see he was struggling with that faith of his.

'You must have been married a long time,' she remarked curiously. 'At least eighteen years.'

'Twenty-four years in August,' he told her. 'Alice was even making plans for our silver wedding anniversary.'

'Plans? A party, you mean?' She couldn't imagine either of them being party people.

'A holiday,' he explained.

'Anywhere special?'

He shook his head. 'I never thanked her,' he said suddenly. 'I think that's what hurts the most.'

'Thanked her for what?' Jill asked.

'For marrying me, for staying with me.'

'Isn't that what love is all about?'

'Alice was a dancer, you know,' he said as if he hadn't heard her. 'She's forty, nine years younger than me.' He spoke in the present tense, Jill noticed. 'When I first met her, she was a talented, fun-loving girl.' He shrugged and smiled at the memory, but the smile quickly faded. 'I loved her passionately and could never quite believe that she could love me, too. But . . .'

He was silent for so long that Jill had to prompt him. 'But?'

'I sometimes think I stifled her. I needed a wife who would support my work. I wanted someone who would be described as a pillar of the community, and a credit to the parish. That was wrong of me, I see that now. Alice was a dancer. She loved music and dancing. She loved to have fun.'

Dance to the Music. Jill was sure that was running at Wolverhampton this evening. It might be worth putting a couple of quid on it . . .

'I always lived with the knowledge that, one day, she'd leave me for someone else,' Jonathan said.

'But she never did,' Jill pointed out.

'No.' He gazed straight at her and Jill saw the moisture of unshed tears in his eyes. 'No, she never did. She was a wonderful wife to me and a wonderful mother to poor Michael. That's how I must remember her.'

The picture Jonathan had painted of his wife was fascinating. The fun-loving dancer bore no resemblance whatsoever to the woman at the party who'd been wearing dull clothes and whose attractive face was devoid of make-up.

'Do you believe Michael killed Alice?' she asked.

'No.' There was no hesitation. 'He's been behaving a little oddly lately, admittedly, but –'

'Oh?'

'Mixing with the wrong sort of people if you ask me. But no, I don't believe he killed his mother. Not that I can think of another explanation,' he said grimly. 'I was there only a matter of seconds after him. My appointment with the bishop was cancelled, and Michael was home early because of problems with the fire sprinklers at school. No one else was there, no one else was seen.' He cleared his throat, adding gruffly, 'According to these people, Alice had only been dead a very short time when I arrived. They can tell from –'

'Yes, I know.'

'I keep thinking about that red van – if indeed there was a red van.'

'Red van?'

'As I was walking up to the vicarage, I heard a vehicle racing along. I turned to look and caught a glimpse of a red van flying past. At least, I think it was a van. It may have been a car. I only caught a brief glimpse through gaps in the hedge.'

'You've told the police about this?'

'Oh, yes. It keeps preying on my mind now. I'm not sure if it was racing along the road or – or if it was speeding away from the vicarage.'

He shook his head, suddenly impatient. 'If only Michael would talk.' He emptied his cup and stood up. 'I must go and pray for him. Thank you for the coffee, Jill. And thank you for listening.'

When he strode off, looking far more purposeful than the man she'd met in the corridor outside the interview room, Jill sat back against the window, closed her eyes and tried to picture the sort of woman Alice Trueman had been.

Despite her good intentions, it was almost six o'clock when Jill left the building that evening. She'd struggled to find a parking spot this morning, but the car park was almost empty now. As she was about to get in her car, Max drove up and parked next to her. She waited for him for get out.

'Are you back with us already?' he asked, surprised.

'No. Phil Meredith phoned and, erm, invited me to lunch.' She waited for a sarcastic comment.

'Right,' was all he said.

'Max?'

'Yes?'

'I'm glad I caught you. I was meaning to mention it to someone but it kept slipping my mind. Last Friday morning, a photo was hand-delivered to my cottage.' She unlocked her car, reached inside for her briefcase, and took out the protective envelope that contained the photograph and the newspaper headline. 'Could you have it dropped in at the lab for me? I doubt there are any prints on it, but you never know.'

He was frowning. 'A photo of what?'

'Me. The one that was in the papers for weeks after Rodney Hill was arrested.'

'Hand-delivered?' He was speaking slowly and deliberately, a sure sign he was forcing himself to keep calm.

'Yes, I was out. When I got home, it was on the doormat with a couple of items the postman had delivered.'

'Last Friday? Some crank sends you a photo of yourself, last bloody Friday, and you don't think to mention it?' His voice was rising.

'I just did mention it,' Jill pointed out calmly, but she knew he had a valid point.

'Any ideas?' he snapped.

'None. Well, someone's taking the mickey, I suppose.'

'It might be someone taking the mickey,' he agreed. 'Be on your guard, and if anything else happens, anything at all, I want to know about it – immediately. OK? And keep that bloody door of yours locked.'

'OK.' Jill was about to get in her car.

'Have you seen our Michael?' he asked.

'Yes, but he's still not talking. I saw his father, too. Apparently, Alice used to be a dancer. It would explain her stunning figure, of course, but it doesn't fit with the woman I met at the party.' She passed over that. 'I've looked through the reports this afternoon – it's funny, isn't it, how both Michael *and* his father arrived home early that day – Michael because the school closed unexpectedly, and Jonathan because his meeting was cancelled? Alice wouldn't have been expecting either of them.'

She broke off as Max's phone rang.

'Yes . . . yes . . . so it's what we thought? Nothing new?' Max was walking a small circle as he listened to his caller. 'You could tell me we were looking for a left-handed dwarf, that might help . . .'

Jill left him to it. If he wanted her opinion, and she wasn't yet sure what that opinion was, he would phone. She wanted to go home and see if Dance to the Music was racing tonight.

Chapter Eight

The Weaver's Retreat was only half a mile from her cottage and instead of driving straight home, Jill pulled into the car park. She'd already stopped to place ten pounds to win on Dance to the Music.

She always bought her eggs from the pub. Having come close on several occasions to killing the hens that wandered at will across the road to the hill opposite, she knew they were as free range as it was possible to get. Meredith had bought her a good lunch, but that was hours ago and a full cholesterol-laden hit of bacon and eggs called.

'Hello, Jill. The usual, is it?' The landlord's hand was already resting on the lager pump. On only her third visit to his pub, he'd asked if she wanted her 'usual'.

'I only wanted some eggs, but perhaps I'll have a quick drink while I'm here. A whisky with lots of ice, please, Ian.'

For a moment, he was thrown, but he soon recovered and filled a tumbler with ice cubes before adding a measure of whisky.

'There you go, love.'

He went to the store at the back for her eggs, leaving Jill to nod to a couple of people she knew by sight.

Ian put the eggs on the counter. 'You won't get fresher than that.'

'Thanks. Business doesn't look to be booming,' she commented, handing him a ten-pound note. Usually, the small bar was packed with locals.

'It were busy at lunchtime,' he told her, 'but it's been

quiet since. What a time, though. The whole village is in shock.'

'Dreadful,' Jill agreed, knowing how this sort of thing affected not only the family involved but also the whole community. Everyone knew everyone else in these small Lancashire towns and villages.

'And fancy them arresting young Michael,' he went on, his voice lowered. 'I can't believe he'd do such a thing. No, I can't have that. Stands to reason. He's a smashing lad. He helped me out last summer – we had the old taproom decorated and he were that helpful. Honest, hard-working – he works at the filling station on Saturdays now.'

'Yes, I know.'

'Idolized his mother,' Ian went on. 'Closer to her than to his dad, I reckon. Not that he don't get on well with his dad. A terrible business all round. But I won't have him down as a killer. I won't.'

A young couple walked in, strangers to Jill and to Ian, and Jill picked up her change and left him to serve them. She sat at a small round table in the corner, next to the fire. People had warned her about the harsh winters endured in this corner of Lancashire, but she'd had no idea those winters arrived so early.

She liked The Weaver's Retreat. It was on the edge of the village, on the Todmorden Road, and was popular with the locals. Ian always had a warm welcome for his regulars; it was a homely place to relax.

Not that Jill was feeling relaxed. She was still trying to picture Alice Trueman as a fun-loving ex-dancer. It didn't fit. Except, of course, she'd had the elegance and grace of a dancer, and those long, shapely legs. She was also curious about the sort of people Jonathan Trueman thought his son was mixing with. What had he meant by that? Kids taking drugs? Or simply kids from the council estate? What would he have made of her, she wondered, if he knew of her lowly beginnings?

'Are you turning to drink?'

Jill looked up, startled to see that Andy Collins was in the bar. He must have come in through the back door.

'I called in for eggs,' she explained with a smile, 'and was tempted to linger in the warmth. Winter's come early.'

'Winter? This is a pleasant autumnal day,' he told her with a laugh. 'Mind if I join you?'

'I'd be glad of the company.'

He paid for his pint and brought it over to the table. Before sitting down, he brushed a couple of specks of mud from his trousers.

'I've been showing a prospective purchaser round Top Bank Farm,' he explained, 'and the chap insisted on walking through the fields. It's ankle deep in mud. Still, a sale is a sale,' he added, downing almost half his pint in one swallow.

'You look as if you needed that,' Jill remarked.

'I can't seem to get going at all at the moment.' He shuddered. 'I keep thinking of poor Alice. I liked her a lot.'

'Dreadful, isn't it? I wish I'd known her better. Did you know she'd been a dancer?'

'Yes. Years ago, she was in one of those groups – you know, like Pan's People or Hot Gossip. Or perhaps that's before your time.'

'She was that sort of dancer?' Jill was amazed. 'I'd imagined her ballroom dancing.'

Andy shook his head.

'She was a real little raver by all accounts. Lovely woman, though. Lovely family come to that,' he said. 'Michael – now I know the police don't arrest people without reason, but I simply can't believe it of him. He's a smashing lad. Jon's the same. He gets on his high horse now and again, but he's a good enough sort. Once you get to know him, you'll find he's a good laugh.' He took another swig of his beer. 'Not that he's got anything to laugh about now.'

'No, poor man.'

'It's the sort of thing you see on the TV,' he murmured,

'not the sort of thing that happens in real life, to real people. And certainly not in a place like this.'

Isn't that what everyone caught up in these situations said? Whether you lived in a sleepy little hamlet or on a bustling inner city estate, it was one of those things that happened to other people in other places.

The door opened and Tony Hutchinson came in.

'Andy! Jill!' he called out. 'Can I get you a drink?'

Jill refused. It was tempting to enjoy the warmth a little longer, but she was hungry. Andy accepted another pint.

'Is this a private party,' Tony asked, 'or can anyone join in?'

'Sit down.' Jill moved round the table to give him more space.

'What a day,' Tony said, taking a drink. 'I had all the kids together for a special assembly this morning, but it's damned difficult knowing what to say to them. They're all so different, too. While we were praying for Alice and the family, one girl of ten was in tears and another girl, the same age, was happily chewing gum and writing "I love Dave" on her arm.'

'That's kids for you,' Andy said. 'Criminals in the making, most of them. I'm glad I don't have your job, Tony. I'd never have the patience.'

'Most of them are fine,' Tony argued. 'They're our future, remember.'

'Then we're all doomed,' Andy said with a rueful smile.

Tony turned his attention to Jill. 'Am I forgiven?' he asked.

'Of course.' She wished he'd shut up about it, and she wished he didn't make her feel so uncomfortable.

'Forgiven?' Andy asked curiously. 'What have you been up to, Tony?'

'Liz told me I was rude to Jill at the party,' he explained. 'It's just that I'm fascinated by her work. It's a bit like that film, *The Silence of the Lambs*, isn't it?'

'No,' Jill said drily, 'it's nothing like that.'

Tony looked embarrassed, and Jill hoped she hadn't made him look a fool.

'The FBI's Behavioral Science Unit is very different to anything we have in this country,' she explained. 'It has to be – you only have to think of the size of the country. And, well, that was a film. My work is – was totally different. Very boring,' she added lightly.

'I bet it's fascinating,' Tony said.

''Fraid not,' she said, managing another smile.

'To think that Alice is gone,' Andy murmured vaguely. 'It doesn't sink in, does it?'

'I've just called on Mary and Gordon,' Tony told them, 'and I saw Jon. He's staying with them, did you know? He seems to be holding up well, considering. Perhaps if you believe in God – well, I mean I believe in God, but if you devote your life to Him, perhaps you see some reason to it. Perhaps you can believe she's gone to a better place.'

At that, Andy looked as doubtful as Jill felt. 'Michael won't be going to a better place, will he?' he said.

'No,' Tony agreed.

'I was just saying to Jill that I can't believe it of him. He'd never do such a thing. Never.'

'Did you teach him, Tony?' Jill asked curiously.

'When he was a youngster, yes. He must have been – let me think – nine years old when the family came to the village so I only had him for a couple of years.'

'What was he like?'

'Bright, a quick learner, polite – the ideal pupil. A little out of it at times,' he added thoughtfully, 'but that goes with the territory.'

Seeing Jill's puzzled expression, he explained. 'As the son of the vicar, you're going to be considered different by the other kids. It's the same for the headmaster's son. Used to be the same for the local bobby's son in the days we had a bobby.' He grinned smugly at her, as if he'd caught her out. 'You're the psychologist.'

Jill supposed he had a point, except she hadn't thought

that applied these days. Perhaps it did in a relatively small village like Kelton Bridge.

'Kids like that go one of two ways,' he went on. 'They either keep to themselves and concentrate on their studies, or they become the local troublemaker, determined to show their mates they're no different.'

'And Michael concentrated on his studies?' she guessed.

'He did. A model pupil.' He thought for a moment. 'He brought an injured blackbird to school once. We reckoned it had got on the wrong side of a cat. During the lunch break, he took it to Betty Taylor's place. She keeps the animal sanctuary on New Road. Eventually, the bird recovered and Betty released it, but Michael called to see that bird every morning on his way to school.' He took a quick swig from his glass. 'I'm with Andy on this. I don't believe he could pull a knife on any living thing and certainly not his mother.'

They fell silent, each thinking, Jill supposed, of young Michael.

'How's Liz?' Jill asked at last.

'Fine, thanks. I expect she'll be along in a while . . .'

Jill didn't stop to find out. She was ready for her bacon and eggs.

It was after nine when Max called at Lilac Cottage that evening. Jill wasn't in the least surprised by his visit.

The cats, despite knowing he wasn't a cat person, gave him a royal welcome. Even Rabble, who didn't approve of visitors, was walking in and out of his legs. It did her no good; he took no notice whatsoever.

'Michael confessed,' he announced grimly. 'Just like that. He asked for a glass of water, then said he'd like to tell us how he killed his mother.'

Jill had liked Michael. She'd warmed to him from the start, and she felt let down. Saddened and let down. Everyone in Kelton Bridge would feel the same, too. Michael was a popular member of the community, the young man who'd been so helpful at the pub, and the lad who had visited an injured bird every day.

'So what's with the long face?' she asked, sighing as Max threw himself down in her armchair as if he'd come home after a hard day at the office.

'His confession's complete crap.'

'What do you mean?'

'According to him, he came home from school, carrying a knife he'd bought from a complete stranger in Rochdale or it might have been Burnley some time ago, saw his mother standing in the hall, looked her in the eye and killed her.'

'So he can't say where he got the knife from?'

'Nope. Or when.'

'Looked her in the eye? She was killed from behind, wasn't she?'

'She was. It doesn't seem as if our Michael's aware of that though.'

'So who is he protecting?' Relief flooding through her, Jill sat in the chair opposite Max. 'We know he arrived home early, and we know he was expecting his father to be out. Was he also expecting his mother to be out? Perhaps he had someone with him? Does he have a girlfriend?'

'He doesn't have many close friends – lots of acquaintances, but not what you'd call real friends. But he couldn't have witnessed the murder,' Max pointed out. 'If he had, he'd know his mother had been attacked from behind.'

'Does his father know?' Jill asked.

'That he's confessed, yes. That his confession is worth diddley squat, no.'

'How did he react?'

'I've just come from there and he's pretty distraught. When it first happened, he was amazingly calm. But he was still trying to resuscitate her when we got there – couldn't accept she'd gone. I thought he was doing OK considering, but he's going downhill.'

'He didn't look too good when I saw him, poor chap. Only the thought of praying for Michael seemed to help.'

Max grimaced. 'He can't accept she's dead, and he certainly can't accept that Michael killed her. His latest idea is that someone was at the vicarage and was still there when we arrived. Either that, or the driver of the mysterious red van killed her and then took off.'

'It's a possibility, I suppose.'

'A very slim one,' Max replied. 'There was blood everywhere. Whoever killed her would have been covered in the stuff, just as father and son were. There's no sign of any by the front door or the back. No shoe-prints.'

Jill curled her feet beneath her, and tried to get things straight in her mind. Michael hadn't seen the murder perhaps, but he had to be protecting someone. Who? It must be someone he cared about deeply.

'What about Michael's mobile phone?' she asked. 'I assume he does have one? Any text messages from girlfriends on it?'

'Nothing visible but it's still being checked.' He gave her one of his coaxing looks. 'Will you come in tomorrow and have a look through his confession? See what you can come up with?'

'I suppose –'

'Thanks.'

He looked at his watch and, with a heavy sigh, got to his feet. 'I need to go home and get some sleep. Oh, and the photo that was put through your letterbox . . .'

'Yes?'

'Clean as a whistle.'

Jill wasn't surprised.

Chapter Nine

He liked the card, found it appropriate. On the front, From Your Valentine *was written amid a mass of tiny, glittering hearts. Inside, it read:* One day you'll be mine. *It appealed to him. Later, he would put it through her letterbox.*

He enjoyed being in her garden, so close to her, and often spent an evening watching her move around. She rarely pulled the curtains across until late. Even then, he liked to see lights go on and off in the various rooms.

Better still, he liked to go inside the cottage. That was best. He liked to walk around the rooms and look at her things. She was neat and tidy, and he approved of that. He had to have order in his life and he guessed she did, too.

Still, it was OK watching from the outside. Funny how he was at home in the dark. He supposed that was one thing he could thank his mother for. Probably the only thing.

He hadn't liked the darkness as a child. Those hours spent locked in the cupboard had filled him with horror. He'd begged and pleaded for a torch but she'd only laughed at him.

'Great baby,' she'd scoffed. 'Not scared of the dark, are you?'

He'd shaken his head, not daring to admit that it terrified him.

He and his mum had shared a bedroom, and he'd hated that, too. It always smelled funny – a mixture of perfume and something else that he hadn't been able to identify for years. He hadn't known it was the smell of sex. All he had known was that he was banished to the cupboard frequently and, although he didn't have many toys, those he did have had to be out of sight before he went to the cupboard.

That smelled funny, too. Dusty and unused. He did nothing in there; there was nothing to do.

It was when the men came that he was sent to the cupboard. Or sometimes, she sent him there when she was angry with him.

She'd never been much of a cook, but for some reason she had enjoyed making biscuits. As she only possessed one cutter, the biscuits were heart-shaped. Once, he helped himself to a biscuit, still warm from the oven, and she was so enraged because he hadn't asked that she sent him to the cupboard. From then on, he was sent to the cupboard whenever she made biscuits.

'You're a thief. You can't be trusted,' she'd said, and no protests from him would change her mind.

'I won't touch them,' he'd cried, tears rolling down his cheeks.

'You won't,' she'd agreed, laughing at her own little joke as she'd dragged him by the arm to the cupboard.

These days, he liked the dark. It didn't take long for his eyes to adjust and then he was fine.

No, he was better than fine. Standing here, at the bottom of her garden, behind the lilac tree after which the cottage had perhaps been named, he saw all sorts of things. Last night he'd seen a sleek, bushy-tailed fox. The fox hadn't seen him. He was as wily as a fox . . .

Her bedroom light dimmed and he guessed she was sitting up in bed with the lamp on. What would she be reading?

He'd watched that policeman, Detective Chief Inspector Trentham, come and go. Some detective he was. Some psychologist she was, come to that. There he was watching them both and they were no nearer the truth than they ever had been.

Still, credit where credit was due. That profile she'd come up with had been close. They'd published it during her glory days when Rodney Hill had been arrested.

Rodney Hill – the very thought of the man filled him with rage. Hill had been a nothing, a nobody. All he'd done was have sex with a whore. Any idiot could do that. During those long hours spent in the cupboard, he'd peeped through the crack and seen hundreds of men arrive, all of them on the verge of wetting themselves in their excitement. They were nothing. Worthless pieces of nothing.

At first, he hadn't known what the men came for. It was Micky Muldoon who told him.

'They have sex with your mum,' he'd said in a matter-of-fact way. 'She's a whore. A dirty, filthy whore.'

He had been seven years old, too young to know the facts of the life, but no one called his mother dirty or filthy. Micky Muldoon hadn't done it again.

His fist had connected with Micky's face and the blood had spurted from his nose.

'Hey, I was only tellin' yer what me mam said,' Micky had yelled.

That was the first time he'd felt the rage and, lucky for Micky Muldoon, he'd raced off to the woods to be alone with it . . .

He'd soon had to accept that Micky was telling the truth. His mum was a whore. She took money from men and let them do filthy, disgusting things to her. He'd seen dozens, no hundreds of men over the years. Men like Rodney Hill.

Had they honestly believed that Hill was Valentine? It was an insult.

He could feel his heart racing with anger, and he had to take a few steadying breaths to calm himself. No good getting angry about it. Hill didn't matter. Valentine was the one they were after. Valentine was the one who had outwitted them. Valentine – as cunny and wily as a fox.

For two pins –

But, no. Later, he'd leave the card for her. It was fun playing games with her.

When he tired of that, he would kill her. That would give the celebrated Detective Chief Inspector Trentham something to think about.

Chapter Ten

Jill was awake early and she dressed quickly, pulling on black jeans and a shirt. She wanted a quick breakfast before heading off to read Michael's confession. No way was she doing it for Max's benefit; she was curious. She was also in a good mood. Dance to the Music had won by a short head last night.

She was halfway down the stairs when she spotted the envelope lying on the mat. It was too early for the postman to have called. This envelope had been hand-delivered. Just like the other one.

Blood began pounding in her ears. Pull yourself together, she instructed herself sharply. Some harmless crank was trying to frighten her, that's all. The strict lecture didn't help.

She walked down the stairs and was about to pick it up when she heard a car slow to a stop outside. A car door slammed and she went to the window to look out. Max was unfastening his seatbelt and getting out.

Relieved, she stepped over the envelope and held the door open for him.

'I've just come from the vicarage,' he said, 'and thought I'd see if you wanted a lift in.'

'Oh, er, yes. Thanks.' She showed him the envelope still lying on the mat. 'I expect that's another photo – or something.'

He scowled at it, opened a pair of tiny tweezers that hung from his key ring, and carefully picked it up. There was no writing on the envelope. No name, no address, nothing.

'Of course,' he said drily, 'it could be a note from the milkman.'

He sliced the envelope open and, using the tip of thumb and forefinger, pulled out the card.

'Shit!'

Jill could have echoed that.

Inside the envelope was a Valentine card. It mocked the crisp, cold November morning. There was no message, just a printed: *One day you'll be mine.*

'I don't like this, Jill. I really don't like it.'

'I'm not thinking of placing an order for champagne and party poppers myself.'

'How do we know it's not Valentine playing games with you?'

'We don't,' she allowed, 'but even if it is, he's unlikely to hurt me.'

'He's put seven women in the morgue.'

'Yes, but all prostitutes. If it is Valentine, and I can't imagine it is, he won't kill me. He'll want to show me how clever he is. And anyway, why now? Why not a year ago? No, it can't be Valentine. It'll be someone playing a sick joke on me. Someone who wants to remind me that I got it wrong.'

'We'll check it out,' Max said, 'and we'll have a look to see who's been released from prison recently. Think back over your old cases. We'll have a word with Rodney Hill's sister, too.'

'It won't be her!' Jill could remember the woman – short, plump, bleached blonde and very angry – screaming abuse at her as she'd left the court. 'She might be a nasty piece of work, but she wouldn't do this. What would be the point? And why now? Why wait all this time?'

'I don't know.' Max put the card on the table and strode through to the kitchen. 'I need some coffee.'

He filled the kettle and switched it on, then leaned back against the sink.

'Jill –'

'No.'

'You don't know what I was going to say.'

'I know exactly what you were going to say. You think I should go back on Valentine's case and the answer is no. I can't do it.'

'I think I know how you feel, but you won't rest, not properly, until he's behind bars. He's taken too much from you.'

'No,' she said briskly, 'and I refuse to discuss it. Have you eaten?' she asked, changing the subject. 'I was going to have cereal but I've got some bacon and eggs if you fancy it.'

'Yeah?' He looked at his watch. 'Thanks, I'll have a bacon and egg butty. I'll even make it myself. Do you want one?'

'No, I'll have cereal.'

Conversation was desultory as they ate. Jill, trying to retain at least some of the good humour she'd woken with, gazed out at her garden. Like everything else about Lilac Cottage it was begging for some tender loving care, but it looked beautiful this morning. The grass was white with frost and an icy cobweb stretched from the old wooden seat to the remains of a clematis climbing the shed.

'We'll get someone watching your cottage,' Max said as he put his plate in the sink. There was no hope of washing up; he'd never mastered that.

'No resources,' she reminded him.

'With some crank playing postman,' he muttered, 'we've got resources. Have you seen anyone or anything? Have any cars driven by slowly? Has anyone been out walking and looked at this place? Have you seen someone with a dog?'

'I haven't seen anything,' she told him, 'but I rarely look out at the front.'

'Get looking and make a note of everything. Get car registrations, descriptions of people walking dogs – anything.'

'I will.'

'We'll get that card checked out but I expect it's clean,' he said.

Jill was sure it would be.

Could it be Valentine? Had he been lurking round her cottage? No, she was being paranoid.

God, she wished they could catch him, though.

Of course, if she were to help, they might catch him more quickly. But could she do it? Could she go through those files again, look at those grisly photographs again, and read Rodney Hill's statement again?

She honestly wasn't sure she could.

Anyway, today she wanted to check out Michael's confession and read the reports. There wasn't time for anything else. She could think about Valentine tomorrow . . .

A couple of hours later, Jill was reading the transcript of Michael's confession. It was a cold, clinical account telling how he'd come home from school, with the knife he'd bought from a chap selling them outside a shop in Rochdale, at least he thought it was Rochdale but it might have been Burnley, lost his temper with his mother and killed her in a fit of anger.

He went into great detail about the new safety equipment at school, how the fire alarm had been going off at irregular intervals for days and how, on the day in question, the sprinklers had come on. Everyone able to go home had done so, and Michael had been lucky enough to get a lift with his friend's mother. No, his friend's mother didn't drive a red vehicle, she drove a dark blue 4×4. No, he hadn't seen any red vehicles near the vicarage.

Only when he reached the end of his story did he break down.

He insisted he walked through the front door and came face to face with his mother. Why was she naked? He couldn't explain that. Why was she standing in the hall? He couldn't explain that, either. What was she doing in the hall? Nothing. Why had he bought the knife in the first place? No special reason.

When asked why he'd been angry with her, he'd said simply, 'The usual stuff.' When pressed, it seemed the usual stuff involved not studying and mixing with the wrong type of people.

That didn't fit with the Alice that Jill had met, albeit briefly, or the Alice villagers spoke of so fondly. That woman had loved Michael, and would have welcomed his friends. As for not studying – no, it didn't ring true. He was the model pupil. His headmaster had said so, as had his teachers, as had Tony Hutchinson, and his school reports proved it. Even if it were true, surely Michael would do what other teenagers did. He would throw a tantrum then sulk for half an hour. He wouldn't kill.

Michael was protecting someone, Jill was sure of it. But who?

Supposing he had a girlfriend and supposing Alice had disapproved. Mixing with the wrong type of people, Michael had said. It's what his father had said, too. Does any mother like it when her only son finds some other woman to love? Supposing Michael had kept quiet about this girlfriend, guessing his mother's reaction would be unfavourable, and had left Alice to suffer the embarrassment and indignity of finding out from someone else?

It was the sort of juicy titbit Olive Prendergast would delight in passing over the post office counter. Jill made a mental note to ask Olive a few questions.

Even if these suppositions were fact, Michael didn't kill her. Could the fictitious girlfriend have done the deed?

To what sort of girl would Michael be attracted? Given the austere nature of his home life, someone different, someone older with more experience of life, someone wild and extrovert would appeal to him. Wild enough to kill his mother? It was possible, she supposed.

There was a pile of paperwork gathered from teachers, schoolfriends and villagers who had spoken about Michael. None of them, not even Olive Prendergast, had mentioned a girlfriend. All the same, Jill would still like a word with Olive. What she didn't know about the residents of Kelton Bridge wasn't worth knowing.

Michael was a member of the school's debating society, along with a dozen more pupils, both male and female, but no one had mentioned any special friendships he might have. It seemed as if his social life was non-existent.

Chapter Eleven

They all looked the same. With their coloured hair, short skirts, fake leather boots, heaving cleavage, heavy make-up and cigarettes in their hands as they stood on street corners trying not to shiver, they looked like his mother.

This one was younger than most, and her hair was red. It wasn't a natural auburn, or even a chestnut, coppery sort of red. No, this was more a plum sort of red, the kind that came straight from a bottle. She had one hand in the pocket of a short, white jacket, and the other held a cigarette on which she dragged as if she needed a hit. Most of them took drugs of some sort or another. Stupid bitches.

He slowed the car as he pulled alongside her and hit the button to wind down the window. There was no one around; it was unlikely anyone would see the car. Even if they did, it wouldn't trace to him. The registration plates were covered in mud, making them illegible.

'How much?' he asked.

'Depends on what you want,' she told him, throwing her cigarette to the ground. She leaned on the roof of the car and looked at him through the open window. 'If you want a blow job –'

'I want more than that.'

On closer inspection, he saw she was a lot younger than he'd first thought. Her skin was fresh beneath the make-up and her teeth were strong and white. How old was she? Eighteen? Nineteen? It didn't matter.

'Get in,' he said, 'and we'll talk about it.'

Even before she got in he could smell her cheap perfume. It was almost overpowering and he kept the window open as he drove off.

'It's a nice evening,' he said, 'and it would be a shame to waste it. I know a deserted spot.' It was a cold but clear night, and a full moon was playing hide and seek with the clouds. 'I'll pay you well for the extra time,' he promised. He took his wallet from his shirt pocket and showed it to her so she could see the wad of notes inside. 'Don't worry about the money. You be good to me and I'll be good to you.'

The sight of the cash loosened her tongue and she didn't stop talking about how badly blokes treated her and how she was saving up to buy her own place. His fingers were white as he gripped the wheel. If she didn't shut up in a minute, he'd kill her. The thought tickled him. That's exactly what he was going to do anyway.

'What's funny?' she asked.

'Nothing.'

'How much further is it?'

'Nearly there.'

They deserved all they got. For the promise of a few quid, they would happily climb in a car with a stranger and head off into the countryside. She'd been in his car for twenty minutes now, but all she was thinking about was the money.

'I'm Annie, by the way.'

Yeah, yeah. And he was Michelangelo.

'What's your name?'

'Micky,' he muttered.

A few minutes later, he pulled the car off the Burnley road and on to a rutted track. It was doubtful if the police would get any decent tyre tracks but, even if they did, the tyres would be long gone by then. They bumped along for a couple of minutes. It wasn't a comfortable ride but at least it kept her quiet.

He'd checked it out – no one ever used it. It led to an old farmhouse but that had been empty for years. Apart from stray sheep that took advantage of the shelter, it saw nothing.

'It's a bit creepy,' she said as he shone his torch inside the empty building. 'Cold an' all.'

'I'll soon warm you up,' he promised distractedly, and she giggled.

He put his torch on the stone windowsill and leaned back to look at her. The torch was powerful, giving off more than enough light, yet he knew it couldn't be seen from outside. He'd checked.

It was this attention to detail that made him so good. Would Hill have checked? No. Why not? Because Hill was a nobody. A simpleton.

The thought of Hill claiming his limelight filled him with rage. It always did . . .

'Let's have a look at you then,' he said.

She licked red lips and grinned at him, then took off her jacket and threw it to the dusty floor. Her top, a flimsy blue thing, was next, and then her skirt, short, denim and grubby.

When she was wearing only boots, stockings, briefs and bra, she stood before him, hands on hips, licking those red lips again.

'Well? Like what you see?'

He loathed what he saw. Filthy, disgusting bitch.

She took a step forward, hands reaching out for the buckle of his jeans, but he stopped her, gripping her tiny wrists in his strong hands.

'Turn round,' he ordered her, and she did, spinning on her high-heeled boots.

She wouldn't have seen the scarf; he was too quick for her. It was tight around her neck before she knew it. She didn't even have time to scream and although her long fingernails were digging into him with a strength that surprised him, he doubted his skin was even marked.

The breath left her body and he felt her go limp.

When he was sure she was dead, he let her fall to the floor.

He pulled the scarf from her neck and was pleased to see that, apart from the marks there, and the way her tongue and her eyes protruded, she looked the same as she had half an hour ago. She looked startled – yes, startled. Not terrified of death, merely startled.

He began taking things from his pocket. First, he put on the disposable gloves and then, very carefully, wiped her wrists with a solution of alcohol. Fingerprints on skin didn't last long, he knew that, and her body was unlikely to be found for days, but it was that attention to detail again. It was his professionalism that made him so good.

He took a cotton bud from his pocket and cleaned beneath her fingernails with the same solution. He had all the time in the world.

Using the small, sharp knife he cut away her remaining clothes, only struggling a little with her tight boots.

When they were off, he walked around, looking at her from all angles. Her clothes were folded neatly by her side, and his torch rested on the pile. Yes, she was ready.

He unsheathed his scalpel but, before starting work, he chopped off a lock of hair. It was the first time he'd done that, and for a moment, he was unsure. He didn't want to spoil her, yet he needed the souvenir. Not for himself, oh no. That was for Jill Kennedy.

The missing hair wasn't noticeable and, satisfied, he began work, cutting the small hearts neatly and carefully. It was slow work, but precision was everything.

Once again, he was in that dark, dusty cupboard listening to his mother making her biscuits. He could almost smell her, that heady mix of cheap perfume and sex. He could almost taste the tiny, heart-shaped biscuits, still warm from the oven . . .

This part, working carefully on her still, lifeless body, was what excited him most. He wished she could watch him and marvel at his skill and precision.

His erection was strong long before he'd finished, but he contained himself. Attention to detail.

Each of the twelve heart-shaped pieces of skin was wrapped carefully in tissue paper and put in a small plastic tub.

He returned the scalpel to his pocket and surveyed his work. Perfect. So perfect it made him want to weep. He often thought Michelangelo must have felt like this when he'd finished painting his ceiling, as if, finally, perfection had been created in an imperfect world.

As he gazed at his work, tears welling in his eyes, he knelt to the side of her, unzipped his jeans and freed his throbbing erection.

He grabbed her skirt – attention to detail again – and wrapped it around his penis. When he came, with huge sobs wracking his body, not a drop of semen touched her body . . .

As soon as he'd caught his breath, he got to his feet, gathered up her clothes, including her soaked skirt, and put them in a bag that he took from his pocket. He double-checked everything, picked up his torch and walked out.

There was nothing to connect him to this.

Now, it was a simple waiting game. Waiting for them to find her.

Chapter Twelve

It was 7 a.m. on Sunday morning, a time when all hard-working people should be sleeping soundly, happy in the knowledge that they could lie in bed undisturbed for at least five more hours. Max, however, had two young boys leaping all over him as they tried to coax him from the warm comfort of his bed.

He wished he had a tenth of their energy. 'How about you make me a coffee?' he suggested.

'OK,' Ben agreed, 'and then can we talk about the dog?'

'It's a deal. You make me a coffee and then I'll tell you again why we can't have a dog.'

Whether the boys heard the last remark, he didn't know. They were already halfway down the stairs.

They were good kids, the best, and he'd love to let them have a dog. Ben, eleven years old and a more gentle soul than his older brother, could think of little else. With their lifestyle, though, it simply wasn't practical. Lifestyle was describing it loosely, Max thought grimly.

He was lucky in that his house had a self-contained flat on the second floor, and even luckier that Linda's mum had been willing to move into said flat to be both mother and father to her grandchildren. God knows what they would have done without Kate.

She'd been there for them all – the wise and caring mother-in-law to Max, loving grandmother to the boys, and friend to Jill.

Kate wasn't a dog person, though, and it was unfair to

inflict one on her. With the kids at school and him at work, she'd be the one left to cope with it.

Life had been much simpler when Jill had lived with them. They'd managed to arrange their working lives around the kids most of the time. For a short time, life had been normal.

Still, it was no using dwelling on that.

The coffee was taking a suspiciously long time. Max was about to rouse himself to investigate when the boys returned. He hadn't known they possessed a tray, but Harry was carrying one laden with toast, butter, marmalade – and coffee.

'Blackmail is a very serious offence,' he told them, and they spluttered with laughter.

Their capacity for fun never failed to amaze him. Their mother was dead, their father was hardly ever home, and yet they still managed to embrace life. He knew a sudden urge to hug them close and never let them go.

'OK,' he said, settling the tray firmly on the bed and buttering his toast, 'let's pretend it's lunchtime on Wednesday. What is this dog of yours doing?'

'Either sleeping off the long walk we'll have given him before we go to school,' Harry said, 'or sitting by the door waiting for the long walk we'll give him when we get home from school.'

They'd clearly rehearsed this.

'Or chewing every stick of furniture we possess,' Max pointed out mildly, 'while peeing on the carpet.'

The boys giggled at that.

'Nan would let him out in the garden for five minutes,' Ben said.

'She'd probably like the company,' Harry put in. 'Look, Dad, we're not kids any more. We know all about responsibility and stuff like that.'

They weren't, and they did. Max couldn't argue with that.

'Don't you think,' he said, taking a sip of strong, black

coffee made just how he liked it, 'that this family is dysfunctional enough without adding even more chaos?'

'Nah,' they scoffed in unison. 'We like chaos.'

'You might,' Max grumbled, 'I don't.'

'You do.'

But he didn't. He would give a lot to come home at a sensible time each day to a wife who was eager to see him and to kids happily doing homework. If life were normal, they'd be able to make plans for the weekend, knowing that his phone wouldn't ring and drag him away to some terrible place.

He had a day off though so he was going to try and push all thoughts of work from his mind. His subconscious could mull things over while he relaxed. Today was for him and the kids.

'We'll think about it,' he said, 'and discuss it next week. Meanwhile, you can take my tray away, thank you, and decide what you fancy doing today.'

As he dressed, he thought of driving out to Southport. It was cold, and a stiff wind was blowing, but the kids would enjoy messing around with a football on the beach. The fresh air would do him good, too. It might clear his head. They could have a McDonald's for lunch. No, they'd stop somewhere decent and have a proper Sunday lunch . . .

A car pulled up outside and, when Max saw that Fletch was driving it, his heart sank. Perhaps work wouldn't wait until tomorrow after all. As he walked down the stairs, he could hear the boys laughing with Fletch.

'And we'll be having a dog soon,' Ben was telling him.

'We'll be discussing *not* having a dog soon,' Max corrected him as he walked into the kitchen. 'Right, you two, scram for a few minutes. Go and see if Nan's OK.'

After saying goodbye to Fletch, they raced upstairs to their grandmother's.

'You don't deserve such good kids,' Fletch told him fondly.

'We always get what we deserve,' Max argued with a grin, 'and I deserve a day off. What's new?'

'Not a lot. I'm on my way home, but thought I'd stop by and let you know that another hooker's been reported missing.'

Max felt his guts clench, but he knew it meant nothing. They came; they went. Sometimes they moved on to a different patch, sometimes they went to work at the nearest massage parlour, sometimes they got so stoned they vanished for days. The possibilities were endless.

'Where from?'

'Burnley. A sixteen-year-old by –'

'Sixteen?'

'Yes. An Anne Levington. We don't know much about her, just that she has a missing drunk for a father, and a mother who kicked her out. She'd been squatting with a gang of misfits. She had a burger with a mate and both of them were going to work the streets for a few hours before meeting up. Anne didn't show and the other girl's worried about her. The girls working the streets are a bit twitchy at the moment.'

'Not twitchy enough to keep them behind closed doors,' Max said grimly.

'It's easy money, I suppose.'

'Risking your neck every time you go to work isn't easy.'

'No, guv.' Fletch shuffled his feet, and Max made a mental note not to be so miserable with people.

'Fancy a coffee?' he asked.

'Thanks, guv, but no. Sandra's got me down for a spot of decorating, and my life won't be worth living if I don't get back soon.' He turned to leave. 'If she turns up, I'm sure someone will let you know. Cornwall's on to it, of course. They're taking it seriously, just in case.'

With Valentine on the loose, every prostitute who was missing for more than five minutes was taken seriously. That maniac had a lot to answer for and, come hell or high water, he would damn well answer for it.

It was nothing to do with him, Max reminded himself. Cornwall was on to it. When they'd pulled Max off the case – 'too obsessed to be objective' – they'd brought in

Don Cornwall with his flash suits and 'fresh ideas'. Max had been reprimanded on more than one occasion for treading on Cornwall's delicate toes.

Max headed for Kate's flat and told himself it was probably nothing. The girls on the streets were as twitchy as the police force right now.

He wondered, belatedly, if Kate had been trying to have a lie-in. It was doubtful, though. She was a lark, not a night owl like Max.

'How's my favourite son-in-law?' she greeted him, dropping a fleeting kiss on his cheek as she moved from table to oven.

'He's just dandy,' he said, 'despite being woken in the middle of the night by this pair.'

'Quite right, too. No point missing the best part of the day.'

She was a lot like her daughter, both in looks and temperament. Linda, too, had been a lark. To her, a lie-in had meant staying in bed until 7 a.m.

'I thought we'd drive out to Southport and mess around on the beach,' he told the kids.

Unsurprisingly, this news was met with a whoop of joy.

'Coming with us, Kate?' he asked.

'Not on your life. Far too cold to shiver on a beach while you mad things chase a football around. In any case, I've too much to do. I'm having a late spring clean of these kitchen cupboards.'

She looked at Max and he wondered what she saw. Was she wondering what her daughter had seen in him? Was she thinking that he hadn't deserved her daughter? Perhaps she was thinking that he didn't deserve her grandsons. Did she think him an idiot for finding another good woman in Jill and then blowing it?

'Enjoy your day, Max,' was all she said.

From the outside, St Lawrence's church was nothing to look at. Part brick and part stone, it could have passed for an old factory or office building if it hadn't been for its impressive tower.

When Jill pushed open the heavy door, it looked as if every member of the parish had turned up for the morning's service. The church was packed.

She slid into an empty pew right at the back and, seconds later, Tony and Liz Hutchinson came and sat beside her. The organist was already playing and they whispered their greetings.

Tony had jogged along the lane past her cottage early that morning. Getting in training for walking the Pennine Way perhaps. He'd said he was a keen runner, and he'd certainly been moving at an impressive pace.

Across the aisle, Bob – Jill didn't know his surname, just knew him as Bob the Builder – was sitting with his head bowed. She made a mental note to have a chat with him after the service if she could. She'd seen and heard enough about the winters in the Pennines to know that her roof needed attention before much longer.

Bob was sitting next to a couple Jill didn't know. She was about to ask Liz to enlighten her but Liz was in a world of her own, her gaze fixed on Bob. Even sitting, he was an impressive figure. He was a wearing a charcoal grey suit that emphasized the breadth of his shoulders. A shaft of light from a stained-glass window gave his blond hair a streak of electric blue.

Gordon and Mary Lee-Smith were sitting in a pew towards the front of the church and Jill made yet another mental note. She'd popped a thank-you note through their letterbox, but she'd catch them after the service and thank them again for the bonfire party. At the same time, she'd see how they thought Jonathan was holding up.

Just then, Jonathan and Michael walked slowly up the aisle.

The police had had to release Michael. His statement was full of inconsistencies and, in the end, he'd said that he hadn't killed his mother, and that he had no idea who had. He'd said he thought people wouldn't believe him innocent as all the evidence pointed to him.

The force, she knew, was divided. Some believed Michael was innocent, and some thought he'd cleverly talked his way out of it. Either way, they had nothing that would stand up in court.

Father and son walked side by side, united in their loss. Jonathan walked tall and erect, the only sign of his grief a ghostly pale face dominated by bloodshot eyes. Michael walked with his head bowed and his hands clasped in front of him. They sat in the empty pew in front of Gordon and Mary. Both looked as if they were attending a funeral.

The funeral was still to come of course.

The stand-in vicar took to the pulpit. He was a young chap – energetic and keen. Not surprisingly, he spoke of the tragedy and guessed the congregation was questioning its faith, something all Christians were called upon to do in times of tragedy. He then asked them all to pray for Jonathan and Michael.

Jonathan knelt to pray. Michael sat with his head bowed and a handkerchief to his nose. Jill wasn't sure if he was sobbing or if he had the beginnings of a cold. Neither contributed a lot to the hymn singing. Jonathan made a token gesture and mouthed the words. Michael stared at a spot straight ahead of him. If it hadn't been for Tony, singing loudly if tunelessly on Jill's right, and Gordon and Mary's stirring performances, the vicar might well have been left to sing alone.

When the service was over, the vicar, Jonathan and Michael all stood at the church door. The vicar thanked everyone for attending.

'I'm sure it's a comfort to the family,' he said, shaking Jill's hand.

Jill didn't argue, but neither Jonathan nor Michael looked comforted.

She walked across the grass to where Gordon and Mary

were standing. They looked as if they were waiting for someone to join them.

'I wanted to thank you for the party,' Jill said. 'I enjoyed it, and it was kind of you to invite me.'

'We're only glad you could make it,' Mary said, adding a whispered, 'Thank goodness we didn't know what lay ahead.'

Jill remembered Alice, how she'd scolded Jonathan for talking religion, how her face had lit up with pride as she'd called Michael to join them.

'Jonathan and Michael returned to the vicarage yesterday,' Mary went on in a lowered voice. 'Jonathan's coming back for lunch, but nothing would persuade Michael to join us. I hate to think of the poor boy alone at the vicarage.'

'Perhaps he needs to grieve alone,' Jill suggested. 'People deal with the grieving process differently. I expect he's trying to be strong and finding it too much effort. Far easier to cry alone sometimes.'

'Perhaps you're right,' Mary agreed.

'You're more than welcome to join us for lunch, Jill,' Gordon put in.

'Of course you are. Where are my manners?' Mary looked beside herself at the gaffe.

'That's very kind of you, but I've made other plans,' Jill said quickly.

It wasn't a lie. She'd just decided to pay Michael a visit. With his father out of the way, he might open up a little. Doubtful, but it was worth a try.

She was heading down the path, away from the church, when she spotted Bob again.

'Bob!' She broke into a run to catch up with him. 'I'm sorry, but I don't know your surname. I don't think I was told.'

He smiled at that. 'I've an even worse confession. I've forgotten your name and you're the celebrity.'

'The celebrity you'd never heard of,' she reminded him with a smile. 'Jill Kennedy.'

'Bob Murphy – at your service.' He took a business card from his suit pocket and handed it to her.

'How busy are you?' she asked. 'There's quite a bit I need doing, and I'd like it done soon. If I leave it much longer, I'll have no roof left.'

'I'm pretty busy at the moment,' he said, 'and that's unusual at this time of the year.' He took a pen and another card from his pocket. 'Give me your phone number. I'll give you a call and make an appointment to have a look. If it's not me, I'll send Len along. OK?'

She scribbled down her name and number on his card. 'I'm in and out a bit at the moment, but you can leave a message on the machine.'

'OK. I'll try and make it for the end of the week, probably late afternoon. I'll give you a ring to confirm.'

'Thanks.' A huge raindrop landed on her nose. 'Oh, great. No car and no umbrella.'

St Lawrence's had been built long before parking had been a consideration and, as it hadn't looked like rain, Jill had decided to walk.

'I'd offer you a lift,' Bob said, 'but I'm in the same boat.' He looked back at the crowd still outside the church. 'There's Len – he's my roofing man. He'll give us both a lift.'

Jill saw that he was referring to the couple with whom he'd shared his pew.

Len and his wife, Daisy, were more than happy to oblige and she and Bob climbed in the back of their elderly car.

'I've been itching to get my hands on that roof of yours,' Len told Jill as he drove them away from the church. 'Nothing bugs me more than seeing a good roof allowed to get in that state. It should have been done years ago.'

'Ah, but old Mrs Blackman didn't have the money,' Daisy reminded him. 'It would have cost more than she paid for the cottage in the first place. Mind, she had the garden lovely, didn't she?'

Len talked roofing, and Daisy talked gardens – at the same time. It was impossible to get a word in. For all that, they were a delightful couple, clearly devoted to each other. Although they'd dressed for church, there was something of the hippy about them. Len had a huge, untidy beard and his thin dark hair was tied back in a short ponytail. Daisy had long auburn hair tumbling this way and that, and bangles, rings and chains on every limb.

Minutes later, Jill was back at her cottage, waving them off. Bob would have to take her place in the conversations.

'Call on us sometime,' Daisy yelled at Jill through the open car window. 'We've got a narrowboat on the canal. Can't miss us . . .'

Jill was still chuckling to herself as she went inside the cottage. What a lovely couple. One of these days, she'd go and find that narrowboat.

Chapter Thirteen

The church clock was striking twelve as Jill parked her car on the drive at the vicarage. Hopefully, Jonathan would be at the manor by now. Not that she had any objection to seeing him, she just thought Michael might be more talkative if she could get him alone.

That, of course, was assuming he answered the door.

She rang the bell a second time.

She could understand perfectly his wish to be left alone. In the same circumstances, not that she'd ever come close to being in those circumstances, she would want to lock the world away, too.

Michael opened the door and stared blankly at her. It was as if he didn't know her, but he'd recognized her at the party.

'Oh, it's you,' he mumbled. 'Sorry, I've forgotten your name.'

'Jill. Jill Kennedy.'

'Dad's out,' he said. 'He won't be back for a couple of hours. Shall I tell him you called?'

He clearly didn't plan to invite her inside so Jill took a step forward, leaving him little option.

'That's OK. I came to see both of you really. To see how you were coping and if there was anything I could do.'

'You'd better come in then.'

She was already halfway in, but she welcomed the invitation. The hall floor was bare and her shoes clattered on the concrete.

'The carpet's – gone,' he explained. 'The police said – erm, it's been painted, too.'

The air was still heavy with the smell of paint, but better that than a murder scene.

There had been blood everywhere, according to Max. Not surprising. Alice's main artery had been slashed when she'd been in a state of panic. Her heart would have been pumping blood for all it was worth.

'Let's go in the kitchen then,' she suggested briskly, leading the way to what she hoped was the kitchen. It was. 'I don't know about you, but I practically live in my kitchen. I'll put the kettle on, shall I?'

A less polite boy would have told her to sod off, but Michael just mumbled, 'Sorry,' and began getting cups from the cupboard.

Cups and saucers rattled in his hands. He was shaking.

The kitchen was large, with a big, scrubbed pine table in the centre of the room. The units were old, but clean and serviceable. Tea, coffee and sugar containers sat in a neat row near the kettle.

'I'd like coffee if that's all right,' Jill said. 'How about you?'

'Mmm? Oh, yes, coffee's fine.'

He wanted her gone, she knew that.

'Are you back at school tomorrow?' she asked, and he nodded. 'I bet your friends are missing you.'

'Er, yes. Oh, I wouldn't think my friends –'

'I bet your girlfriend is,' she put in quickly.

'Girlfriend? I don't have a girlfriend.' But the hot blush that spread across his face told Jill otherwise.

'Come on, you don't have to be shy with me!' She nudged him in an all-pals-together sort of way. 'Besides, I saw you with her.'

'Oh.'

So he did have a girlfriend.

'I was exactly the same at your age,' she rushed on, knowing she had never been like this vulnerable young man. 'If I so much as mentioned a boy's name to my parents, they'd want to know it all. Then, knowing it all, they would decide he wasn't right for me. In the end, I kept quiet.'

He listened politely, but didn't comment.

'So what's she like? Lovely, I bet. Does she go to the same school?'

He gave her a suspicious look. 'No. Er, she's older.'

'Really? I only saw her from the back. Is she pretty like your mum?'

'Yes.' He smiled shyly.

Their coffee ready, Jill made herself comfortable at the table, leaving him little choice but to do likewise. Except he didn't look comfortable.

'I wish I'd known your mum better,' Jill said. 'I only met her at the party, but she seemed a lovely woman. Very pretty, too, and a stunning figure. I envied her that. Comes of being a dancer, I suppose. Your dad said she'd written me a note, inviting me to lunch. That was so kind of her. She was a kind lady.'

'Yes. We miss her.'

His immaculate manners would drive Jill crazy. He knew something, she was sure of it.

'Any news?' she asked. 'Have the police come up with anything? What about that red van your dad saw? You didn't see it, did you?'

'I don't remember seeing anything on the road.'

'Your dad arrived only minutes after you, didn't he?'

'Yes.' He cleared his throat. 'Look, I'd rather not talk about it if you don't mind.'

'Of course. Sorry.'

The house was freezing and she shivered. She was glad she'd chosen to wear a thick jumper.

'You must come to me for lunch one day,' she said. 'No need to make it lunch, either. Call in any time. I'm a good listener and sometimes it helps to get away from home, doesn't it?'

'Thanks.'

'My cooking's pretty dire,' she told him, 'but I always

have plenty of cakes and biscuits, tea and coffee. There's always a can of beer or a bottle of Scotch, too,' she added with a smile. 'Call in, Michael. I don't get many visitors and the cats would like the company.'

'Cats?'

His world was disintegrating yet the mention of cats had sparked his interest. Jill supposed the subject offered him an uncomplicated, easy escape from his problems.

'I knew you had one cat,' he added. 'I've seen it about.'

'I've got three. One's sixteen, a black and white female who keeps the other two in line. The other, Sam, is eight now – a big, fat, lazy tom. And the third, a pretty black and white tuxedo, adopted me. When I lived in Preston, I knew a cat was coming in at night and stealing food. Sometimes, if I crept into the kitchen, I'd be in time to see a black tail vanishing through the cat flap. After a week or so, I found her sitting on the kitchen chair. The poor thing was too tired, too ill and too hungry to escape.'

'Ah, shame.' At least she had his interest. If she could gain his trust as well, she might get somewhere.

'I took her to the vet and he gave her a shot of antibiotics for an infection. While she was there, he found she had a microchip. I was hoping that some poor person had lost the cat.'

'Did they trace the owner?'

'Yup.' Jill grinned. 'Officially, Tojo is stolen goods.'

'How come?' He was smiling, too.

'Later that day, I had a phone call from a woman who said, "I believe you've got my cat." She didn't sound very friendly. Anyway, it turned out she only lived at the back of my place. Her kitchen window was always open so the cat could have gone back any time. She asked if the cat was still with me, and I lied. I said she'd run off as soon as I'd got back from the vet's. I even promised to call the woman if I saw the cat.'

He laughed at that, and Jill wondered if it was the first time he'd laughed since his mother had been murdered.

'It's a special feeling to be chosen by a cat,' she said

thoughtfully. 'Anyway,' she went on briskly, 'you must come and see her. She's a gorgeous little thing. Not that she's little now. She's fat. The others are, too. They love visitors though.'

'I will. Thanks.'

'Promise?'

There was a long pause as he made up his mind.

'Promise,' he said at last.

'Good.' Jill got to her feet. She'd done all she could for now. There was no point alienating him. 'I'm truly sorry about your mother, Michael. I don't have your dad's faith in God, so I can't offer any help in that direction, but I do know that time heals. It's a trite saying, one that probably infuriates you now as everyone will be telling you that, but it really is true.'

'Thanks,' he said gruffly.

'I'll be off then. No need to see me out. I'll see you soon, Michael. Hey, bring your girlfriend too. The more the merrier!'

As she walked away from the vicarage, she thought of all she'd learned. The main thing was that Michael had a girlfriend. How much older was she? Was she twenty? Perhaps she was in her thirties even. If that were the case, there was no doubt that Michael's father would disapprove strongly. Alice, no matter how much she loved her son, and no matter how easy-going and fun-loving she was, would have hated that, too.

The main thing at the moment was gaining Michael's trust and she was fairly confident he'd be a visitor at Lilac Cottage before long.

Chapter Fourteen

'So what was she like?' Max asked.

Jim Brody, the Truemans' gardener, had been interviewed before. Grace thought they were wasting their time, but Max thought it worth talking to him again, mainly because the cleaner had said he got on well with Alice Trueman.

'Alice would spend hours talking to him,' the Truemans' cleaner had said.

No one liked to speak ill of the dead, but usually someone had something unkind to say about some member of the family. Not the Trueman family it seemed. As yet, not one person had said a bad word about any of them.

'I've told your people all this before,' Brody pointed out.

Max ignored the expression on Grace's face. 'I know, but humour me, will you?'

Brody sighed, and he was struggling to look Max in the eye.

They were in Brody's lounge, an untidy, cluttered room, but homely for all that. It was a homely sort of house, old and detached, with an enviable garden. One would expect the garden, Max supposed, as it was a good way of advertising a trade, yet this one was more peaceful than showy.

Constantly in the shadow of Brody's feet was a dog, a sleek black and white border collie that Ben would have killed for. Her eyes never left Brody's face, and she was poised and alert for any move he might make.

'Alice was always good to me,' Brody said at last. 'Not

like some I've worked for. She was one who'd invite you inside to shelter from a sudden downpour, or bring you a cold drink on a hot day. Some folk look down on you, but not her.'

'Are you married?' Max asked, and Brody stared at him in amazement. 'Just curious,' Max explained.

'No,' Brody told him.

'How did Alice get along with her husband?' Max asked.

'All right, I imagine. Look, I was only the gardener.'

'I know that, but you must have formed an impression. I didn't know her, yet I've been given a picture of a fun-loving woman who used to love dancing.' He scratched his head. 'I can't imagine a woman like that living with a man like Jonathan Trueman.'

'Because he was a vicar?' Brody scoffed.

'Partly, I suppose. But vicar or not, he doesn't strike me as a party animal.'

Brody shrugged. 'I wouldn't know.'

'According to the cleaner, Mrs Trueman used to spend a lot of time talking to you.'

'So what? Plenty of folk have an interest in their gardens. Not much point me putting an area to grass when what they wanted was a rose garden, is there?'

None at all, Max thought, but surely they wouldn't have spoken only of the garden. Max was no gardener, far preferring to have a big lawn that only needed mowing once a week, and he couldn't believe there was that much to discuss.

'You must have talked about other things. She must have said something in passing. People do.'

'No.'

Call it intuition or gut instinct, but Max was convinced Brody knew something.

He wished people would talk, it would make his job much easier. This case should be cut and dried by now. They didn't talk, though. Villagers looked out for their own. They knew all there was to know about their neighbours, but wouldn't divulge anything to outsiders. And Max was an outsider. Worse, he was a copper. He'd have liked to get Jill more involved, but even she was an outsider. As the new woman, she wouldn't be trusted. Bloody villages. Max hated them.

'You must have liked her,' he pushed on, 'so you must want her killer put where he belongs.'

Brody didn't comment.

'Are you sure there's nothing you can tell me? Someone who disliked her? Some family problem?'

'Nothing.'

Max knew he would get nowhere. 'Give me a call if you think of anything,' he said.

'I will.' Brody was quickly ushering them out of the house, eager to get rid of them, but Max stopped in the open doorway.

'Lovely garden,' he remarked.

'Thanks.'

'Kelton Bridge is a decent village, isn't it?' Max persisted, turning to look at him. 'A friend of mine has just moved here, Jill Kennedy. I assume you've met her?'

'Kennedy?' Brody shook his head. 'I don't think so. Where is she? Up on the estate?'

'No. She's along Pennine View. Her place, Lilac Cottage, is at the end of the lane.'

'Ah, that'll be Mrs Blackman's old place. I knew someone had moved in there. How's she settling in?'

'She loves it,' Max said, wondering why Brody was friendlier and easier to talk to when he wasn't discussing the murder of Alice Trueman.

Brody's dog nudged Max's hand and licked his finger.

'Lovely dog,' Max said, bending to stroke the animal's head.

'Holly's a good one,' Brody agreed. 'She doesn't usually take to strangers. I suppose she's a one-man dog. I've had dogs all my life, but never one like Holly. I don't know why she's like that.'

Max, feeling honoured, fussed the dog some more before leaving.

'While we're here, Grace,' he said, 'we'll have another word with the Truemans' cleaner. She works mornings, and should be at the vicarage till twelve.'

'Right,' Grace replied, voice clipped to register her feelings on the matter.

Molly Turnbull was indeed at the vicarage.

'There's only me here,' she said as she opened the door to them.

'It's you we've come to see,' Max told her.

There was an exception to every rule and, in Kelton Bridge, Molly Turnbull was that exception. She loved to be the centre of attention. The other villagers might close ranks, but Molly loved to talk.

'We've been chatting to Mr Brody, the gardener,' he explained, 'and thought we'd have another chat with you while we were in the village.'

'You'd better have a cup of tea then,' she said.

While she clattered around, she talked non-stop. None of it was of any interest to Max, but he let her ramble on for a while.

'Mr Brody says he and Alice only used to talk about the garden,' he got in eventually.

'Is that so? Well, it's not my place to contradict him but I can't believe that.' She lowered her voice to a whisper. 'The only times I heard Alice laugh were when she were in the garden with him. Can't see that talking about the garden would make her laugh, can you?'

'Not my idea of a joke, Molly.'

'Quite. She had a soft spot for Jim Brody, you mark my words.'

'Are you sure?'

'I suppose there's only her would know that,' Molly allowed, 'but she were always eager to go and chat to him and, like I said, he used to make her laugh. The rest of the time, she were quiet – lonely, I always reckoned. Of course, Mr Trueman were out and about all the time doing his good deeds in the parish. Perhaps she were different when he were home. Perhaps he made her laugh.'

'Perhaps he did,' Max agreed.

Molly pushed a plate of biscuits in front of them, and Max took a couple of chocolate ones.

'How big a soft spot do you think she had for him?' Grace asked.

'A big one, I reckon,' Molly said. 'Not that she would have done anything about it. She wasn't the flirty type if you know what I mean.'

Max and Grace nodded to indicate that yes, they knew what she meant.

'What about Brody?' Max munched on a biscuit. 'How do you think he felt about her? Did he realize she had a certain fondness for him, do you think? Did he look forward to their chats?'

'I always thought so. I never saw anything improper, but I reckon they had a certain way of looking at one another. Put it this way, I wouldn't want my Ronnie looking at a woman like that.'

'Really?'

As Molly told them all about her Ronnie, Max's mind went through the possibilities. How would Michael have felt if he'd seen the glances between his mother and the gardener? Would he have been angry with his mother? Angry enough to kill her? Was there more than a certain fondness on both sides? Was Michael jealous? He was a strange kid, no doubt about that.

'My Ronnie reckons I read too many Mills & Boons,' Molly was saying. 'I told him I thought Alice were a bit too friendly with Jim Brody, and he laughed at me. Said I were talking nonsense, and that I were too much of a romantic. Perhaps he's right.'

'There's nothing wrong with a touch of romance, Molly,' Grace said.

Max, surprised the word romance even existed in Grace's vocabulary, helped himself to another biscuit.

'A friend of mine's just moved to Kelton Bridge,' he remarked casually. 'Jill Kennedy. Have you met her yet?'

'No, but I've heard all about her. Moved into old Mrs Blackman's place, used to be one of them psychiatrists but gave it up.'

'Psychologist,' Max corrected her.

'All the same to me,' Molly said, and Max had to smile. It was all the same to most people.

'Andy Collins sold the cottage to her,' Molly added. 'Nice spot there, so long as you don't mind being a bit cut off.'

'It is,' Max agreed.

'Anyone new comes to the village and people talk about them until the next person moves in,' she said. 'So yes, I've heard all about her.'

'And what are people saying about her?'

'Pleasant enough, clever, keeps herself to herself. Nothing scandalous,' she added with a laugh, 'but that'll come later. If they can't find any skeletons in her cupboard, they'll invent a few. That's village life for you.' She was about to pour them a second cup of tea, then paused. 'Ah, I remember now. It was her were in the news when you lot thought you'd caught that serial killer, weren't it?'

'Yes.'

'Now who were telling me about that?' She poured them each a cup of tea. 'Can't remember. Perhaps it were Tony Hutchinson. Yes, I reckon it were him. I clean there, too. A couple of afternoons a week.'

'Tony Hutchinson?'

'Headmaster of the primary school,' Molly explained. 'His wife Liz has a drink problem.' That last came in a hushed whisper.

'Does she?'

'Yes. Mind you, I reckon I'd turn to drink if I were married to him. He's all right, I suppose, but a bit of a know it all. Reckons he's cleverer than the rest of us. S'pose he is, but no need to rub it in, is there?'

'There isn't,' Grace agreed.

By the time they left the vicarage, they'd heard the life stories of most of Kelton's residents.

'Don't tell me,' Grace said, as they got in the car, 'we're going to see this Hutchinson chap.'

'May as well,' Max replied.

Tony Hutchinson had already been questioned and his story about being at the school when Alice Trueman was murdered checked out. Max was curious, though. No one had bothered Jill for a year. Now, just when she moves to Kelton Bridge, someone starts paying interest. Some creep was trying to frighten her, and it had to be connected with her move to Kelton Bridge. As far as he could discover, the only person who'd mentioned her work had been Tony Hutchinson when chatting to Molly Turnbull.

Max would have liked to talk to the man at home, he always preferred speaking to people on their own ground, but he didn't want to hang around Kelton Bridge all afternoon so he drove them up to the school.

Dozens of kids were chasing each other round the playground when they arrived yet, at the sound of a bell droning out, they formed two orderly lines and walked back into the building. Max was impressed. He was also surprised at how many kids attended the village school. Kelton Bridge was bigger than it looked, though. Two large estates had been built within the last ten years, which must have doubled the village's population.

After a quick word with the school secretary, they were immediately shown into the headmaster's office. The school building was old, and the office, with its modern desk, state-of-the-art computer, and executive leather chair came as a surprise.

'I assume you've come about poor Alice,' Tony Hutchinson said when they'd shaken hands. 'A terrible thing. I don't think anyone has come to terms with it yet.'

'I'm sure everyone wants the culprit found as much as we do,' Max agreed. 'It's difficult to move on until then. Now, I know you've spoken to us before, but I'd be grateful if you could tell me all you can about Alice. At the moment, we're hoping that someone can think of something and put us on the right track.'

The office window overlooked a large field with a rugby pitch and hockey pitch marked out. No children were making use of the facilities on this damp, grey day.

'Does Jim Brody look after this?' Max asked, nodding at the pitches.

'No. Our groundsman is ex-Man United,' the headmaster informed him with a touch of pride. 'Here, take a seat.'

Max and Grace pulled lightweight blue chairs close to his desk and sat.

'I've thought and thought about Alice,' Tony Hutchinson said, 'and yet there's nothing – well, nothing of importance. She was a very popular woman, the sort any husband could be proud of, the sort that got on well with the other women in the village. Always willing to help. A very unselfish person.'

'What about friends? Or enemies?'

'I can't think of a single enemy.' Tony fiddled with his pencil. 'Do you know, I've never heard anyone say a bad word about her.' He smiled. 'And that's rare in a village like this.'

'Yes, I'm sure it is.'

'But friends – she didn't really have close friends. Or none that I knew of. She wasn't the type to go on girls' nights out or anything like that. She seemed happy enough with her family. I always believed that was enough for her.' He put his pencil down on the desk. 'I'm sorry I can't be of more help, but there's nothing else I can say.'

Molly had called Alice Trueman a saint, and Max was beginning to believe it. No one's life was this squeaky clean.

'When was the last time you saw her?' Grace asked.

'Ah, that's easy. Mary and Gordon Lee-Smith live at the manor and they'd invited us to a bonfire party. Alice was there with Jon and young Michael.'

'I've heard about the party,' Max said. 'A friend of mine was there. Jill Kennedy. Did you meet her?'

'Oh, yes.' Hutchinson's face lit up. 'We had a lovely long chat. Of course, you'll have worked with her when she did that profile for the serial killer?'

'Yes, that's right.'

'Fascinating work – hers and yours.'

The last thing Max would call his work right now was fascinating. Soul-destroying was more accurate. All it consisted of was talking to hundreds of people, one of whom might have something of interest to say, and wading through endless paperwork. He was dog tired and getting nowhere.

'My wife thought I made a nuisance of myself,' Hutchinson added. 'She didn't think I should have sounded so enthusiastic about Jill's work. After all, she must have felt bad when that chap hanged himself. You all must.'

Felt bad? He wouldn't be surprised if Jill still had nightmares. Not that she'd admit it.

'There was evidence linking the man to the murders,' Max said carefully.

'And he matched Jill's profile. Fascinating stuff.'

That word again – fascinating. Few people found it fascinating. Most were appalled that the killer was still on the loose. Many drew comparisons with the Yorkshire Ripper and the force's inability to catch him, too.

'This party at the Lee-Smiths' place,' Max said, changing the subject. 'How did Alice appear?'

'Her normal self,' Hutchinson said. 'She looked happy enough, didn't seem to have a care in the world.'

'She was with her husband, yes?'

'Yes, and Michael. They all seemed happy. But why not? They were just a normal family.'

Life in a normal family didn't involve having your throat cut from ear to ear. Well, not in Max's experience.

'What colour car do you drive, Mr Hutchinson?'

'What?' He laughed at what he considered the absurdity of the question. 'Grey. A dark grey BMW. Why?'

'Just curious. Do you know anyone who drives a red van?'

'I do,' Hutchinson replied, still laughing. 'The postman!' More serious, he went on, 'Drives like a maniac, too. Always in a hurry, that lad.'

'So I believe.'

That lad was Carl Astley. He was twenty-six years old and enjoyed the challenge of delivering mail in record time. When Alice Trueman was murdered, however, he'd been on a fortnight's holiday in Cyprus with his girlfriend.

'Dead cheap at this time of the year,' he'd told Max, 'and still lots happening.'

His replacement was Wilf who was coming up to retirement. On the day Alice was murdered, he'd finished his round early and had been on his allotment, with witnesses, when Jonathan Trueman saw the red vehicle.

'Can you think of anyone else who drives a red van or a red car?' Max asked.

'How long have you got?'

'I'd be grateful for some names,' Max told him, ignoring his sarcasm.

Hutchinson wrote down half a dozen names and handed the slip of paper to Max. However, there was nothing else to be learned and they left soon afterwards.

'That was a waste of time, guv,' Grace complained.

Not entirely, Max thought. At least he'd found someone who, to him at any rate, had an unhealthy interest in Jill's work. A fascination even.

Chapter Fifteen

Jill couldn't sleep. She'd put the radio on quietly, hoping that would take her mind off things, but the inane chat between the presenter and his female guest was so irritating that she'd switched it off. She tossed and turned, thumping her pillow into shape, but it was no use. Her mind was too full.

She still hadn't visited her parents and the guilt was really kicking in now. Perhaps next weekend. She owed them. Given different parents, she could have turned out like Anne Levington, a sixteen-year-old prostitute.

The River View estate had bred more than enough wastrels. It brought a whole new meaning to that old joke, What do you call a scally in a suit? Answer: The accused. If you came from River View, it was too close to the truth to be funny.

Without her mum pushing her at school and constantly reminding her that education was the only path out of River View, things would have been very different for Jill. Mum had worked at every job going – cleaning at various places during the day and pulling pints at night. At the time, Jill had been closer to her dad. It was to him she'd gone for fun and laughter. It was he who'd shown her the thrill of doubling or, more often, losing her pocket money on racehorses. Dad she had idolized, yet Mum was responsible for the person she was today. Her education, her qualifications, her work, her cottage – without her mum, she'd have none of that.

Sadly for Anne Levington, she hadn't had a mum like

Jill's. She'd had an absent drunk for a father, and a mother who'd kicked her out. She was sixteen! Just a kid. But perhaps that was in her favour. Valentine's victims had all been in their early thirties. Jill thought he was fond of children. If he'd been abused as a child, or if his siblings had, either physically or mentally, it was likely he'd have an affinity with them. Perhaps she was wrong about that, too.

What exactly drove Valentine? God, how many times had she asked herself that?

He was strong, they knew that much, and the victims never had long to fight for their lives. Other than the marks of strangulation, and the hearts cut from their skin, there were no bruises or lacerations. He treated their dead bodies with a degree of respect. It was as if, once he killed them, they were no longer prostitutes and therefore objects of hatred to him, but decent human beings again. He was cleaning up the world single-handed.

Oh, she hoped young Anne was safe. The thought of Valentine attacking her, a child, made her sick to her stomach. The photo given to the media had shown Anne in school uniform. There weren't any more recent photos. None had been taken in the last two years.

'Her hair's red now,' her mother had said in an emotionless TV interview. 'Or it were the last time I saw it.'

Jill switched on the bedside lamp and glanced at the clock. It was nearly midnight. She picked up the phone and hit the button for Max's mobile. It was answered almost immediately.

'Hiya.'

'Sorry, did I wake you?'

'No, I've only just got in. What has you awake at this time of night?'

'Anne Levington.' She got straight to the point.

'Ah.'

'What do you know about her?'

She could hear the chink of a bottle hitting a glass, and then liquid being poured.

'She has three sisters, aged eight, nine and eleven,' Max told her, 'and they're all at home. I gather it was left to Anne to look after them all – the mother was pretty much out of it. However, the father seemed to hold the family together until he was made redundant, lost his own father and discovered his wife had had an affair – all in the same week. He went on a drunken binge and left the lot of them. He's been living in Ireland, but he's on his way back to England. The mother's a nasty piece of work, and threw Anne out. Told her it was time she fended for herself and stopped relying on handouts. Anne started begging, then turned to prostitution.'

Jill shuddered. How on earth was a sixteen-year-old expected to cope on the streets? Apart from anything else, it was the middle of November and bitterly cold. Her heart wept for the girl.

'It's not like Valentine to choose such a young victim,' she pointed out.

'I know,' he agreed, 'but sixteen-year-olds look a lot older these days. Her eleven-year-old sister could pass for sixteen.'

Jill heard him take a swallow of what she suspected was whisky.

'She is young, and that's in her favour,' he went on, 'but I don't like it.'

Jill didn't either. So long as Valentine was on the loose, and God, he was proving difficult to find, there would be more missing girls to worry about, more lives snuffed out.

'What do you know about Tony Hutchinson?' he asked, and the change of subject took her completely by surprise.

'The headmaster? Not a lot. He's not a person I could warm to. I gather his wife has the same problem,' she said, 'as I sensed some bitterness and resentment between them. Mind you, I've only seen them together once, at the party at the manor, so they might have had a tiff or something that night.'

'I wasn't too keen, either. He seems interested in you, though.'

'How do you mean?'

'I don't know,' Max admitted. 'He just seemed to have an unhealthy interest in you and your work.'

'Oh, that. He's just a general pain in the arse. He started a psychology course apparently. He's harmless enough.'

'Sure?'

Now she came to think of it, Jill didn't know what to make of Tony. That evening at The Weaver's Retreat, she'd felt distinctly uncomfortable in his presence. Could he be the crank sending her photos and cards? If it was him, it would be a relief in a way. Better Tony Hutchinson than Valentine. But why would he do such a thing? Because he was jealous of psychologists and the glamorous way they were portrayed in newspapers and TV dramas? Did a headmaster's lot seem dull by comparison? Did he feel he was twice as clever and could have caught Valentine single-handed by now?

'I'm sure he's harmless,' she said slowly, 'but you're right, he is very interested in my work. He's another *Silence of the Lambs* fan,' she added with a sigh.

'He's a cocky sod.'

'Yes, he is.'

'So,' Max said slowly, 'what's keeping Anne Levington on your mind? Are you thinking of taking Meredith up on his offer?'

She didn't know. All she knew was that there was no hiding from Valentine. Until he was caught, there would be no peace for any of them.

'I keep feeling I should help if I can. Meredith's right. I've got good qualifications and a lot of experience behind me.'

'Exactly!' Max sounded pleased.

'Hopefully, Anne Levington will turn up safe and sound,' she said.

'Hopefully,' he agreed. 'But until Valentine's caught, there will be others who don't.'

On that chilling note, Jill said goodnight.

Chapter Sixteen

Jill had been sitting with her laptop on her knees, typing up all she could remember of Valentine. Amazingly, despite trying her damnedest to forget, she knew the case by heart.

When she answered her door to find Michael Trueman standing there, she couldn't have been more pleased.

'A visitor! Wonderful. Just the excuse I need. Come in, Michael.' Again, she was going to do most of the talking and hope that, by doing so, she could coax him to relax with her.

She switched off her computer, put it back on the desk, and took him into the kitchen.

'If I've come at a bad time, just say so,' he murmured shyly.

'You couldn't have chosen a better time. It's lovely to see you, and to have some company. Some days, I get so involved in my writing that I don't speak to a soul all day. I'll be getting cabin fever if I don't watch out.'

He was already stooping to stroke a cat.

'That's Tojo, the one who adopted me,' she explained. 'She doesn't look so sorry for herself these days, the fat thing. When I got her, she'd already been spayed, but she often looks as if she's about to give birth to half a dozen kittens.'

'She's lovely,' he said, and he sounded wistful.

Perhaps no pets had been allowed at the vicarage.

'Sam's upstairs, asleep on my bed,' she went on, 'but he'll amble down to see you in a minute. And Rabble, the old one, is eyeing up birds in the garden. She's far too old and stiff to catch them now, thank heavens, but she still likes to sit and scowl at them.'

He smiled at that, then stooped to pick up Tojo. The cat, always delighted to be the centre of attention, sat happily in his arms, purring loudly. Tojo loved rough and tumble, and enjoyed nothing more than a boxing match with Sam, but Michael was infinitely gentle with her and she responded by giving his fingers a touchingly light lick.

The scene reminded her of the story Tony Hutchinson had told her, of the way Michael had worried about the injured bird he'd found.

Michael was a gentle, sensitive person who needed a lot of love. He needed to feel secure, yet he looked very frail and vulnerable right now. More than that, he looked ill. He had a green, washed-out look about him, like someone who'd spent the last eight hours being seasick.

'Do you have any pets?' she asked.

'No. Mum always wanted a cat, and we had one for a while, a stray kitten that used to call for food, but my father doesn't like them.'

An only child with no pets must have a lonely existence.

'What about friends? Do you see any of their pets?'

'Not really.'

He was more interested in Tojo than anything else and, probably without thinking, wandered into the sitting room and sat in the armchair. Tojo was more than happy to sit on his lap.

'Tell me about this girlfriend of yours then,' Jill suggested lightly, sitting on the floor facing him. 'When do you manage to see her? Does she work?' She saw his hesitation. 'Don't worry, my lips are sealed. Not even Olive Prendergast manages to wheedle gossip out of me.'

His smiles when they came were worth waiting for. They changed his whole demeanour, making him look like a young man who would enjoy fun – if only he were given the chance.

'Her name's Becky.' He spoke in little more than a whisper. 'She works in the baker's, on the counter.'

Not a job that would go down well with his father.

'In the village? The shop with all the scrummy cream cakes in the window?'

'Yes. Green's.'

Jill, always a sucker for freshly baked bread, often shopped there. Whenever she'd been inside, there had been two women serving behind the counter. One had to be in her fifties. Joan, was she? The other was probably about thirty.

The shop's van was often parked outside. A red van. Coincidence? It was a red van with 'Green's, Bakers of Distinction' and a phone number printed on the sides.

'Did you meet her at the shop?' she asked.

'Yes. Well, almost. She has a cigarette break and stands outside to smoke. We got talking one day.' He looked embarrassed.

'That's nice.' Nice probably wasn't how Jonathan Trueman would describe it. 'Does she live in Kelton?'

'No, she lives in Bacup. Her uncle owns the baker's in Kelton, and she's helping him out while she looks for another job.'

'Oh? And what does she want to do?'

'She hasn't decided yet.'

Jill pictured the two women in the baker's. Both seemed highly unlikely candidates for Michael's affections, but he had to be talking about the younger one.

'She's very attractive, isn't she? Tall, too. And I really envy her long blonde hair'

He blushed. 'Yes, she is pretty.'

One thing was clear at least, Alice Trueman would have disapproved of the relationship almost as much as the Reverend Jonathan Trueman. Almost.

Jill hadn't spoken to Becky, it was always the other woman who served her, but young Becky looked as if she ought to be taming Eminem. She'd swallow and spit out the likes of Michael without even noticing. Of course, she could be doing the girl a grave injustice. Perhaps she was just as sensitive and gentle as Michael. Jill doubted it.

'She's, erm, quite a bit older than me,' he admitted.

About twelve years, Jill guessed.

'She's thirty.'

Spot on.

'Really? Well, that seems a lot now, but the gap always appears smaller as you get older. Some friends of mine have been happily married for more than ten years now and they share the same age gap. Karen is twelve years older than Peter.'

'We're only friends,' Michael said and, again, he sounded wistful.

'Does she get out and about? Do the deliveries? I think I've seen the van about.'

'No.' His expression was guarded. 'She just serves in the shop.'

Rabble chose that moment to wander inside and while Michael leaned out of his chair to make a fuss of her, Jill wondered if he'd got as far as kissing Becky. She doubted it. Perhaps that was no bad thing, but he desperately needed a friend.

Predictably, as Rabble was being fussed, Tojo jumped off Michael's lap and wandered off to the kitchen.

'She's very fickle,' Jill explained.

Michael was stroking Rabble with a hand that was shaking violently. Had talk of a red van brought that on?

'I don't know what to do,' he burst out. He looked to Jill as if she might have all the answers.

No hope of that. She didn't have the questions let alone the answers.

'You talk,' Jill said urgently. 'If you know anything about your mother's murder, and I believe you do, you have to talk.'

'I'm sorry,' he whispered. 'So sorry.'

'Don't be hard on yourself, Michael. You've lost your mother and I'm sure you were very close. Everyone expects you to grieve; everybody knows the pain you're in. You don't have to wear a brave face all the time, you know.'

'I don't know what to do,' he said again, his voice thick with anguish.

She knelt on the floor in front of him.

'Talk, Michael,' she urged him. 'You have to talk – for your sake and everyone else's. You've enough to deal with without bottling that up. You can talk to anyone – another vicar, the police, your GP, your father, me – but you need to talk.'

He seemed to recoil when she suggested talking to his father, but perhaps it was the idea of talking to anyone. For the moment, he was choosing to keep things to himself.

'Can't you talk to Becky?'

He shook his head. 'I'll have to go.' He got to his feet, rubbed his handkerchief around his eyes, blew his nose on it, and returned it to his pocket. 'Thank you for – Thanks, Jill. I'll see you again.'

Damn.

'Make sure you do.' She had to rush to the door to get there before he was gone. 'And if you need to talk, I'm here. Day or night,' she called out.

He turned to wave as he walked down her path.

Chapter Seventeen

Jill had given in and accepted Andy's invitation to lunch. It was a means of escaping Michael's problems, and a chance to forget about Valentine for a while.

She had arranged to meet Andy at The Ram, midway between Todmorden and Burnley. Jill had been there before. It had the relaxed atmosphere of a pub coupled with the welcome addition of a varied menu and delicious food.

'Have you had a chance to speak to Bob yet?' Andy asked when they'd ordered.

'I have and he's coming out tomorrow afternoon to look the place over and give me a quote.'

'He won't let you down. It'll be a fair price and he'll do a good job.' He laughed suddenly. 'I'll bet he's glad to be doing the work, too. Mrs Blackman was forever getting him to price up the work, and she never got as far as having it done.'

'She was getting on a bit, though,' Jill pointed out. 'I expect it was too much hassle.'

'Yes, that's one reason she moved down to Devon, I think. She wanted to be nearer her family – two of her daughters live down there now. There's the money involved, too,' he added with an amused shake of his head. 'She and her late husband bought your cottage for eighteen hundred pounds and –'

Jill laughed at that.

'It's true,' Andy went on. 'She couldn't believe it when I told her what it was worth. The thought of spending more than that on getting the roof fixed was too much for her.'

Jill remembered being told much the same thing when Daisy and Len had given her and Bob a lift home from the church.

Jill wanted the work done as soon as possible. Then, when she didn't have to worry about loose tiles being torn off in the gales, or old windows falling out, she might be able to sit back and enjoy life in the village.

Their food was put in front of them.

'This looks delicious. I'm starving.' Jill immediately began tucking in.

'I have to eat out regularly or I'd starve,' Andy admitted with amusement. 'I expect I could cook if I put my mind to it, but I can never see the point. It's a lot of fuss when there's only one to cook for. Do you find that?'

'I certainly do. I hate cooking and exist on stuff out of packets. If I can't take something out of the freezer and slam it in the microwave, I'm not interested.' She grinned at him. 'You need a wife. Why haven't you married?'

'Why haven't you?' he retorted.

'I have.'

The laugh died on his face to be replaced by embarrassment and shock. 'I had no idea. So you're divorced?'

'Widowed.'

'I am so sorry.'

'It was a while ago.' She couldn't deal with sympathy. If Chris hadn't got himself shot, they would have been divorced by now. Sympathy seemed out of place given the circumstances. 'Why haven't you married?'

'I've never met the right woman,' he said at last. 'It's as simple as that.'

'Ever come close?' she asked.

'Nope.'

'Hey, this is delicious.' It was a long time since she'd had a traditional roast on a Sunday.

'Isn't it? It almost makes me wish I was still living with my mother,' he said with a smile. 'She always made a big thing of Sunday lunch – roast beef with all the trimmings followed by a mouth-watering apple pie and thick custard.'

'Couldn't you visit her on Sundays?'

'Not really. Besides, now she lives on her own, she doesn't bother.'

'Your father?'

'He died.'

'I'm sorry.'

He didn't elaborate and Jill didn't want to pry. This was supposed to be a relaxing lunch with a friend. She was still wary of getting too involved yet she did want to settle in the village and make friends.

'I would like to,' he said, confusing her.

'To what?'

'Meet the right person,' he said softly.

Jill's fork, with a tender piece of beef on it, hovered midway between her plate and her mouth as she tried to figure out if she was being chatted up. What would her sister make of him? Married with kids, and beginning to believe there was something wrong with Jill, Prue would probably suggest she snap him up before someone else did.

He was certainly husband material. Good-looking, a steady job that gave him a decent lifestyle . . . Perhaps, like her, he was 'too picky' as Prue was always saying.

'Then I'm sure you will,' she said briskly.

'Marriage is a funny business, though,' he went on. 'You only have to look round Kelton to see that. There's Tony and Liz for a start. I'm sure they're madly in love but they spend half their time quarrelling.'

'Do they? What about?'

'I've no idea,' he said, 'but I suspect Liz's drinking doesn't help.'

'Does she have a real problem?'

'I've heard she has a bottle of vodka most days, and that's before she goes out in the evening.'

Jill grimaced.

'And, of course, Tony's into this keep fit lark,' Andy went on.

'It doesn't seem to be doing him much harm,' Jill replied. 'I see him running past my cottage most days. He's in great shape for his age.'

'Yes, he is.'

Jill gained the impression he wasn't too keen on Tony, either.

'What about Jonathan and Alice Trueman? They had a good marriage, didn't they?'

'I imagine so, yes. Who knows what goes on behind closed doors, though?'

'True.'

'Jon said you were there – with the police, I mean – when Michael was being questioned. Are you working with them again?'

'No. Well, not yet.' But she would be. She had no choice. 'I was visiting friends there,' she explained.

'Will you help them catch the serial killer? They're still no closer to catching him, are they?'

'Not that I've heard.'

'Will you work on that again?'

'Oh, I don't know.' There was no need to discuss it with him.

'Liz – Tony's wife – was saying that she was getting too scared to go out at night. I told her she's safe enough. His victims have only been prostitutes, haven't they?'

'Are far as I know, yes.'

'That's what I told her. Silly for someone like her to worry.'

He didn't say so, not in so many words, but he seemed to have the 'only prostitutes so it didn't matter' attitude and Jill realized, sadly, that he'd just slipped in her estimation. Anne Levington, the sixteen-year-old who'd had such a terrible start in life, was more than 'only a prostitute'.

'Every woman should be on her guard,' Jill said, putting down her knife and fork, her plate empty.

There was no saying that his next victim would be a

prostitute. People assumed that Valentine was mentally unstable, 'a nutter' as one police officer had described him, but in his own way, Valentine was clever. The murders were all planned to the last detail. He wasn't careless or sloppy. Each murder was carried out with precision. And a killer, like anyone else in a different profession, developed and grew. Just as an office clerk would seek promotion, so a killer would get more and more ambitious.

'Then we'll have to hope they soon catch him.' Andy smiled at her. 'God, this is gloomy talk for a Sunday. Tell me about yourself. Where do you come from originally? I mean, I know you moved from Preston, but you don't come from that area, do you?'

'Liverpool,' she told him, glad of the change of subject. 'My parents and my sister and her family still live there.'

'Older or younger sister?'

'Younger. And married with kids, as my mum never fails to point out. What about you?'

'There's only my mother. She lives in Manchester and I don't see much of her. Dessert?' he asked and, laughing, she shook her head.

'I couldn't eat another thing. Coffee would be good, though.'

Over coffee they talked of books, films and music they enjoyed and Jill was amazed to discover their tastes were similar.

'I love the old black and white films,' she told him.

'Me, too. What about *Casablanca*? That's probably my all-time favourite.'

'Mine, too. Oh, I weep every time. I only have to hear the music.'

Andy laughed. 'I remember watching it with my mother. She used to cry long before they got to the end. What about more modern films?'

Jill thought for a moment. '*Sliding Doors*, I just love. And *The Fisher King*.'

'Ah, *The Fisher King* brings the odd tear to my eye, I must confess.'

He went back up in Jill's estimation. He loved *The Fisher King*, he must be OK.

'Another coffee?' he asked.

'I can't,' she said, somewhat reluctantly she was surprised to discover. 'I've got a stack of work that I really must do.'

'OK. Perhaps we can do this again sometime?'

'I'd like that. Thanks, Andy.'

As they walked outside to their cars, Andy's hand rested in the small of her back. There was something almost possessive in the gesture, but it wasn't altogether unpleasant.

'I'll call you,' he said.

'OK,' she said, non-committal as she unlocked her car.

She sat there for a few moments, watching as he slid behind the wheel of a gleaming red Lotus. She'd spent a pleasant couple of hours with him, she thought he found her attractive – so why couldn't she be more enthusiastic about seeing him again?

Pushing the question aside, she fired the engine and drove off. She thought of the work she needed to do, but she wasn't in the mood. Ever since moving in, she'd been promising to unpack all her books and find homes for them. She'd bought another small bookcase in the week, one that just fitted on the landing, so perhaps she'd fill that up instead.

When she pulled up at the cottage, she was in time to see Kate hurrying down her path to her car.

'Kate!' Jill jumped out of her car and ran to hug her. 'What a lovely surprise. Why didn't you call me?'

'I should have,' Kate said, laughing. 'I wasn't sure if your doorbell worked so I've been hammering on your door. I have the bruises to prove it.'

'Yes, the doorbell works. I've been out to lunch with a friend.' Jill dashed back to lock her car.

'Male or female?' Kate asked.

'Male,' Jill told her, 'but he's only a friend.'

'Things must be looking up then,' Kate said, but she couldn't quite hide the quick flash of disappointment.

Jill knew that Kate still hoped she and Max would get back together, no matter how many times Jill told her it wouldn't happen.

'I overdid the baking – again,' Kate explained, changing the subject, 'so I thought I'd have a ride out here and see if your freezer had any space. It was a bit impulsive and I didn't stop to think about your being out. I should have phoned.'

'It doesn't matter. Come in.'

Jill unlocked the front door, pushed it open and froze at the sight of the small white envelope lying on the mat.

Chapter Eighteen

'That'll be the milkman's bill,' Jill said quickly, picking up the envelope and putting it on the table. No point worrying Kate by telling her that some maniac was stalking her.

'You have a milkman? How civilized. Now then, let me bring these things inside. There are a couple of cherry pies, and a fruit cake for the freezer and a sponge.'

'You're a gem,' Jill told her, managing a smile.

They chatted about Jill's cottage, the weather and a dozen other things as they unloaded Kate's car and filled up Jill's freezer.

'So how are the boys?' Jill asked at last. She missed them so much.

'Badgering Max to let them have a dog,' Kate replied with amusement. 'They're making his life hell. Serves him right.' She sighed. 'He's working too many hours, as usual, so they don't see nearly enough of him.'

'It's difficult,' Jill agreed.

'I think I'll have to get on their side,' Kate said with a wry smile. 'I'm not keen on dogs – too much hair and dirt about.' She sighed as Rabble jumped into the cardboard box that had been emptied of pies. 'I'm not keen on cats either,' she said with a laugh, 'but I think a dog might do Ben good. He's not as outgoing as Harry. He still misses his mum. He misses you, too, Jill.'

Not as much as she missed him, Jill suspected. He was one of those kids who was permanently sticky. You could scrub his hands twenty times a day, but he'd still be sticky. How she'd loved his sticky hugs, though.

'You'll end up taking the dog for walks,' she pointed out, preferring not to comment on Ben's problems.

'I know.' Kate was resigned to that. 'But yes, the boys are fine. Harry's fed up with school, although he's happy enough on the sports field so no change there. He's in the school football team, which is good going for a thirteen-year-old. Mind you, I expect that'll involve me freezing to death on the sidelines.'

Jill had to laugh. Despite Kate's comments, she knew just how much she loved the two boys. If Max didn't know what he would have done without Kate, Jill shuddered to think how Kate would cope without Harry and Ben. Divorced, and with her only daughter dead, and her only son living in America, life for Kate revolved around the boys.

She sat down at Jill's table. 'So tell me all about this male friend of yours.'

'There's nothing to tell,' Jill replied with amusement. 'He's the estate agent who sold me this place. Nice enough. He's good-looking, very good-looking in fact, charming and thoughtful. But he doesn't set my heart beating any quicker.'

'I wonder why,' Kate mused, voice heavy with sarcasm.

'No idea,' Jill said airily. It had nothing to do with Kate's son-in-law.

'Max said he'd seen you,' Kate went on, 'and he thought you might be back at work soon.'

Now it was Jill's turn to sigh. 'It looks that way. I can't seem to say no.'

'Call me a bluff old cynic, but that could be because you love the work so much. It wasn't your fault that chap hanged himself, Jill.'

'I know that.'

She did; it was absurd to think anything else. A profile could be spot on, yet the police still needed at least a shred of evidence before arresting a suspect. There had been plenty of evidence too. What Rodney Hill did was not her fault . . .

'Call in sometime,' Kate said as she was leaving. 'The boys haven't seen you for ages. It wouldn't hurt just to call and say hello, would it?'

'It wouldn't, no. Yes, I will. Maybe next weekend.' Except next weekend, she really would have to visit her parents.

'I'll expect you on Saturday morning. Max is sure to be working so you can help me entertain those boys of his . . .'

As soon as Kate's car was out of sight, Jill walked over to the table and looked at the white envelope.

How many times had she seen her father go through this pointless exercise? He would stare at a letter, turn it over, inspect the postmark and hold it up to the light while wondering aloud who could have sent it. Jill, her mother or her sister would cry, 'Just open the damn thing!' Inside would be a bank statement or an offer of cheap insurance.

Somehow, Jill doubted if her own envelope was as innocent.

'Shit!' She jumped a foot when her phone rang out.

'Hello?' Nerves made her sound wary.

'Jill, it's me, Ella Gardner. We met at Gordon and Mary's party.'

'Yes, of course. Hello, Ella. How are you?'

'Feeling fat. I'm just about to go and walk off my lunch. But that's not why I'm calling. The history group has invited a lecturer from Liverpool University to speak to us next Wednesday evening and I wondered if you'd like to come along.'

'Wednesday evening? Is it in the hall?'

'That's it. It should be interesting. He's bringing old photos showing an early Kelton Bridge and surrounding area.' She laughed softly. 'Interesting or not, it's my job to try and drum up business. Usually, there are only six at most at our meetings and that's embarrassing if we manage to get a speaker. Do try and come if you can.'

'I will. Thanks, Ella.'

'So how are things with you?' she asked.

'Fine, thanks. I've had a big lunch myself, and ought to be walking that off, but I need to get on with some work. Shame really.'

'I'm surprised Tony Hutchinson hasn't persuaded you to go out running with him,' Ella said, chuckling. 'He's developed a bit of a thing for you, my dear.'

'Me? What on earth do you mean?'

'Since meeting you, he's changed his running route. He always used to run up towards the moor, but now he runs along the lane, past your cottage, and out towards the Rochdale road. I can't see any reason for that other than seeing you, can you?'

She laughed at Jill's surprised silence.

'Don't worry. Our Tony's a terrible ladies' man, and I don't know how Liz puts up with him, but he's harmless enough.'

'Perhaps he'd like to deliver my paper on his way past,' Jill said lightly.

While Ella chatted about the unreliability of the paper boys and girls, Jill's heart raced. Was Tony responsible for sending those silly photos and cards? She glanced over at the envelope still sitting on the table. If he ran past when she was out, it would be easy enough to put an envelope through the letterbox without being seen. Neither her short driveway nor her front door was overlooked.

Perhaps she'd have to drive her car into the village, leave it there, walk back via the fields, get in the house through the back door and lie in wait for him. Then, when he put an envelope through the door, she could confront him . . .

'Anyway, must dash, Jill. Hope to see you on Wednesday night. Seven o'clock.'

'Yes, OK, Ella. Thanks for that. Bye.'

Jill put down the phone and picked up the envelope. If

it was a note from the milkman, and she was sure it wasn't, it wouldn't matter about fingerprints. If it was from the crank taking great delight in hounding her, then the envelope would be clean.

Heart racing, she opened the envelope – and nearly dropped it when she saw the contents.

For a moment, she thought she would vomit, and she had to pace around her sitting room, taking deep, calming breaths. She still wanted to scream.

Anger had her hands shaking as she picked up the phone again.

She hit the button for Max's mobile and was relieved when he answered it immediately.

'I've had another envelope pushed through the letterbox,' she said breathlessly, 'and this one – oh, God, Max!'

'What? Calm down, love. What is it?'

'There's a lock of hair inside.' Sharp, angry tears stung her eyes and she had to blink them back. 'A lock of red hair!'

Chapter Nineteen

It was a weird sensation, switching on the television and seeing that prostitute's face staring back at him. He only caught the end of the report, '. . . and said that hopes of finding the girl alive are fading.' She looked different on the screen, mainly because she was wearing a school uniform and her hair was a mousy brown colour. For all that, she was easily recognizable.

The newsreader went on to speak about the appalling weather, and the floods that had hit the north-west. He switched off, not interested.

That was it then. The lock of hair must have convinced them she was dead. He'd checked it carefully; there was no follicle, nothing from which they could obtain a DNA sample.

They hadn't found the body, though. Sometimes, he thought he ought to put up signposts and give them a helping hand. God, they were stupid.

He wished he could have watched Jill Kennedy open that envelope to find the lock of hair.

Was she wondering what Valentine had in store for her? Oh, he hoped so.

He still wasn't sure what to do with her. It was so very tempting to kill her now, and send that Detective Chief Inspector Trentham a lock of her hair, but then half the fun would be over. Eventually he'd kill her, of course, but meanwhile he was enjoying playing with her. With the police so slow and dim, it helped to pass the time.

He would visit her cottage this evening.

She was dim, too. Despite the fact that her cottage was being watched – that is, a patrol car drove past slowly two or three times a night – he delivered his little surprises to her in broad daylight and she was none the wiser.

Valentine was too clever for her, for all of them. He was a perfectionist.

Chapter Twenty

'Well?'

Jill looked up from the computer's screen, rubbed her tired eyes to bring Don Cornwall into focus, and stretched her neck and shoulder muscles. It was late and she was tired. She'd spent over nine hours in front of this computer in the windowless office, and she was ready to go home.

'Well what?' She wasn't Cornwall's number one fan. He was ambitious, insensitive, abrupt and would sell his soul for an arrest. Or perhaps he simply wasn't Max. He wasn't on her wavelength.

'What are you doing?'

'Starting over,' she said. 'I'm going back to the beginning and plotting Valentine's crimes in chronological order on the map – again. I'm seeing where the girls went missing and where their bodies were found.' He came to look over her shoulder at the various coloured dots on the screen. 'He gets about a bit, though,' she said thoughtfully. 'The murders all take place at night. Either he works during the day or there are more prostitutes on the streets at night. Not much help,' she admitted, seeing his scornful expression. 'The thing is, though, a criminal will commit crimes in an area in which he feels safe. He's used to the towns in Lancashire – could be a salesman who covers Lancashire, a delivery man, something like that. Yet the bodies are always found in remote places. So he drives them away to the open countryside. And that's another thing. There are no signs of a struggle so they go willingly. And they're in his car for one hell of a long time.'

'So he pays them well?'

'It's more than that,' Jill replied. 'He'll be well spoken, smartly dressed and driving a decent car.'

'Like Brad Pitt in that film?'

Jill had no idea what he was talking about.

'Millionaire, hooker, Ferrari,' Cornwall said impatiently.

Perhaps their star signs were incompatible. Whatever, she wasn't happy working with him. As usual, his dark suit was immaculate and, today, was teamed with a crisp white shirt and dark blue and grey silk tie. His aftershave was over the top, though. He was younger than Max, probably eight or ten years younger.

'It was Richard Gere, not Brad Pitt. Richard Gere and Julia Roberts in *Pretty Woman*. And yes, it's a bit like that in that the girl will believe he's a cut above her usual customer. He won't drive a Ferrari or anything showy, though. That would draw too much attention. He'll drive a high end of the market saloon – a model that's smart yet popular. A year, two years old at most.'

She thought for a moment. 'So he's well spoken, high IQ, smartly dressed, good car. He offers them a good sum of money for a full night.'

'That's easy enough. They can even hold the cash while he drives.'

'Exactly. Hold the cash and dream of other nights – maybe days and weeks with him.'

'What's with the open countryside?' he asked. 'Why drive them miles away?'

'He needs to feel safe. The fact that he's killing them away from the towns makes me think he's used to open spaces and feels happier in them. You're looking for someone who lives, or at least was brought up in the country. A farmer perhaps. A farmer's son.' She rubbed her eyes again. 'God knows,' she said on a long sigh. 'I'm going round in circles again.'

'He's a clever bastard,' Cornwall muttered.

'He is. The fact that he's leaving no trace makes me think he's clued up on forensic procedures. Another thing, he chooses his victims in busy towns yet nothing has ever been caught on CCTV. He thinks of everything. So, forensic procedures –'

'We could be looking for someone who works on the force,' Cornwall said wryly, 'if we could find anyone who knows what a night off is.'

'Or someone who's been arrested before, perhaps served time. Not murder – and I don't think it would be a sexual crime – but I think he could have a police record, and I think it might have something to do with prostitutes. Perhaps he roughed one up. I don't know, but he's certainly ridding the world of them now. Perhaps he fell in love with one and couldn't get her to give up her work. Perhaps his mother, sister, wife was one. No, not his wife. He's not married. He's not in a long-term, stable relationship. I'd stake money on his mother being a prostitute and his being starved of love as a child. It's not the men visiting them he hates, it's the women themselves. The men are nothing to him. Yet, although he resents prostitutes, he spends time cutting hearts from their skin.'

'A real romantic,' Cornwall muttered, eyebrows raised.

'It must take a lot of time and care, though. He cares for women. He probably has a great deal of respect for them when they're dead. To him, they'll be clean and pure again.'

She stared at the screen. 'A map is all very well, but I'm working on the geographical and our killer will be working from his mental map.'

'Uh?'

'The two are very different,' she explained. 'If I were asked to draw a map of Preston, say, and you were asked to, our maps would be very different. Because I've lived in Preston, the centre of my map would be more or less where I'd lived. You've worked there so yours would have a place of work as its centre. A city like London, which is clearly divided by the Thames, is a better example. Some people in London live north of the Thames and haven't been south. Their map would show just a tiny part of

London as being south of the Thames. We draw our own mental maps.'

He didn't comment on that. 'Meredith told me you were good,' he said instead.

'I am!'

'You'll need to be if you aim to get one over on Valentine. The man's a genius.'

'The man's a killer,' Jill corrected him.

He's also sending me presents, she added silently, but Cornwall hadn't seemed unduly bothered by that.

'That lock of hair –' she began.

'What about it? There's nothing to say Valentine sent it.'

'No, but –'

'More likely to be someone reminding you that you cocked up – that the whole force cocked up.'

'Maybe, but –'

'We're looking into it,' he promised, dismissing it. 'We're also searching open fields within a five-mile radius of Burnley. That's an awful lot of fields. If there is a body out there, and it looks likely there is, we'll find it.'

Jill knew it was an impossibly large area to search, especially when they could be way off the mark. Valentine might have taken his victim six miles away.

'That's another thing,' she said. 'When he takes his victim to the place of death, he'll take them in the direction of his base – where he lives. So that's what I'm working on, the place of death.' She looked at him. 'It's definite the victims haven't been killed and then moved to these places, isn't it?'

'Yup.' With that, he walked out of the office leaving her to it.

'Ignorant so and so,' Jill muttered.

Another hour, and then she'd go home.

Max had done his best to get her to leave her cottage, but she refused to do that. All the same, she felt uneasy when she was inside and hated opening the door when she got home. She'd had extra locks installed on the doors and windows, a couple of officers were keeping an eye on the place, and getting access to Fort Knox would be easier, but she still felt on edge.

Right, back to work.

Looking for the clues a criminal left was so much easier when going through crimes that had already been solved. That was fascinating work, deducing clues from known facts. Now, she felt as if she were working completely in the dark, like a watchmaker trying to mend a watch up a chimney.

Chapter Twenty-One

His church was cold, but Jonathan didn't mind. It wasn't as cold as the look in his son's eyes as he'd left the vicarage earlier. Jonathan had no idea where Michael had gone. 'For a walk,' was all he'd said.

Jonathan loved everything about his church, including the temperature that had always made Alice shiver, and the smell of the place, a mixture of musty prayer books, polish and wax that had made her wrinkle her nose and pull a face.

The lights were on, yet he'd felt compelled to light a few candles.

Built in 1644, St Lawrence's wasn't a particularly old church, and Jonathan could still recall his first sight of the building and the disappointment he'd felt then. That, however, was perhaps mainly due to the fact that he'd hoped for a larger parish. Eleven years had passed since then, and now this felt like home. He wouldn't want another parish.

The main body of the church was built of red brick, with darker, almost black bricks laid to make crosses. The west tower, stone-faced and topped by small but impressive battlements, had been added in 1720. On the south face was the large clock that told the people of Kelton Bridge the time of day.

The inside, in Jonathan's view, was far more impressive. Over the years, Jonathan had seen many visitors to the church stand in awe beneath the stained-glass window near the font that celebrated the baptism of Jesus. The nave, with its single aisle leading to the chancel, was broad and majestic, and the pulpit was one of the largest Jonathan had seen. Standing in that pulpit, gazing down on his flock, it was possible to believe he was God and not merely passing on the Word.

This evening, however, he paid scant attention to his surroundings. He sat in the front pew for a while, then knelt. His eyes were open, his hands clasped tightly beneath his chin.

'Father, forgive me,' he whispered.

He stared at the window high above him, where Jesus, carrying his weighty cross, stared straight back at him. His eyes were a deep blue and as pure as the open sky.

Jonathan shivered.

The Lord had given his only son to save the world; Jonathan had almost given his only son to save his own skin . . .

'What else could I do?' he whispered.

The silence was awesome and it would have been possible to hear the scurrying of the proverbial church mouse.

'Alice, you understand, don't you?'

He wanted – *needed* – some sign of forgiveness. If only Alice was here to pat him on the shoulder and say, 'It'll be all right, Jon. Your God will understand.'

Always his God. Never hers.

He had never heard her say so, but he knew her faith had not been strong. Only last year, before the Christmas service, she'd said, 'They'll be there in their droves – the one service of the year that people attend.'

'Once a year is better than nothing,' he'd said feebly.

'Is it, Jon? Or are those who don't come, those who are too busy doing things for others less fortunate, the better people?'

Of course they were.

What would she say if she could see him now? What would she have said if she could have seen Michael being interrogated by the police? Would she have found it in her heart to forgive him?

Somehow, Jonathan doubted it.

She had loved that boy with every breath in her body, as Jonathan did, and she would have given her life willingly to spare him an hour's sadness.

Jonathan hadn't been able to meet his son's gaze since. Every time he looked at the boy, he saw accusation in his eyes. It was justified. How could he have left Michael alone to face all those questions?

What would his parishioners say if they knew he'd let his own son be suspected of murdering his mother, when all he'd had to do was tell the truth? He was supposed to take care of his flock, to guide them, to lead by example, and he had let them down.

'Oh, Lord, I am so unworthy.'

He had come here this evening to be quiet with God. Instead, his mind was filled with Alice. He had loved her more than anything, more than God even, from the moment he first saw her, and he would still love her more than anything when he drew his final breath. It was her forgiveness he needed. It was her voice he needed to hear.

But Alice was gone and, somehow, Jonathan had to make a life for himself without her. He had to. For his own sake, and for Michael's, he had to carry on without Alice by his side.

He must talk to Michael, too. They would discuss the subject of Michael's future and Jonathan vowed to make that future bright. It was what Alice would have wanted. If Michael didn't want to go to university, and Jonathan strongly suspected he didn't, and that he was only contemplating it to make his father proud, then together they would think of alternatives. What did it matter whether he went to university or not?

The silence was broken. Someone had slammed the outer porch door. Or perhaps the wind had increased.

Jonathan got to his feet. He turned to face the door, expecting to see Olive Prendergast or perhaps Mary Lee-

Smith with fresh flowers for the church, but no one came. It must have been the wind.

That's what he would do next, he decided suddenly. While the people of the parish were united in their grief, he would start a fundraising campaign so the roof could be repaired. He would do it for Alice. Mary Lee-Smith had plenty of contacts and she loved fundraising. He would enlist her help. For his own part, he would work tirelessly.

There was another noise, one he couldn't identify.

'Who's there?' he called out.

There was no answer. It must have been the wind.

He walked towards the sound of the noise, and swung back the large oak door that opened on to the porch.

'You? What are you doing here?'

Chapter Twenty-Two

Pennine View was unlit and it was reassuring to drive along it with Max's headlights behind her.

As soon as Jill pulled on to her drive, the front security light came on and that, too, offered reassurance. There were shadows created by a couple of bushes, but it was as well lit as it could be. Max had to park on the lane, and she waited for him to catch her up before getting out of her car and locking it.

'You OK?' he asked.

'Fine,' she replied automatically, but she was glad he was there.

She unlocked her front door, pushed it open and groaned at the amount of mail lying on the mat. They stepped over it, and Jill closed the door before picking it up and flicking through it. It was mostly junk mail.

'Nothing of interest,' she told him.

'Good. A coffee would be welcome,' he said hopefully, already striding off.

He checked downstairs first, then went upstairs. She heard him in the bathroom, then opening and closing wardrobe doors. She even heard him check the attic.

'Just you and three cats,' he said, coming back to the kitchen.

She hadn't expected him to find anything else. To say she was relaxed would be a lie, though.

It was difficult now to assume that some crank was playing games with her. Valentine must have delivered that lock of hair. Jill had thought they could get it tested, and was surprised to learn that there was no DNA on cut hair. 'You need a follicle,' she'd been told. Nevertheless, she was convinced it was a lock of Anne Levington's hair. She was also convinced Valentine had sent it.

The kettle had boiled and she spooned two generous helpings of coffee into each mug. Instant would have to do. Let's face it, after the sludge that came out of the machine at the station, anything would taste good.

Neither took milk or sugar so, after giving it a quick stir, she handed him a mug. He must have noticed the way her hands shook.

'I wish you'd get out of here, Jill. If you don't want to stay at my place, stay with Kate. Or stay in a hotel.'

'We've been through this before, Max, and my answer's still the same. I refuse to be driven out of my own home by this creep. I have the cats to think about and –'

'Sod the bloody cats!' Max exploded.

'Even if it is Valentine,' she said, 'and even if he did get to me, which is highly unlikely, I don't think he'd harm me.'

'I expect other girls have had that same thought. A pity they ended up in the morgue.' He took a deep calming breath. 'Unless you've got a new sideline I know nothing about, you're not his usual type,' he admitted.

'Exactly.'

'So how are you getting on with Cornwall?' he asked.

'Badly.' But perhaps that was her fault, not his. 'He's too ambitious for my liking, and he doesn't listen. I'm sure he thinks I'm a waste of space.' She gave him a wry smile. 'Other than that, we're getting along just dandy.'

There was a knock on her door and even that had her heartbeat going at an alarming rate. She had to calm down.

Michael Trueman was standing on her doorstep, his usual shy expression on his face.

'Hey, what a lovely surprise.' She grabbed his arm and dragged him into the kitchen. 'This is Max. I expect you remember him.'

'Yes.' Michael shook hands with Max. 'Good to see you again, sir.'

Max would be the last person he wanted to see, but that was typical of Michael. He was polite to a fault, and it was never forced. He respected good manners.

'Sorry, I didn't realize you had company, Jill,' he said. 'I'll come back another time.'

'Nonsense,' she said briskly. 'Max is just leaving.'

Jill gave Max a pointed look and was relieved to see him drink his coffee. If Michael had things on his mind, he was far more likely to offload them to Jill if she could keep his trust. He'd clam up with Max around.

'Yes, I'm off,' Max said. 'Be seeing you, Jill. Night, Michael.'

Jill closed and locked the door behind him, then returned to the kitchen where Michael was stroking Rabble.

'Fancy a drink?' she asked. 'I don't know about you, but I'm going to have a Scotch. Fancy one with me?'

'Whisky? I've never tried it,' he admitted.

'Then try it. Have a Scotch and ginger ale with me. I think you'll like it.'

She poured small measures into two glasses and added ginger ale.

'I'm also starving,' she told him, as she handed him a glass. 'Will you eat with me?'

'Oh, no, really. I don't want to put you to any trouble. I only called in to say hello.'

Left to his own devices, that's all he would say.

'How about an omelette?' She checked the fridge. 'I've got plenty of eggs, but it'll have to be cheese or mushroom. Fancy either of those?'

'Cheese?' he asked.

'OK. You grate the cheese, and I'll whip up the eggs.'

They moved around the kitchen companionably and then sat at the table to eat. Michael looked less edgy as time went on and it was good to see him relax a little. Or perhaps that was the whisky. He'd almost emptied his glass before the omelettes were even cooked. She hoped she didn't get him into trouble with his father. Would

Jonathan Trueman approve of her plying his son with alcohol? She doubted it.

When they'd cleared away the plates, Jill walked into the sitting room, giving Michael little option but to follow.

'So how are things?' she asked, sitting on the floor next to the fireplace. 'How's your dad?'

'OK.' He sat down, and Jill could sense the inner debate he was having. There was something he wanted to say, she was sure of it.

'Do you want to talk?' she asked. 'I've told you before, I'm a good listener.'

'I don't know what do.' That was becoming Michael's stock phrase.

He was immature, and more vulnerable than other lads of his age. No way could he cope without someone to talk to. What in hell's name did the streetwise Becky make of him? Perhaps his vulnerability was part of his appeal.

'What about your girlfriend? Surely you've talked things over with Becky?'

'No. She's not – I mean – well, I expect I read too much into that. I haven't seen much of her lately.'

Which probably put Becky in the clear.

'Try telling me and I'll see if I can help. You know what they say, two heads are better than one.'

He was silent for what, to Jill, seemed an age, but she was reluctant to disturb him.

'When Mum was killed . . .' he said at last.

Again, this long silence. Jill wasn't *that* patient. 'Yes?' she prompted.

'It didn't happen like that – like my father said it did.'

He referred to 'Mum', yet it was always the more formal 'my father'.

'Oh?'

'I got home just after two o'clock that day because the school closed. They'd had trouble for days with the fire alarms and sprinklers. That day, the classrooms and everyone in them were getting soaked so they sent us home. I had a lift with Jack's mother. Jack's in the same class as me.' He took a quick swallow of his drink. 'My father was already there and Mum was already dead. It was my father who was standing over her with the knife in his hand. Not me.'

Jill's mind raced with questions, but she kept her voice calm. 'What did your father say?'

'His first words were "You're early."' Michael shook his head, as if, even now, he couldn't believe that. 'Erm, then he said he had to ring the police and the ambulance. He threw the knife down – it landed on Mum – and then he called 999.'

'What did you do while he did that?' Jill asked.

'I knelt down by Mum to see if I could find a pulse. I thought she must still be alive.'

There had been two sets of fingerprints on the knife, Michael's and his father's.

'There was a lot of blood,' he said, eyes closing as he relived the memory. 'I was covered in it. Then people started arriving, and the police wouldn't let us move her. I was still holding her. I didn't want to let her go. My father was trying to resuscitate her and the ambulance men had to drag him away from her. People were talking to my father and he said he'd arrived home and found her – and me – like that.'

He opened his eyes; they were filled with panic.

'Why?' Jill asked calmly. 'Why do you think he said that?'

Samuel wandered in and, despite not being a lap cat, promptly jumped on to Michael's lap for some fuss.

'I was too shocked to ask him at the time.' Michael absently stroked the cat. 'Afterwards, when the police let me go, he acted as if that was what happened. He gets angry, furiously angry if I talk about it, so I don't mention it now. It's as if he believes it really happened that way.' His eyes suddenly filled with moisture. 'She didn't have any clothes on.' A huge sob shook his body.

'I know,' Jill said quietly.

All was silent except for the kitchen clock ticking loudly. Jill had never noticed it before.

'I don't know what to do,' Michael said yet again. 'At

first I said nothing, and that was wrong. Then, when I thought it would be easier if I told them it had happened just like that and that I'd killed Mum, it was even worse. They keep asking questions, day in, day out, and I can't say anything right.'

'Michael, do you think your father killed your mother?'

He was a long time answering. 'I don't know.'

'OK,' she said briskly, 'you have to tell the truth.'

'Who would believe me?' he demanded.

'I do.'

'Yes, but you're different.'

'Michael, the police knew you hadn't killed her.' Some of them had known it. 'They can gather all sorts of information from the scene of the crime and your story didn't fit. The only story that will fit is the correct one. You have to talk to the police and tell them exactly what happened.'

He shook his head and Jill couldn't blame him. The police had hounded him, and he'd had enough.

'Detective Chief Inspector Trentham didn't believe you killed her,' Jill said gently. 'Right from the start – well, almost the start, he didn't believe it. He's a good man, Michael. You can trust him. You must talk to him.'

He hesitated.

'I'll give him a call,' Jill said. 'I can ask him to come here and you can talk to him here. You'll need to make a formal statement, but it will be fine.'

'I can't. My father will –' He broke off, not knowing what his father would do. 'It's my word against his. Who's going to believe me? He's a bloody vicar, for God's sake. Thou shalt not lie and all that.'

If the situation hadn't been so serious, Jill would have smiled at that. It was the first time she'd heard him swear, and the context amused her.

'Why did he lie, Jill? Why did he tell them I did it?'

The poor, poor boy.

'I don't know,' she replied, 'but it's not your word against his. It's the truth and the evidence against his.'

As far as Jill could see, Jonathan Trueman had lied to protect the killer. And that killer was himself. She could be wrong, but she'd bet her cottage that Jonathan had killed his wife.

'I can't tell the police,' Michael said flatly.

'You have to.' Jill reached for her mobile. 'I'm going to phone Chief Inspector Trentham and ask him to come over.

Michael slumped back in the chair, resigned. And scared.

It was forty minutes later when Max arrived.

'It will be better coming from you, Michael,' she said, giving his shoulder a reassuring squeeze. 'He won't bite. Truly.'

Michael looked doubtful but, very slowly and hesitantly, he told Max exactly what he'd told Jill. And to give Max credit, he managed to listen without interrupting and without losing his calm.

'Michael's worried that no one will believe his story,' Jill said.

'I believe you,' Max told him.

'Thank you, sir,' Michael said quietly.

'Right.' Max was on his feet. 'I'm going to visit your father, Michael. I want you to stay here. OK?'

Michael looked at Jill. 'Is that all right?'

'Of course it is.'

When Max had gone, they could settle to nothing. Jill had another drink, and Michael made himself a cup of tea.

'Max will phone as soon as he's spoken to your father,' she told him.

At least, she hoped he would. It would be typical of Max to haul the man off for questioning and forget all about them.

Jill made up the spare bed, and they sat watching television for a while. She had just decided they might as well go to bed when Max phoned.

'Has Michael been out of your sight this evening?' he asked.

'No, of course not. Why? What's his father said?'

'Nothing,' Max said grimly. 'Jonathan Trueman is dead.'

Chapter Twenty-Three

The Pennines looked dark and menacing as Jill drove to the post office. She normally walked, but the sky was heavy with rain. She'd lived in the shadow of the Pennines long enough to know that when the rain came, it tended to be heavy and horizontal, making umbrellas more of a hindrance than a help.

There was a queue at the counter and she was tempted to call back later. She only needed postage stamps, and she guessed Olive would be gossiping. Given the shocked state of the village, there was plenty to keep her tongue busy.

The post office, like most of those to survive the village cutbacks, sold everything from groceries and cigarettes to a motley collection of fading birthday cards.

Jill was on the point of leaving when Ella walked in.

'Jill, I was going to phone you,' she said. 'Tonight's meeting has been cancelled.' She pulled a face and dropped her voice to a whisper. 'In view of what's happened, it seemed the only thing to do.'

Jill had forgotten all about the meeting.

'No doubt Olive will supply all the gory murder details,' Ella went on, her voice so low that Jill struggled to catch the words. 'I would have given her and her tongue a wide berth, but I need to get this parcel off today. It's for my niece in the States and it'll struggle to get there for her birthday as it is.'

'I was about to walk out, too,' Jill said, her voice low, 'but now I'm here, I may as well wait for my stamps.'

'How's young Michael?' Ella asked. 'Have you heard?'

'His aunt's at the vicarage with him.' Jill liked Ella, and instinctively recognized her as someone to be trusted. Her quiet acceptance of things was enviable, and her genuine concern for Michael was touching. People often forgot Michael in all this.

'That's a good thing. That will be Alice's sister, Eve. I've met her a couple of times. She's a lovely lady.'

'That's her.'

It was still difficult to believe what had happened. Max had told her that the vicarage had been deserted so he'd wandered across to the church to see if Jonathan Trueman was there. Max had found his body in the porch. Someone had shot him five times.

It was Jill's turn at the counter.

'A dozen first class stamps, please, Olive.'

'I was just saying,' Olive remarked, her voice a dramatic whisper for all to hear, 'that I'd always thought Jonathan Trueman a strange one. Someone else must have thought the same thing.'

'People don't get killed for being strange, Olive,' Jill pointed out.

'Who knows? I'll tell you this, though, Jim Brody is another strange one.' Her fingers hovered above the postage stamps. 'I wouldn't have bothered giving him the time of day if I'd known I'd get my head bitten off for my trouble.'

Jill suspected Jim Brody had been fully justified.

'I expect he's miffed because he's lost his job,' Olive went on, 'unless the next vicar wants his garden doing the same, but there's no need for him to take it out on me.'

'Indeed. Sorry, Olive, but I'm in a bit of a hurry.'

Olive sucked in her breath at what she interpreted as a snub, gave Jill her postage stamps and took the ten-pound note Jill gave her.

Her change was slapped down in the metal tray. Jill grabbed at it.

'Thanks, Olive. Bye.'

Olive didn't respond, which caused Ella to chuckle.

'I'm in a hurry, too,' Jill heard her tell Olive as she left the post office . . .

It wasn't raining yet, so Jill popped into the baker's next door. She needed some bread, and she wanted to see if Michael's girlfriend was about. However, there was no sign of the girl. Molly, the Truemans' cleaner, was there, being served by Joan. It was clear that Molly had been crying, poor woman.

'I can't stop thinking about it,' she was saying as Joan put a couple of custard tarts in a paper bag.

'That's what happens when strangers come to a village,' Joan said. 'All these holiday homes – you can't get to know people so you can't trust them.'

Molly turned, saw Jill, and asked, 'What harm did they do anyone, eh? First poor Alice and now . . . What's the world coming to, that's what I wonder?'

Before Jill or Joan could respond, Jim Brody walked into the shop and everyone fell silent. Confidences were being shared among women and Jim Brody had broken the circle.

'Hello, Jim.' Molly was first to speak. 'This is a rum do and no mistake.'

'It is, Molly.'

'Of course, you were never that keen on him, were you? You were friendly with Alice, not Jonathan.'

Jim Brody shrugged. 'I never rated church, so rarely had cause to see the man. There are enough problems in the world without adding religion to 'em. And he left the garden to Alice.'

'You saw him the other night,' Molly reminded him. 'I heard the two of you arguing.'

'Dear God,' Jim snapped. 'You can't breathe in this damn place without everyone needing to know about it. D'you know what I had for my breakfast an' all, Molly? If you don't, Olive Prendergast is sure to be able to tell you!' With that, Jim turned on his heel and slammed out of the shop.

'What did I say?' Molly asked in astonishment.

'In light of what's happened, I expect he's regretting his disagreement with Jonathan,' Jill suggested. 'In the heat of the moment, we all say things we regret.'

'I didn't think of that.' Molly looked suitably contrite for a moment. 'He's a funny one, Jim, but he soon forgets. The next time I see him, he'll be as nice as pie, as if nothing happened.' Cheered by this knowledge, Molly turned back to Joan. 'And a small cottage loaf if you've got one, Joan.'

As Nice as Pie? That was running at Haydock Park this afternoon. It didn't have a hope of winning. The distance was against it, as was the going. Added to that, this would be the horse's first outing after recovering from a virus. No, it didn't stand a chance.

All the same . . .

'The village is changing,' Molly was saying, 'and not for the better. These young kids – they hang around outside the old library drinking and think nothing of throwing the cans on the ground. You can't tell 'em. They'll mug you as soon as look at you.'

'It's the driving that gets me,' Joan confided. 'You can't sleep for young men racing cars through the streets. I was walking past the church and –' She broke off and grimaced. 'Ooh, that'll have been around the time Jon was being – killed. Thank God I didn't know that at the time.'

'What happened?' Jill asked.

'Some idiot in a van nearly knocked me down, that's what happened. I thought at first it were Nigel as drives our van, but it weren't. Don't know who it were, but if I catches 'im –'

'A red van?' Jill butted in and Joan nodded.

'Going hell for leather, it were.'

Chapter Twenty-Four

Andy hated Christmases and birthdays. His own birthdays had always been joyless affairs, but he hated his mother's birthdays far more. So many hints were dropped that he always felt honour bound to take her out for a 'nice meal' and buy her something extravagant and frivolous. This year, he'd bought her a silk dressing gown, flowers and chocolates and, amazingly, Melanie Collins had approved.

She always sent a card and enclosed a book token on his own birthday. When he phoned to thank her, she always said the same thing: 'It's no use me buying you a proper present when I don't see you for months at a time.'

She saw him a lot more often than Andy liked. His life wouldn't be worth living if he didn't see her on Mother's Day, at Easter, today for her birthday and then, three weeks later, for Christmas. Given the choice, he'd never see her again.

'This soup could be warmer,' she said now.

'Mine's fine,' he replied.

'Mind you, the restaurant could be warmer. Looking at the prices they charge, you'd think they could provide some heat for the customers.'

She'd probably only looked at the prices to make sure he was treating her right.

'Put your cardigan on if you're cold,' he suggested, teeth gritted.

God, she was hard work, and they had another two courses and coffee to get through yet. She would be on a diet, she was always on a diet, but it wouldn't stop her ordering a sweet.

She was wearing a maroon, floral-patterned dress and, after a moment's consideration, must have decided the cardigan wouldn't show it off to its best. Give her her due, she was still an attractive woman. She kept herself in shape, and always spent whatever it took to keep her hair looking good. Naturally dark, you'd never catch her looking anything but blonde. Andy sometimes thought she would rather die than let anyone see her with dark roots showing.

'I might in a minute,' she said.

The restaurant was plenty warm enough, thanks to several radiators and two roaring fires, one at either end of the large dining area.

She was staring at him. 'Your father used to do that,' she said, and the criticism was there for all to hear.

'Do what?' He was eating soup.

'Frown,' she explained. 'Wore a permanent frown, that man did.'

Andy couldn't blame him for that. He'd never known him; the mystery man had made an escape several months before Andy was born. He was never entirely convinced his mother knew who his father was, either.

'Sorry,' he said, giving her a broad smile. 'So what have you been up to, Mum? Still doing your dancing?'

'What would I have if I didn't do that?' she demanded. 'I'm not like some people who always have family popping round.'

'At least you have plenty of friends.'

'It's not the same as family. Maud – you know Maud who I go dancing with – she has six to lunch every Sunday without fail. At least six.'

Andy let her talk about the lucky Maud. Compared to her, everyone was 'lucky'. His neck was feeling tense already. He could feel the muscles tightening up. Soon the conversation would progress to his single status.

'Are you listening?'

'Of course,' he assured her, but he hadn't a clue what she was talking about.

'Anyway, she's got another baby on the way,' she went on. 'Funny that. She spent six years with you and couldn't decide if she wanted to get married or not, and then within a year of meeting that Frank, she's married with a kid.'

So she'd managed to work the conversation round to Tanya already. Usually, she waited until they reached the dessert stage of this ordeal to give voice to her disapproval. It wasn't Tanya who caused the disapproval, it was what she saw as his failure to be like her friends' children. Without exception, they were married with the obligatory two point four children.

He and Tanya had been together for six years but, for the first three years, it had been a very casual relationship. They'd gone to the cinema or out for a meal once a month or so. Neither of them had wanted marriage, despite occasionally mentioning it as something they might do in the future, yet Andy's mother always insisted on laying the blame for their break-up squarely on Andy's shoulders.

In reality, Tanya had arranged to meet him for lunch unexpectedly one day, and told him she'd met someone else.

'His name's Frank,' she'd said, 'and I love him.'

At the time, Andy had felt something akin to relief.

'When I was at the hairdresser's the other day,' Melanie Collins said, dabbing a napkin to her lips, 'I read an article in one of these trendy magazines, *Cosmopolitan* or one of those, and it reckoned that most women leave their men because the sex isn't much cop.'

'Mother!'

'I'm only telling you what I read.'

'I'd rather not know,' he snapped.

'I'm sure you wouldn't.' She smiled slyly. 'Course, we both know that you like to treat your women a bit rough.'

'I do not!' Confound the bloody woman. 'Now, have you finished with that? The girl's been across to the table twice to try and clear away our plates.'

'I've finished.'

He kept talking until they were tucking into their main course – her a lemon chicken and him a good-sized rare steak.

'Don't know how you can eat that,' she muttered. 'You get all sorts of problems from eating food that's not cooked properly.'

'It *is* cooked properly.' His neck was even more tense now and his jaw ached from gritting his teeth. He took a couple of deep breaths and forced himself to relax.

'Your Tanya,' she persisted.

'She was never my Tanya.'

'Whatever. Did she know about your police record?'

'Mother, the charges were dropped.' He took a swallow of his wine. If he had enough, perhaps he'd drive them both into a ditch. 'Besides,' he added tightly, 'that was years ago, when I was at university.'

'Yes, at least you had the good sense to do it away from home. Well? Did she?'

'Did she what?'

'Did Tanya know about it?'

'Yes,' he lied. 'Why shouldn't she? It was all a silly mistake.'

'Anyway, she's happy now. Another baby on the way.'

'So you said.'

'People talk, you know. If I tell people you're thirty-five and still not married, they think there's something wrong with you. Most reckon you must be gay. That's all the rage these days.'

She clearly expected some comment from him, but he refused to give her the satisfaction.

'That chap you lived with –'

'I shared a flat with other men after uni,' he said heavily. 'People do. It doesn't mean they're gay.'

'Oh, we know you're not that.'

Andy refused to rise to her bait.

'You're not, are you?'

'No, Mother, I'm not gay. I'm busy, I have lots of good

friends, some male and some female. I simply haven't yet met a woman I'd want to spend the rest of my days with.'

He was tempted to invent a girlfriend. He could tell her about Jill Kennedy, and how he'd taken her out to lunch, but it wasn't worth it. Far better to eat as quickly as possible and then drive her home.

Christmas was only three weeks away, and he'd have to suffer this agony again then, but after that, with any luck, he wouldn't need to endure her company until Mother's Day in March.

Chapter Twenty-Five

Bob Murphy arrived on the dot of ten o'clock on Saturday morning, just as he'd said he would, and Jill couldn't have been more pleased to see him. Last night, her bedroom window had been rattling in the wind again. In the end, she'd given up and slept in the spare room. Not that she'd slept much. Her mind had been too full.

Michael's aunt, his late mother's sister, had come to the vicarage as soon as she'd heard the news, to take care of Michael.

Eve was a lovely woman with five children of her own. All were older than Michael, though, and all had left home, and Jill thought she saw Michael as someone to mother. She forgot he was eighteen and an adult. For all that, she was a delightful, kind, warm-hearted person. As executor of her sister's will, written many years earlier when Michael was still a child, it was, she'd said, her duty to take care of Michael. Jill had assured Michael he was welcome at the cottage any time he liked, and he'd chosen to spend most of his spare time with her until the future was more settled. He'd done that without hurting Eve's feelings, too.

This morning, he had a friendly word with Bob, and then went back inside to his music and his solitude.

'How's he doing?' Bob asked.

'Amazingly well,' Jill said truthfully. 'He has his moments, of course, but he's coping.'

'It's a dreadful thing. Bad enough to lose your parents in

an accident or something, but this must be even worse. I mean, to have both parents – murdered.'

'I know.'

'It doesn't sink in, does it?'

That was the essence of it; the horror simply didn't sink in. It was one reason Michael was coping so well, it hadn't sunk in, and one reason the local residents were managing to go about their daily business.

'They say trouble comes in threes,' Bob murmured. 'It makes you wonder what's coming next.'

Funnily enough, exactly the same thought had occurred to Jill. Perhaps that was simply because they were all on edge, all trying to make sense of life.

'Still,' he went on grimly, 'we should be safe enough. There are more police than residents in Kelton at the moment.' He stepped back to look up at the cottage's roof. 'Now then, what are you needing here? Ridge tiles replacing? Guttering renewed?'

'Yes.'

'There are a few slipped tiles and a couple of cracked ones that need sorting out. What's the back like?'

They walked round to the back of the cottage and the list of priority jobs grew alarmingly.

'I'd like all the windows replaced as soon as possible,' Jill told him, 'but one, that one there –' She pointed to her bedroom window. 'It's driving me mad. It rattles in the wind and keeps me awake.'

'I'll have a look at that while I'm here, if you like. I might be able to do a temporary job.'

'Would you? I'd be grateful.' She looked at the other windows. 'They all need replacing soon, though, don't they?'

'They do, yes. Don't look like that,' Bob added with a rare smile. 'I'll work out the cost before we start work.'

'I'll probably need a lottery win. I'm having some plans drawn up for the extension,' she went on, 'but there's no hurry for that. I would like the roof making good as soon as possible, though.'

'No problem.'

'Come inside, Bob,' she suggested, 'and I'll show you the sort of new front door I want.'

They discussed the options for Jill's cottage, and Bob almost made her faint by telling her how much her front door would cost.

'How long have you been in business?' she asked.

He smiled. 'Long enough to know what I'm doing.'

'Oh, I didn't mean –'

'I know you didn't. Only joking. It'll be ten years now. I did my apprenticeship as a bricklayer, and then started out on my own. It was just me and a van. I like to keep it small, and I still only employ four others. They're all good, hard-working chaps. You've met Len, my roofing man. He'll do your roof.'

They could hear the sound of Michael's music coming from upstairs.

'Len did the roof at the vicarage last year,' Bob remarked, as if Michael's music had reminded him of more unpleasant things.

'That must have been a big job. It's a huge house.'

'It is, but I like plenty of space.'

'So do I until it comes to cleaning.'

Rabble wandered into the kitchen and immediately went to investigate their visitor.

'How old is she?'

'Sixteen,' Jill told him, 'and revelling in all the fuss she gets from Michael. I've got three about the place. You'll see them, or Len will, when you start work, but I don't think they'll be a nuisance.'

'Don't worry about that. Len's got a zoo. Two dogs, a cat and a cockatiel at the last count.'

'What a combination!'

'A nightmare on a narrowboat.'

Jill still hadn't visited Len and Daisy's narrowboat. She must.

'There's a stray cat keeps coming round to my place,' Bob said. 'Quite a young thing. She calls by, has some food, and then goes off for a couple of days. I've had cats before and I'd quite like another. We'll have to see if she moves in on a more permanent basis.'

This was probably the longest conversation Jill had had with Bob. He really was a man of few words.

'Right, I'll have a look at that window for you.'

'Thanks.'

She took him upstairs and showed him the problem.

'The frame's loose, but it'll be OK for a bit,' he told her. 'The opening light is causing all the problems, and I should be able to tighten up the catch and the hinges. Hang on a minute, and I'll get a screwdriver . . .'

Ten minutes later, her window had been fixed temporarily.

'It's not perfect,' Bob warned her, 'but you should notice an improvement.'

'Thanks.'

'No trouble. I'll have a look at this lot, and drop in some prices so you can see what you think. If they're OK, give me a ring and we'll get round to starting work.'

He noticed her newspaper opened at the racing pages and his eyebrows rose as he spotted horses' names ringed. 'Don't tell me you like a flutter on the horses.'

'Occasionally,' she admitted. 'You?'

'I've been known to dabble,' he replied, grinning. He frowned at a horse she'd circled. 'Nemesis? I'd thought of backing that, but –'

'I know, the going will be too heavy.'

'Yeah, that's what I thought. Are you going to back it?'

'I might.'

'Mm. It might be worth an each-way bet. Don't put too much on it, or you'll never afford to pay me. Right, I'd better be off . . .'

Jill watched him drive away, and felt vaguely cheered. It would be good to get the cottage sorted out. Then, hopefully, she could settle down and enjoy her new life in Kelton Bridge. She couldn't settle to anything now, though. What with worries about Anne Levington, Valentine's persona to try and unravel, the shocking death of Jonathan Trueman to come to terms with . . .

And just as Bob had said, the village held its breath as it waited for something else to happen.

Bob hadn't exaggerated too much when he'd said there were more police than residents in the village, but they hadn't found the murder weapon. They were still searching the locality for it, as well as carrying out house-to-house enquiries. It was a long, painstaking job.

Jill had thought Jonathan must have killed Alice. Now, she wasn't so sure. But why would anyone want to kill Alice *and* Jonathan? Two more harmless people it would be impossible to meet.

Had Jonathan killed his wife? Had the same man or woman murdered husband and wife? Was it possible that Kelton Bridge had seen two killers? Surely not. It was odd to kill one person with a knife, and kill them very cleanly, and then kill another with a gun. The two murders had been completely different. Alice had suffered one swift cut to the throat and would have died almost immediately. Jonathan, on the other hand, before receiving the fatal shots to his head, had been shot twice in the leg. The killer had wanted him to suffer. Why?

Perhaps she'd try to forget it all for a while. Michael might fancy a walk in the fresh air. Probably not, though. He was as comfortable seeing people as they were seeing him. No one knew what to say to him and, if they did say something, he didn't know how to respond.

Time might be a good healer, but it was a painfully slow one.

She sat down with her newspaper and studied the day's runners. Brixnmortar appealed to her. She smiled to herself. What was the point of studying form when she behaved like a complete ignoramus and backed a horse with a name that appealed? On the other hand, Nice as Pie had fought off the opposition and romped home with energy to spare.

Chapter Twenty-Six

Later that afternoon, Jill had a phone call from her sister.

'Steve's away this weekend and his mum's volunteered to have the kids so I thought I'd come and have a night with you.'

'Really? Oh, that's fantastic!' Jill felt the sudden unexpected sting of tears. A visit from her sister was exactly what she needed right now.

'Can you cope with a girls' night in?' Prue asked

'I can think of nothing I'd like better.' And it was true.

Jill loved her sister dearly, even if they did have nothing in common. Prue was mother to Charlotte, Zoe and Bethany – and that was it. Life revolved around her kids.

Jill spent the next two hours cleaning and generally setting the cottage to rights. It was amazing, she thought, how one person could get a place in such a mess.

At just after seven that evening, Prue entered the cottage like a whirlwind. Bottles of wine clanked as she put carrier bags on the floor and Jill glimpsed a huge box of Thornton's chocolates. Oh, yes, this was going to be a real girls' night in.

'This place is the back of beyond,' Prue said, giving her a hug. 'I got lost twice.'

Prue had only visited the cottage once before, and she'd got lost then.

'But isn't it gorgeous?' Jill said.

'Well, yes, but what happened to civilization?'

'This is civilized enough for me.' Jill had never understood how Prue could live on River View, how she'd never longed for escape. She hadn't, though. Despite their mother's pushing, Prue had left school at sixteen, walked straight into the local salon to train as a hairdresser, set her eyes on Steve, a lorry driver, married him and started breeding.

'Civilized? Two people have been murdered here within the last month. That's one a fortnight.' Prue pulled a face. 'I know you reckon River View's rough, but better that than a village like this. All the residents are inbred in these back-of-beyond places. You take a look at their feet, and I'll bet they've got six toes.'

Jill burst out laughing. 'It is so good to see you, Prue. You talk complete rubbish, and I love it. Right – glass of wine after your journey? How's Steve and those gorgeous nieces of mine?'

'They're fine, thanks, and yes, a glass of wine would be welcome.' Prue picked up the carrier bags and followed her into the kitchen. 'Steve's working all the hours God sent so no change there, and the kids couldn't wait to be rid of me. It's a treat to get away, though. I'll just go and freshen up . . .'

Smiling to herself, Jill took their wine into the sitting room. It was wonderful to see her sister, but she guessed it would be just as good to wave goodbye to her.

'Nothing interesting in your bathroom, I see,' Prue complained as she joined her.

'Such as?'

'Oh, aftershave, razor, that sort of thing.'

Jill rolled her eyes.

'You're not turning into a hermit, are you, Jill? Ever since you and Max split – well, you're like one of these frumpy old –'

'Thanks very much!'

'You know what I mean. How's that estate agent chap, by the way?'

'I assume Andy's very well. We had lunch a couple of weeks ago and he was fine then.'

'Lunch?' Prue's interest was grabbed. 'And?'

'And nothing.' Jill knew that a vivid description of an afternoon's wanton, abandoned passion would earn her a few Brownie points, but she resisted. 'He does nothing for me.'

'But you said he was nice. Good job, and good-looking, you said.'

'Yes, he has a good job and he's pleasing on the eye. There's more to life than that, though.'

Prue, clearly unable to think of anything more, shook her head in a despairing way. 'What about Max? I assume you're still giving him the cold shoulder?'

They'd been through this before, too. The way Prue spoke, it was obligatory for a man to have an affair. Jill would like to see her face if Steve had one. Second thoughts, she wouldn't. It was too painful to wish on her worst enemy.

'Actually, I've seen quite a bit of him lately,' she said. 'I'm back at work, temporarily, on the serial killer case.'

'Oh, no.' Prue threw herself down in the armchair, and groaned. 'So you discuss murder and mayhem together? That must be *so* romantic.'

Even Jill had to smile at that.

'Seriously, love,' Prue went on, 'all these murders in Kelton Bridge –'

'Two,' Jill pointed out quietly.

'That's about two per cent of the population.'

It wasn't, there were over four thousand people in Kelton Bridge now, but she did take Prue's point.

'And when you're not living in a place where people are getting murdered on a daily basis, you're working in a job where people would be out of work if all the killers were locked up.' She sighed her frustration. 'It's unhealthy!'

'I'm happy enough.'

Prue gave her that all-seeing gaze of hers. 'Are you?'

Jill rarely thought about it. People might complain about being depressed or fed up, but it was rare that someone decided they were happy. Thinking about it, though, she thought she was as happy as could be expected, considering the man she'd once loved had betrayed her and considering that some crank, possibly a serial killer, was making use of her letterbox . . .

'Yes, I am,' she said firmly. 'I enjoy my work, I love my cottage, I love this village and the people in it, I love the cats – yes, I am happy.'

'You're not getting any younger, Jill –'

'Oh, God.' Laughing, Jill got to her feet. 'I'd better bring the bottle in. You're right, Prue,' she called from the kitchen, 'I'm not getting any younger, but the British Museum isn't interested in me just yet.'

'I was thinking of children,' Prue said when she returned.

'I know what you were thinking. We've had this conversation before. Perhaps I don't want children.'

'Of course you do,' Prue scoffed.

She was right; Jill did want children. The trouble was, whenever she imagined those children, they were all miniatures of Max.

A sudden thought struck her. 'Why is Steve's mum having the kids? How did she beat off Mum?'

The expression on her sister's face had Jill's stomach churning. 'Prue?'

'It's probably nothing,' Prue began.

'Oh, my God! What is it?'

'She hasn't been feeling well,' Prue explained, eyes firmly fixed on the rim of her wine glass as if she were having to concentrate on a well-rehearsed speech. 'You know she can't shake off that cough? Well, now she's got a pain in her shoulder.'

'Oh, no. Those bloody fags of hers!'

'It might be nothing,' Prue insisted.

'And it might be –' But she couldn't say the c-word. Couldn't even think it. Certainly couldn't think of life without their mum.

'It might be a muscular thing,' Prue said firmly.

Jill guessed that, like her, Prue was too frightened to think otherwise.

'She went to the doctor's yesterday,' Prue told her.

'Lord, she must be ill.'

'He's sending her for an X-ray. I was impressed. She's having that on Monday.'

Jill wasn't impressed; she was terrified. To move so quickly, the doctor obviously thought it important.

'I keep meaning to visit,' Jill murmured.

'She knows how busy you are.'

'I'm not *that* busy.' How could she be too busy for her own mother? The thought disgusted her.

'Let's talk about something else,' Prue said firmly. 'Zoe's got a boyfriend, did I tell you? He's four years old and he gave her a birthday kiss.'

They talked about the children, even managed to laugh, but Jill knew they were both thinking of X-rays and the overflowing ashtrays that had been a part of their childhood.

The phone rang and Jill got up to answer it.

'Hi, it's Bob. Bob Murphy. Just wondered if you'd backed Nemesis?'

Jill laughed. 'I didn't.'

'Phew. That's OK then. I still stand a chance of getting paid.'

'You do,' she told him easily. 'I backed Brixnmortar.'

'Never! The outsider? 25–1, wasn't it?'

'Yep. I just wish I'd put a couple of grand on it.'

'I wish I'd put my business on it,' Bob said, 'but as it was, I backed – let me see – Blue Mountain –'

'Oh, dear.'

'Flame Thrower –'

'Oh, dear, oh, dear.' She spluttered with laughter.

'And a couple of others who should reach the finishing post before midnight.'

'I'd better be careful then or you'll be upping your estimate.'

'I might at that,' he said with amusement. 'Perhaps I'll have better luck next week. I'll be in touch anyway. Night.'

'Night, Bob.'

She was still smiling as she replaced the receiver.

'Bob? Who was that then?' Prue asked curiously.

'Bob Murphy – the builder who'll be doing this place.' Before she could go into detail, someone rang her doorbell and then hammered on her door.

On her way to answer it, Jill wondered if Prue had noticed the way she'd jumped in shock at the sound. Probably. Prue didn't miss much.

'Oh, hi, Andy.' Had her sister's willpower brought him to the cottage?

'I thought I'd drop by with the brochure you wanted,' he explained.

Jill had forgotten all about it. A nearby farm was being sold and the farm's contents were being auctioned separately. According to Ella, there were some lovely pieces going under the hammer. 'The Wrights are giving up farming and retiring to Spain,' Ella had told her, 'and most of their furniture is being sold. They've some lovely knick-knacks . . .'

'Thanks, Andy.'

She would have to ask him in, yet he looked exceptionally handsome this evening in a dark suit, pale blue shirt and silk tie. Prue would probably eat him.

'Come in. My sister's here – we were having a natter over a glass of wine.'

She'd hoped he would refuse the invitation, but he didn't. On the other hand, it would at least show Prue that there were a few decent men in Kelton Bridge. Well, one at any rate, and even Prue wouldn't think of counting Andy's toes.

'This is Andy,' she introduced him. 'He's the wonderful chap who found this lovely cottage for me.'

Prue, she could see, was mentally calculating the cost of his suit and shoes and eyeing up his broad shoulders. He passed the test quickly, and Prue soon had him sitting on the sofa next to her, a glass of wine in his hands. She then proceeded to fire questions at him.

'I couldn't live anywhere else,' Andy said in answer to

one of them. 'It's a great place. Everyone's very neighbourly, people look out for each other.'

'If someone had looked out for the vicar and his wife,' Prue pointed out quietly, 'Kelton Bridge wouldn't be mentioned on every news report.'

'I can't argue with that,' Andy replied. 'A terribly sad business all round. In all the years I've lived here –'

'How many is that?' Prue wanted to know.

'I lived here for a year when I was a kid – my mother liked to move around a bit – and I came back here when I was twenty-five. So that's eleven years in total. In all that time, we've never had so much as a Mars bar stolen.'

'What did your mother do, apart from move around a lot?'

Heavens, Prue was nosy.

'Oh, this and that. Any job that took her fancy really.'

'Lovely,' Prue said. 'A friend of ours was like that. You remember Diane, don't you, Jill? She picked grapes in France, waited on tables in Spain, and became a lifeguard in Australia. So romantic.'

Smiling, Andy nodded.

'You're not married then?' Prue pushed on, knowing full well he wasn't.

'Take no notice of her, Andy,' Jill told him. 'Before you arrived, I was on the receiving end of the high time you settled down and had kids lecture. Personally, I think she's just jealous of our freedom.'

They chatted for another hour or more. Andy was driving so he stuck to one glass of wine, but Jill and Prue made up for it.

Eventually, Andy glanced at his watch. 'It's time I was off. Lovely to meet you, Prue, and I hope we meet again. I'll look forward to seeing you at the auction, Jill, and thanks for the wine.'

As soon as he'd gone, Prue threw her arms wide in a dramatic, and slightly tipsy, gesture. 'I have died and gone to heaven. He is drop dead gorgeous, Jill. Dear God, girl, get a doctor to check you out. You must be dead from the neck down. He's –'

She broke off as Jill's mobile phone rang.

Jill welcomed the distraction until she saw who was calling.

'It's me,' Max said. 'I think we've found Anne Levington.'

'Alive?' But she knew the answer to that from Max's voice.

'No.'

'Where?'

'An old ruin of a farmhouse on the Burnley to Todmorden road. Cornwall's out there, but it's on my patch so I'm on my way there now.'

Chapter Twenty-Seven

On Monday morning, Jill was at work in the small, windowless office. The traffic noise was constant, and welcome. At least it hinted at signs of life outside.

Cornwall strode in. 'Well?'

He always greeted her with that 'Well?' Never 'Good morning' or 'How are you?', always 'Well?'

'I'm writing up a brief report,' she told him. 'According to my reckoning, our man lives on this side of Lancashire, either Todmorden, Rochdale or Rossendale.' He might even live in Kelton Bridge, she thought, and the knowledge brought an involuntary shudder. 'The most likely area, according to this, is Rossendale. I also reckon he'll live out in the wilds. He won't live on an estate, but on the edge of a village or a town. He'll be close to open countryside.'

'Or he could live in a tower block in Manchester,' he scoffed.

Jill leaned back in her chair. 'Does being this grouchy come naturally or do you have to work at it?'

He looked up, surprised, and then, amazingly, gave her a small smile. It was the first time she'd seen him smile. 'Sorry. Bad weekend.'

'Oh?'

'My car wouldn't start so I had to call out the AA, the wind blew a ridge tile off the roof that missed the car by inches, the washing machine flooded the kitchen, and my lottery numbers came up and I've lost the damn ticket.'

Jill gasped at the latter.

'Only a tenner,' he said, 'but it's not the point.'

'Could have been a lot worse then,' Jill said, grinning. 'The ridge tile might have missed your car and hit you instead, and your numbers might have come up for the jackpot.'

'True.' He didn't look cheered. 'Let me see your report asap. By the way, we found a piece of chewing gum at the scene.'

'What? From Valentine?'

'Who knows? I'll keep you posted,' he said, closing the door after him.

No, you won't, she thought grimly.

Jill didn't get too excited. Valentine wouldn't leave chewing gum around. He was far too careful. She concentrated on the changing areas of Lancashire that were coming up on her display. Valentine *could* live in Kelton Bridge.

That begged another question, one she hardly dared ask herself. Was he responsible for the deaths of Alice and Jonathan Trueman?

Valentine was a killer – fact. He killed working prostitutes. As he'd killed Anne Levington, they had to assume he was responsible for the lock of Anne's hair that was delivered to Jill's cottage.

Anne's father had formally identified her body. She'd been left in a crumbling old farmhouse in the middle of nowhere that hadn't been occupied for many years. True to form, she'd been left naked with only a couple of strangulation marks on her neck and the usual hearts, twelve in all, cut away from her young, pale skin.

As yet, no clues had been found at the scene – other than that piece of chewing gum. Officers were still carrying out a fingertip search, but no one was hopeful. It was uncanny how Valentine left no clues.

So – Alice and Jonathan Trueman. The killings weren't Valentine's style. The first had involved a knife, and although Valentine was skilled with a scalpel, he liked to strangle his victims first. Alice had been naked, but she wasn't a prostitute. For Jonathan's murder, the killer had chosen a gun and that certainly wasn't Valentine's style. It was too messy, and too risky. Valentine didn't prolong death; it was always over quickly.

Had Alice ever been a prostitute? Surely not. She had been a dancer and – what had Tony called her? – a real little raver? What if she'd used the casting couch method to gain a place in the dance group? They needed to delve very deeply into Alice's past.

But perhaps the killings weren't linked.

Jill stood up to stretch her legs, then decided to get herself a coffee.

It was good to get out of that cramped, airless room and see people rushing along corridors. Stuck in her office, the world could end without Jill being any the wiser. Here, there was constant noise – people running, shouting and talking, and phones ringing.

She was at the machine, waiting for it to pour some sludge into a white plastic cup, when Max came striding along.

'Any news?' he asked her.

'How would I know? Cornwall doesn't confide in me. Although he did say something about finding chewing gum out there.'

Max's eyes lit for a brief second but then he shook his head. 'Valentine's not that daft.'

'That's what I thought. I know it's nothing to do with you, Max, and Cornwall would have me flogged at dawn if he knew I was discussing it with you, but I think Valentine's most probable dwelling is in Rossendale.'

His eyebrows rose at that.

'It could even be Kelton,' she said, suppressing a shudder. 'Now, do you think he's responsible for Alice and Jonathan Trueman's deaths?'

'No!'

'But if –'

'Never in a million years, Jill. There's nothing whatsoever to connect them. They're totally different.'

'Yes,' Jill agreed, knowing all too well that Max wouldn't want the crimes connected, 'but they just might be linked. I was thinking about Alice. She was a dancer, and I heard her described as a real little raver in her youth. Who's to say she didn't sleep with the odd director to get on TV?'

'That was years ago.'

'I know.' At least she had his attention. 'But it's possible.'

'No. Jonathan Trueman killed his wife, I'm sure of it. Whoever killed him was out for revenge.' He put some coins in the machine and gave it a thump. 'Let me see this report you're doing on Valentine, will you?'

'I will.' Sod Cornwall.

Back in her office, a plastic cup of sludge in her hand, Jill thought about Valentine. Several times she'd wondered if the envelopes had been delivered to her cottage because Valentine wanted to be caught. He was famous now, yet he couldn't reap the benefits of that fame. Was he eager to grab his glory?

If she was right about him living in the Rossendale area, that would narrow it down to, oh, a mere twenty thousand people. Even if they got lucky and that chewing gum did belong to Valentine, a blood test of twenty thousand men didn't bear thinking about. And, of course, Valentine would make sure someone else went along in his place.

Meanwhile, he would kill again. And again.

The computer had analysed everything and Jill was as certain as it was possible to be that their man lived in the Rossendale area – Rawtenstall, Haslingden, Waterfoot, Stacksteads, Bacup, Irwell. It was a big area, but they *had* narrowed it down. He would also live on the edge of a community so they could forget the centre of Rawtenstall or Haslingden, and the main road running through the valley.

The dates of the attacks. She needed to compare the dates and times the victims were first reported missing, the dates and times the pathologist believed the victims were killed and the dates and times the bodies were found. The latter wouldn't tell her much, but you never knew. It was just possible that the computer might find some link.

Every millimetre of CCTV footage was being checked, but that was a long, slow process, especially when they had no idea what they were looking for. A glimpse of Anne Levington's last movements would be good. According to the pathologist, Anne had died around three hours after eating that burger with her friend. If only they could see her on CCTV at some point during those three hours. Even better if Valentine slipped up for once and they saw her getting into his car. And how unlikely was that?

Chapter Twenty-Eight

There were four faces waiting to greet Max when he arrived home that evening. Two faces looked wary, one looked exceedingly sheepish and the fourth . . .

Words failed him.

'I can explain, Max,' Kate offered, still wearing her exceedingly sheepish expression.

'I don't need an explanation,' Max told his mother-in-law, scowling at the four-legged creature that was staring back at him. 'All I need to know is when it's going back to wherever it came from.'

'Well –'

Before Kate could proffer this information, the four-legged creature wandered over to Max, had a quick sniff and promptly lifted his leg and urinated on Max's trousers.

'Oh, Lord! Boys, get your dad a drink – half an inch of whisky. I'll, er, get the disinfectant.' Kate looked at Max. 'Why don't you change? Give me your suit and I'll deal with it. I can pop it into the cleaner's in the morning.'

The boys headed off, whispering.

'Make that an inch,' Max called after them. 'A big inch.'

Max went upstairs, vowing with every step that he would not get talked into this. He loved his kids more than life itself, and he knew how much they wanted a dog, but it wasn't practical. He had no idea how this creature had found its way into the house, but it would leave by the same route. And fast.

It was huge, too. Big, yellow and boisterous, it was half

Labrador and half collie, Max suspected, which would make it neurotic, greedy and stupid.

What the devil was Kate thinking of?

He switched on the bedroom light and pulled the curtains across to shut out the dark, damp evening. Perhaps Jill was doing the same. The difference was that Max's house was set back from a busy road where streetlights illuminated the shadows. Jill's cottage was remote. Anyone could lurk along that unlit lane.

Why wasn't Cornwall taking her stalker seriously? Because he was confident it wasn't Valentine? Because he thought some small-time crank was responsible, one whose arrest wouldn't further his career?

Perhaps he was right.

Then again, perhaps he wasn't.

Max pulled on jeans and a sweatshirt and went downstairs.

'Right,' he said, as he walked back into the lounge. 'Let's hear this explanation. And if that damn dog wants a pee, he can use someone else's leg.'

Harry handed him a glass, in which was a good inch of Scotch.

'Thank you. But don't think this will win you any favours. He can't stay here – not even for a night.'

'Max –'

'I'm serious, Kate. The boys and I have discussed this a dozen times, and we all know that a dog is out of the question.'

'Will you let me explain?'

He stood by the mantelpiece, trying to be patient. 'I'm all ears.'

While Ben hugged the dog in a way that said he would die rather than be parted from the creature, Kate sat on the edge of an armchair.

'A couple of weeks ago,' she began, 'we called at the rescue centre. I thought it would be a good idea for the boys to see that a dog was a huge commitment, and to see exactly what changes would be needed before they could have one. I guessed the staff at the centre would have plenty of good advice.'

'What? All they want to do is offload the dogs.'

'Rubbish,' she scoffed. 'They check out potential homes. They won't allow them to go anywhere, you know.'

'Right, so having garnered all this wonderful advice . . .?'

'We met poor Fly,' she explained.

'Fly? This creature is called Fly?' Apparently, it was. At the mention of his name, a huge tail swept half a dozen unread newspapers off the coffee table and on to the floor. 'And why *poor* Fly? Oh, don't tell me, let me guess. He was unloved, unwanted, uncared for, probably abandoned on the motorway –'

'The RSPCA found him. He'd been neglected and tied up near a disused railway line.'

'My heart bleeds,' Max said, 'but he's not staying. We can't have a dog, and that's that. They're too much of a commitment.'

'Ben, Harry, take Fly upstairs,' Kate said firmly. 'If you're careful, you can throw his ball across the landing.'

Ben's bottom lip was trembling as they left the room, Max noticed.

Kate rose to her feet and walked over to Max. She stood for a moment, running her fingers over a glass paperweight that sat on the mantelpiece between various framed photographs.

'I have always tried not to interfere, Max,' she said at last, her voice like steel. 'I've tried to stand back and say nothing as you've made a complete mess of your life. Sometimes, I've even gone along with the nonsense you dish out. When you first introduced me to Jill, I went along with your story about only having met her recently – yet I knew damn well that you'd known her a long time.'

Max couldn't hide his shock.

'Oh yes, I knew there was someone else in your life, Max. I haven't blamed you for that. These things happen and, thankfully, Linda was too wrapped up in the boys to notice.'

Max felt himself redden. Even the tips of his ears were hot with shame.

'I can't say I approve of your life,' Kate went on. 'You live in a nasty world, you still drink too much, and you can be arrogant, selfish and downright stupid.' A sudden, reluctant smile softened her words. 'But I do love you, Max, and I know how much you love the boys.'

Max paced the length of the room, her words making him uncomfortable. He'd had no idea she'd known about Jill. In his naivety, he thought she'd always seen him as the model son-in-law.

'Harry and Ben don't live in your nasty world, Max. They live in the same fun world that most people do. They don't know about killers, and I'm damned if I'm going to sit back and watch them find out. They'll learn about the darker side of life in good time. Meanwhile, they need fun, laughter and happiness.' She paused. 'Ben still misses Linda, you know.'

'Yes, I know that.'

'He misses Jill, too. The boy was ready to accept Jill as a replacement mum.'

'I know that, too,' Max said grimly.

'I'm not suggesting for a moment that you attempt the impossible and find him a mother,' Kate said lightly. 'I do think he would benefit greatly from a dog, though. He needs someone or something to love, someone or something that is always there for him.'

Max knew that. As soon as Ben had left the room, with his bottom lip trembling, Max had known he would have moved mountains for the boy if it would put a smile back on his face.

Of course, there was another reason he was so against having a dog in the house. Despite all evidence to the contrary, he still harboured the faint hope that Jill would come back to them. She wouldn't leave her cats, and no way could anyone survive in a house that contained three cats and a dog. It was as if Max had to say goodbye to that hope . . .

'OK, Kate, you win.'

Kate slipped her arm around him, and he felt her gentle sigh as she rested her head on his chest.

'You're doing a great job with the kids,' she said softly, 'you know you are. Harry's fine, he's like you, but Ben – sometimes my heart breaks for that boy.'

'You know something, Kate? Sometimes mine does, too.'

'Yes, I know that.'

They could hear the sound of the boys' laughter drifting down from Harry's bedroom. Heavy paws pounded across the landing.

'And sometimes,' Kate added quietly, 'my heart breaks for you, Max.'

Chapter Twenty-Nine

Liz Hutchinson had a glass in her hand as she showed Max and Grace into her lounge. It might have contained water, but Max doubted it. Her husband, Tony, was sitting reading a newspaper, but he happily put it aside and got to his feet as soon as they entered. Max suspected he would dine out for weeks on stories of how the police had come to him for help. What a character he was. Nothing fazed him. Even the knowledge that his missing shotgun might have been used to kill Jonathan Trueman hadn't shaken him. Although what they had to say to him today might wipe the smile from his face.

'Hello, there, what can we do for you? I've already –'

'I know,' Max cut him off, 'but I have a few more questions, if you don't mind. Could we have a word?' He looked at Mrs Hutchinson and gave her a smile. 'Alone?'

'There's nothing Liz can't hear,' Tony declared.

'This could be a little delicate, sir.'

'Nonsense. We've no secrets, have we, Liz?'

She pulled a face, as if even the sight of his cajoling smile was distasteful to her.

Fair enough, Max thought.

'So,' he began, 'will you tell us again when you discovered your gun was missing?'

'Sit down,' Liz offered. 'Can I get you both a drink?'

Max and Grace sat.

'Thanks,' Max said, 'but I'll save the drink for another time if I may.'

'Not for me, either.' Grace had a quick sympathetic smile for Liz Hutchinson.

Liz stood at the window, facing them. She looked tense, Max thought. Tense, angry and ready to snap in two. Tony Hutchinson looked his usual confident self.

'Mr Hutchinson?' he prompted.

'As I've already told your chaps, I hadn't noticed it was missing until they came looking for it. I used to be a member of a club, you see. The licence is in order, though,' he added hurriedly.

'Yes, we've checked that.'

'Let me see – Jon was killed on the Monday. On the Tuesday afternoon, when I returned from the school, your people were waiting to talk to me. I told them I owned a gun, and when I went to the cabinet, I found it had been stolen.'

'You're sure nothing else was taken?'

'We've checked and yes, we're sure.'

'And you've no idea when the gun was stolen?'

'None. I remember cleaning it just after the summer break. Late September, I'd say. Since then –' He shook his head. 'I haven't even opened the cabinet since then.'

'How many people know you own a gun?' Grace asked, and Tony Hutchinson smiled at that.

'Most people. Anyone who comes here.' He rose to his feet. 'Come with me.'

Max and Grace followed him to the dining room where several trophies were displayed on beech wood shelves.

'Everyone is curious about these.' Tony was bursting with pride. 'I was a pretty good shot, even if I say so myself.'

Smug bastard.

'So most people around here would know you had a gun?' Max asked. 'And would they know where it was kept?'

'Oh, yes. People liked to see my guns. At one time, I had four, but I sold the others. It's a great sport, although sadly I don't have time for it these days.'

They returned to the lounge. Liz was still standing with her back to the window but, during their absence, she'd refilled her glass with what Max assumed was vodka.

'How about knives?' Max asked, preferring to stand now.

'Hey, I don't go in for knives.' Tony looked appalled by the suggestion. 'Listen, you don't think I had anything to do with this, do you? Jon and Alice were my friends – our friends. They used to come to dinner parties.'

'I'm just trying to get a clear picture in my mind,' Max told him. And I don't like you, he added silently. He didn't warm to the man at all. He was too smooth, too showy and too damn cocky for his own good.

Liz suddenly let out a cackle of laughter. 'Him? Kill Alice? More likely to kill himself trying to get into her knickers.'

'Liz, for God's sake.' Tony cringed. 'Take no notice of her, Chief Inspector. She's apt to get a little jealous when she's had a drink.'

With due cause, Max thought grimly.

'Did you have an affair with Alice?' he asked casually.

'Of course I didn't. I told you, they were our friends.'

'On the night Jonathan Trueman was murdered –'

'Monday,' Tony said, as if Max needed reminding.

'Where were you?'

'I was at the school.' Tony was getting agitated, as well he might. There was a thin line of perspiration on his upper lip. 'I've already told your chaps that.'

'And what time did you arrive?'

'I've told you. I was there all day. It didn't seem worth coming home when the school day ended only to go back in the evening.'

'I see,' Max said, frowning. 'The thing is, we've done a little checking of our own. You haven't lost your credit card as well as your gun, have you?'

'My –? Er, no.'

'What does his credit card have to do with anything?' Liz asked curiously.

'Well, now,' Max explained cordially, 'it seems that either your husband, or someone using his credit card, checked into a hotel in Manchester just after 2 p.m. on Monday afternoon.' He turned his smiling face to Tony. 'Would that have been you, sir?'

Before Tony could respond, Liz marched across the room and threw her vodka in his face. She then stormed from the room, slamming at least four doors on her way upstairs.

'And the lady you checked in with,' Max went on, as if nothing had happened. 'Would you give us her name and address, please? We'll need to speak to her.'

'Is this necessary?' Tony demanded, no longer smiling. 'God, I'll own up to being in the blasted hotel. There's my alibi. What more do you need?'

'To speak to the lady in question,' Max replied. 'If you'd give us her address, sir, I'd be very grateful.'

Tony Hutchinson gave them the necessary contact details for Mrs Pamela Struthers. Max remembered the name; she was the school secretary. Very cosy.

'Thank you. Right, hopefully we won't need to bother you again. As soon as we find your gun, we'll let you know. Oh, and in the unlikely event of it turning up, perhaps you'd be good enough to give me a call.'

'I will,' Tony snapped, his voice angry and sarcastic.

'Thank you. We'll show ourselves out.' Max paused in the doorway. 'I'm sorry your wife's upset. Perhaps you should go and talk to her.'

'I think I'm best qualified on how to deal with my wife, don't you?'

'Of course. Thank you for your time. Goodbye.'

Max and Grace let themselves out.

'We'd better have a word with the lucky Pamela, boss,' Grace said.

Lucky?

'Do you like him?' Max asked curiously.

'He's OK, yes. Nice-looking in a way. Too old for me, of course, but yeah, he's OK.'

It must be a gender thing, Max decided. He detested the man.

Chapter Thirty

Seeing Max's car pull up outside was getting to be a habit. On this particular Saturday morning, however, Jill saw two young boys jump out. That wasn't fair.

She opened the door, and Ben raced into her arms, his legs still moving when he reached her. He felt warm, and sticky, and she loved him. Harry came more slowly, but he was still young enough to be hugged. She stood at the door, an arm around each of the boys, and couldn't speak for the huge lump wedged in her throat.

'Dad said we could show you our dog,' Harry explained, and still Jill could only nod.

'He's in the car,' Ben said, 'in case he chases the cats. Where are they?'

'Erm . . .' Jill cleared her painful throat. 'They're about, but I'm sure the dog will be OK. Go and fetch him, eh?'

Max was standing to one side.

'They bring tears to my eyes, too,' he said softly as they ran back to the car for the dog.

'Bastard!' she muttered.

'Tsk! And my dad always speaks so highly of you.'

The cats raced off at the first sight of the tail-wagging bundle of energy that invaded the cottage, and Jill was tempted to join them. Then Rabble, recalling days from her youth perhaps, suddenly turned and delivered a swift right hook strong enough to make the dog's nose bleed.

'He won't chase cats for a while,' Max said with amusement.

They took Fly into the garden, and spent a hectic time throwing a stick for him.

'Right, you two,' Max said, 'keep that dog amused. I need to talk to Jill.'

'He needs training,' Jill remarked breathlessly.

'He needs a lot of things,' Max retorted. 'Tranquillizers, concrete boots, humane killer.'

Fly was a lovely dog, though. His only fault, as far as Jill could see, was his enthusiasm for life. That could hardly be deemed a fault.

Jill followed Max inside and, without conscious thought, they stood in the lounge at the window overlooking the garden where they could watch the boys.

'No more envelopes?' Max asked, and Jill shook her head. 'Seen anyone? Anything?'

'Nothing. As far as I know, only Ella Gardner has walked up the lane this morning. She called to tell me about a history group meeting. Oh, and Tony Hutchinson ran past early. He does that most days because he's getting in training for walking the Pennine Way.'

'It always comes back to him, doesn't it?'

'How do you mean?' she asked curiously.

'I don't know, but he keeps cropping up. His gun has been stolen –'

'I didn't even know he had one!' Jill was amazed.

'A shotgun. He used to be a keen member of a shooting club.'

Yes, that would appeal to him. A competitive man, Tony would have to be the best.

'We checked out licences,' Max explained, 'and when we went to see this gun, he realized it had been stolen any time between the end of September and now. It may or may not have been used to kill Jonathan Trueman.'

'You're joking!'

'Er, no,' Max said drily, never one to joke about murder. 'He has an alibi for the night Jonathan Trueman was shot. Having spent the afternoon in bed with his mistress, he attended a meeting at the school.'

'God, poor Liz. Does she know?'

'She does now. And she said something telling. She reckoned he was more likely to want to sleep with Alice Trueman than kill her. Do you think he and Alice ever had an affair?'

'I wouldn't know,' Jill said thoughtfully, 'but I'd doubt it. I can't see him being Alice's type.' Not that she had known Alice. 'And surely, he wouldn't sleep with anyone in the village. As Jim Brody said, you can't breathe in this place without everyone knowing about it.'

On the other hand, Tony was an attractive man and an incorrigible flirt. A woman like Alice, living her quiet life at the vicarage, might have been taken in by his charm. She'd spent a long time being treated as a wife. Even Jonathan had admitted to stifling her. Wasn't it likely that she'd enjoy being treated as an attractive woman?

'I don't know,' she said again, 'but it's possible, I suppose. He's not your killer, though. For one thing, he has damn good alibis.'

'Mmm. He also has reasonably strong alibis for a couple of the nights Valentine struck.'

'Oh, come on, Max. He might be a pain in the arse, but he's not out there killing prostitutes. And anyway,' she reminded him, 'you were pulled off Valentine's case, remember?'

'Mm. It doesn't hurt to check people out, though. Anyway, on the night Anne Levington was murdered, he was at a conference in Birmingham. The local paper took a photo of them all at dinner, and his face is easily recognizable.'

'That's more than a reasonably strong alibi,' Jill pointed out.

'It depends how long it would take him to get from Birmingham to Burnley. Two hours at a push late at night. He was there the next morning to check out of the hotel, but he could have got to Burnley and back easily enough. Whether he'd have enough time to kill her, and then cut those sodding hearts from her skin, I don't know.'

'He's not a killer. He doesn't –' She was about to say Hutchinson didn't fit her profile, but changed his mind. They both knew what had happened to the man who had fitted that profile. 'He's not a killer,' she said again.

Max shoved his hands in the pockets of his jeans and Jill could almost hear his brain working.

'What do you know about Andrew Collins?' he asked suddenly.

'Andy? He's the estate agent who sold me this place. Nice enough. Seems popular with people.' She remembered Prue's description: drop dead gorgeous. 'You need to speak to Prue,' she told him. 'He called in when she was visiting and you know what Prue's like. She mentally calculated the cost of his suit, shoes and watch and decided I ought to marry him.'

'What did he call here for?'

'God, Max, I do have friends, you know. As it happens, he brought me a sale brochure for an auction being held at a local farm, but I often see him. We've been out for lunch.'

She enjoyed that. It was confirmation that, like Max, she could attract good-looking partners. Confirmation that she could enjoy life without him.

'Did he tell you he'd been accused of rape?' Max asked.

Jill's head flew up. 'Rape? Never!'

'He was twenty, and the charges were dropped,' Max allowed, 'but there's no smoke without fire.'

'When he was twenty?' she scoffed. 'So some girl fancied him, and he's a very good-looking bloke, and decides she'll accuse him of rape? That hardly makes him a murder suspect.'

Thinking about it, though, she realized she knew very little about him.

'He is a bit cagey about his past,' she admitted. 'This is Prue again. She was trying to get his life story from him, and she failed miserably. His father's dead. He and his mother lived here in Kelton for a year when he was kid, but moved around the country a lot. He's lived here for about the last ten years.'

Max looked at her long and hard.

'If you're planning any more cosy lunches with him,' he said at last, 'be on your guard.'

'In case he tries to rape me? Or in case he tries to murder me?'

Max ignored the sarcasm. 'Watch Tony Hutchinson as well,' he went on. 'I don't like him.'

Jill didn't either.

'I'm planning an off-the-record chat with his wife on Monday when he's at school,' he added.

'That shouldn't be too difficult. I don't think Liz is that keen on him.'

'She isn't now she knows he's been playing away.'

'No, it does tend to put women off. Funny that.' She gave him a sweet smile that didn't even begin to hint at the rush of pain, anger and hurt she felt. 'I expect the boys are getting hungry. I'll go and see if they want something to eat.'

Chapter Thirty-One

Max and Grace were at Tony and Liz Hutchinson's house soon after nine o'clock on Monday morning.

Liz Hutchinson opened the door to them, and she looked how Max felt – tired, hungover and not quite sure what day it was. She was wearing dark blue satin pyjamas.

'Tony's at work,' she told them. 'Or is it me you've come to arrest?' she added with a smile.

'We're not here to arrest anyone,' Max told her, returning her smile, 'but I'm curious about this stolen gun of your husband's. I was wondering if we might have a chat with you and see if you can remember anything.' He'd love to have a good look round this house, and find something to pin on Hutchinson, but a chat with his wife would do for now.

'I can't, but you're welcome to ask questions.'

'We can come back later if you like,' he offered, but she was already showing them inside.

'No need. I doubt I'll be sober later. Would you like a drink?'

It struck Max that she was lonely. She was even glad of their company.

'Yes, that would be good, thanks. What are you having?'

'Vodka.'

Even if Max touched the stuff, which he didn't, it was too early for vodka.

'If I wasn't working I'd have one with you,' he said, 'but as I am, is there any chance of a coffee?'

'My culinary skills aren't great but, yes, I can manage that.' She looked questioningly at Grace.

'Coffee for me, too, please. Can I help you with it, Mrs Hutchinson?'

'If you like,' Liz answered vaguely. She motioned towards the dining room. 'Your people have already decided there's no sign of a break-in but you're free to look. You know where it was kept.'

'Thanks. I'll take another look, if I may,' Max said.

Grace, who reckoned Max was wasting his time and hers, followed Liz into the kitchen, leaving Max free to poke around.

It was rare Max came across anyone so obliging. If people had something to hide, it was obvious they weren't going to welcome him with open arms, but even the most innocent tended to follow them around. Not Liz Hutchinson. She had more or less given them free reign to delve wherever they chose.

The dining room wasn't of much interest to him. A door off that room led into a study and that showed far more promise. It was crammed with books and the modern desk in the centre of the room had six drawers, three either side. He listened, heard Grace talking to Liz Hutchinson in the kitchen, and tried the drawers. One side was locked, but the other three were filled with paperwork that had been thrown in rather than filed neatly. There were bank statements, credit card statements, and mortgage statements. He'd thought this house came with the job, but no, it had a hefty mortgage on it.

There was nothing of interest on the bank statements or the credit card statements. The latter were paid off in full each month. There were a couple of hotel bookings, a fairly large amount to a jeweller's, but nothing of great interest. They already knew he had a mistress.

'I thought we'd lost you,' Liz said, coming into the study just as he was browsing the books on the shelves. 'Coffee,' she said, handing him a mug.

'Thanks.'

Still wearing her pyjamas, she leaned against the edge of the desk. 'Have you found anything?'

'I'm not sure what I'm looking for.' That at least was true. What he'd like to find was some damning piece of evidence that would put Tony Hutchinson behind bars. Why? Because he didn't like the man? No, there was more to it than that. Tony Hutchinson was raising far too many questions for Max's liking.

'Tony isn't a killer,' Liz said, 'if that's what you're thinking.'

'That's good,' Grace said with a smile.

Liz Hutchinson would make a good prison visitor, Max thought. Despite the hungover look, she was attractive. She'd liven up any prison. If she had any sense, though, she wouldn't bother visiting her husband.

'And no,' she added, 'there's not much love lost between us. God knows why we stay together. I suppose he stays with me because he'd find divorce distasteful – a man in his position and all that. He's very fond of what he calls his position.'

'Why do *you* stay with *him*?' Grace asked.

'He keeps the drinks cabinet stocked,' she answered simply.

Max pointed at the glass in her hand. 'You drink too much. And I'm allowed to say that because I drink too much, too.'

'One dipso to another?' She laughed, and he thought that in a happier relationship, she'd be a special sort of woman.

'Something like that.'

'It passes the time,' she told him, 'and after a bottle of vodka, even Tony looks appealing.'

Max could sympathize. Most things would look better after a bottle of vodka.

As he spoke, he'd been idly glancing at the books on the shelves. There were dozens of thrillers and murder mysteries – P.D. James, Ruth Rendell, James Patterson, Agatha Christie and what looked to be a complete set by Arthur

Conan Doyle. There were also a couple of books on Jack the Ripper.

'Good bedtime reading,' he said with a wry smile.

'He used to be a member of the Jack the Ripper Society or whatever they call themselves,' Liz told him. 'Perhaps he still is. I remember him dragging me round London once. That was years ago. You can go on the guided tour and see the murder spots. He loves stuff like that.'

'Really? God, he knows how to show a girl a good time.'

She laughed again, a light-hearted tinkling sound that made Max smile.

'He doesn't have the balls to kill anyone though,' she said. 'If he had, I'd have been pushing up daisies for years.'

Max pointed at the desk. 'Does he do a lot of work from home? I suppose he does. They reckon teaching is all paperwork these days. A bit like my job.'

'He works late quite often, but he doesn't bring stuff home. Well, he says he works late,' she corrected herself, her tone bitter, 'but who knows what he's doing?' She attempted to open the drawers, and seemed surprised to discover that one side was locked. 'That'll be to keep the cleaner out,' she explained. 'Molly Turnbull cleans here a couple of afternoons a week. You'll have seen her up at the vicarage.'

'Nosy, is she?'

'No more than most,' Liz said, 'but Tony likes to keep things from her. The trouble is, he's always too lazy to fetch the key so he ends up shoving stuff in the unlocked side. It's just crap – bank statements and stuff like that. I'll get the key for you. Not,' she added with a grin, 'that you'll find his shotgun in there.'

While she was gone, Max studied the books more closely. As well as the fiction, there were a couple on forensic psychology.

It might not be the lightest reading material, but you couldn't arrest a bloke for that. They already knew he'd started a course in psychology and they knew he was a fan of Jill's work and films like *The Silence of the Lambs*. All the same, it didn't sit comfortably with Max.

'Here you are,' Liz Hutchinson said, dangling a small key from her fingers.

Grace took the key from her and unlocked the drawers.

'I'll go and put some clothes on,' Liz said, leaving them to it.

It was almost as if she wanted them to find some incriminating piece of evidence. In fact, if she'd known they were coming, she might even have planted something. She hadn't known they were coming, though. He was being fanciful.

Max looked in the drawers and, this time, all the financial statements were stored neatly in folders in the top drawer. There was a lot more paperwork but none of it interesting – TV licence, house and contents insurance policies, receipts for a DVD player and an electric fire.

In the bottom drawer was what at first glance looked to be unused school notebooks. On closer inspection, Max saw that newspaper clippings had been stuck in.

'Good God, look at this, boss!' Grace jabbed a finger at one of the clippings, a grainy photograph.

It was poor quality, but Jill was easily recognizable. A good quality copy of the same photograph had been hand-delivered to her cottage.

Chapter Thirty-Two

Ella was relieved to see Tom in his chair in front of the TV. She hated leaving him for long, but he was sound asleep, looking relaxed and comfortable.

This morning, she had caught the train for Manchester to meet up with Gemma Thornbury. They'd had a long chat over afternoon tea at the Lowry Hotel. Sitting grandly alongside the banks of the River Irwell, the five-star hotel was dubbed Manchester's most fashionable venue. Ella didn't doubt it.

It would have been a thoroughly enjoyable day if not for worries about Tom, and frustration when her train was delayed. She'd toyed with the idea of taking the car, but she hated driving in Manchester these days. Traffic often had the place at a standstill and Ella swore they changed the one-way system on a daily basis.

Still, she was home now and Tom was with her. He was snoring softly. Smiling, Ella sat back in the armchair, slipped off her shoes, stretched her legs and closed her eyes. She was shattered.

It was funny, she thought, how a mental picture of someone could be so far off the mark. She and Gemma had corresponded several times by email and she'd imagined Gemma almost the same age as herself. It had come as a surprise to meet a young woman in her thirties. Also, in her emails, Gemma had appeared a brisk, businesslike type. She had been lovely and Ella could have chatted to her all day.

Gemma was researching her family tree and had wanted

to pick Ella's brain. It had been exciting to share her knowledge of Rossendale with Gemma, and to be able to give Gemma a photograph of the girl's great-great-grandfather, a local mill worker . . .

Ella was nodding off herself when Tom woke.

'How have you been, love?' she asked, determined to keep her tone light and unconcerned.

'Fine.' He smiled that gentle smile of his. 'How was your day?'

'Interesting.'

She told him of her day, about chatting with Gemma over tea and cakes in the hotel.

'And you'll never guess who was on the train,' she added.

'Charles and Camilla?'

'Tony Hutchinson and some girl.' Ella thought back to the disturbing encounter. 'I've no idea who she was. The type my mum would have said was no better than she ought to be, whatever that means. Early twenties, I suppose. A brassy-looking girl. Showing too much cleavage and wearing a skirt that should have been sold as a belt.'

Tom laughed. 'Your powers of description never fail to amaze me.'

'I wonder who she was.'

'Heavens, Ella, it was probably a friend or relative of his and Liz's.'

'Never. If that were the case, he would have introduced me. When he saw me, he went so red in the face I thought he was going to explode there and then. He was up to no good, you mark my words. If looks could kill, I wouldn't be sitting here now.'

'You and your imagination.'

'Before he knew I was there, he handed her an envelope. They looked close,' Ella said thoughtfully, 'but not happy to be with each other if that makes sense.'

'None whatsoever.'

Ella laughed. Perhaps Tom was right, and she was reading something into nothing. With so much on her mind lately . . .

There was only one thing on her mind, losing her beloved Tom. Somehow, and she had no idea how, she had to face up to the fact that soon he would be taken from her. She wouldn't think about it now, though. He was here with her, and that was all that mattered. They would take things a day at a time.

'Gemma showed me her family tree,' she rushed on, changing the subject, 'and it was fascinating. She's a proper detective, that girl. But what did fascinate me – of course, Gemma wasn't interested in this – but what fascinated me was that her aunt fosters children. Have you heard Bob Murphy mention his Aunt Jenny? His foster mother? Lives in Stockport? Well, this Jenny is Gemma's aunt. What a small world we live in.'

'I knew he'd moved here from Stockport, but no, I don't know of Aunt Jenny.'

'Oh, I knew he'd been fostered. According to Gemma, his mother died in a house fire. Anyway, I must remember to tell Bob about young Gemma.'

'He's done well for himself has Bob,' Tom said. 'A cracking little business he's got there and plenty of friends.'

'No real family, though,' Ella said, 'and a good business can't take the place of family.'

'That reminds me,' Tom said suddenly, 'we'll have a word with him and see if he'll do that front wall. I don't know why we didn't get him to do that when he did the work on the kitchen.'

'I'll give him a call in the week,' Ella promised, amazed that Tom could worry about garden walls when his life was ebbing from him.

Her mind drifted back to her meeting on the train with Tony Hutchinson. Even allowing for an over-active imagination, there had been something odd about that. The way he'd handed over that envelope had been shifty. He'd looked about him and then, just as he was handing it over, spotted Ella.

His face had quickly broken into a smile. It had been a cold, forced smile that had stopped a long way short of his eyes.

Ella wondered about Liz and, not for the first time, her heart filled with sympathy. No wonder Liz had a drink problem. Everyone in the village knew that Tony was an incorrigible flirt. Ella guessed it went deeper than flirting, too. It was none of her business, but she suspected Liz had a lonely existence.

That woman he'd been with was too young to be his mistress. What nonsense, she scoffed. No one would be more thrilled than Tony to discover he could still attract someone so young.

She could have been one of those escorts, she supposed. Ella had no idea how the system worked, but didn't men pay to have young women accompanying them? That would explain the envelope he'd handed over. And didn't those women often perform sexual favours?

Ella smiled to herself. She had no idea; and she wasn't sorry about that.

'What's amused you?' Tom asked curiously.

'That woman with Tony Hutchinson,' she told him. 'I'd just mentally booked her as one of those escorts. The sort that are paid to go out with men. I then wondered if these men had their wicked ways with them.'

'And do they?'

'I've no idea what they do,' Ella chuckled, 'and I'm way too old to find out.'

Chapter Thirty-Three

It was the Sunday before Christmas, a bright, crisp, clear day. It was getting chilly now, but the sun had made it pleasantly warm during the day.

Jill had bought a book giving details of easy, moderate and difficult walks in the area and today she'd chosen a moderate one. Unfortunately, the author's idea of moderate wasn't quite the same as Jill's. Her legs were protesting and she still had quite a trek home. Perhaps she couldn't blame the author for that; she'd spent too much time in front of a computer lately and was out of condition.

There was another reason she couldn't blame the author; she had a feeling she'd strayed from his route. She'd had a vague idea of where she was, though, and when she came to New Line reservoir, she knew exactly where she was, about to head out on to the Bacup to Rochdale road.

She walked by the side of the lake and smiled at the way the ducks and geese spotted her and rushed over.

'If I had any bread,' she told them, 'I'd be eating it myself. I'm starving – duck with orange sauce sounds good to me.'

With disgruntled quacks and squawks, they swam or flew off.

Jill wished she'd brought her camera. The sun was sinking fast, leaving everything bathed in warm light, and the scenery was stunning. The hills rose behind the lake, the steep fields separated by old stone walls. Sheep were white spots on the hillside.

She'd visited her parents yesterday and had been

shocked by her mother's appearance. Since her last visit, three or four months ago, Mum had aged. Yesterday, she'd looked grey, tired and old. Her X-ray had revealed something on her lung and, although Mum was reluctant to discuss it, that constant cough had spoken for itself. She was having an exploratory operation in the morning.

Jill refused to think about it. The whole purpose of this walk had been to take her mind off it.

She was about to continue on her walk when she spotted someone heading for one of the benches. Again, the ducks and geese gave this person a noisy welcome. This time, they were rewarded.

She watched the person throw bread on to the water for a full minute before she realized it was Ella Gardner. She walked across to join her.

'Jill! What are you doing out here?'

'I could ask the same of you. I'm out for a walk and think I probably took the wrong turning. What about you?'

'I've been doing some last-minute Christmas shopping,' Ella explained, 'and I often stop here on the way home. Today, I even remembered to bring the stale bread.'

Ella looked tired. She also looked as if she had the problems of the world on her shoulders.

'You OK, Ella?'

'Mmm? Oh, yes, I'm fine.' She smiled, but it looked a little forced to Jill.

'Isn't it lovely here?'

'A gorgeous spot, isn't it?' Ella agreed. 'Did you see that film – *Whistle Down the Wind*?'

'That's one of my all-time favourites. Alan Bates is the escaped convict and Hayley Mills one of the children who believes he's Jesus.'

Smiling, Ella nodded. 'I love it, too. Some of it was filmed round here, you know. One of the tunnels was used. Of course, the tunnels are either blocked up now or used for storage. And there's a good view of the old mill's chimney . . .'

They chatted about other films they'd both enjoyed but Jill still thought Ella had things on her mind.

'You sure you're OK, Ella?'

'Yes. It's just that – well, you'll know the police have been questioning Tony Hutchinson?'

Jill inclined her head slightly, not sure she could discuss the matter with Ella. 'They're bound to.'

'Because his gun was stolen, yes.' Ella was thoughtful. 'I saw him on the Manchester train the day before yesterday. He was with a young girl. I didn't recognize her, but he looked shifty, Jill. He handed her a well-stuffed envelope and then he spotted me. The way he looked at me –' Ella shuddered. 'I told Tom all about it and made light of it for his benefit, but it made me quite nervous. It was more than anger, somehow.'

Jill was intrigued. She guessed it would take a lot to unnerve Ella.

Ella recounted the incident and gave Jill a good description of the girl involved.

'Are you telling me this in confidence, Ella, or can I pass it on to someone who might be interested?'

Ella thought for a few moments. 'Pass it on, Jill. It's probably nothing at all, but you never know. Right,' she went on briskly, 'you'd better have a lift home with me. We've chatted so long, we'll be in the dark in a minute.'

'The exercise would do me far more good, but hey, I'd love a lift, thanks.'

They left their bench and walked back to the picnic area's car park. Only Ella's car was there, a small yellow one, and Jill had to laugh as she got in.

'Are you prepared for every known emergency, Ella?'

'Pretty much,' Ella replied with a chuckle. 'I've maps, water, sweets, a change of clothes, tissues, at least three umbrellas, a first aid kit, a couple of books in case I get stuck in a jam, binoculars in case I see some rare bird, a flask – empty, sadly . . .'

Ella was a slow, careful and very courteous driver. No one could have felt less than safe with her.

'I hear on the grapevine that you've been out with Bob Murphy,' Ella remarked.

'Out? I have not. Oh, I called at The Weaver's Retreat for a drink at the same time Bob called in. We didn't arrive or leave together,' Jill replied, amazed at how effective the grapevine was.

'Nice chap,' Ella said.

'Yes.' They'd spent a pleasant hour talking about horses.

Ella was right; as she pulled up outside Lilac Cottage it was quite dark.

'Will you come in for a tea or coffee, Ella?' Jill hated going inside on her own when it was dark. She dreaded seeing another envelope lying on her doormat. Who was she kidding? She was dreading far worse than that. Envelopes she could cope with.

'Thanks, but I'd better make it another time. I need to get home and see how Tom is.'

'Oh? Isn't he well?'

Ella hesitated. 'He's been a bit under the weather, that's all, love. We'll save that cuppa for another time.'

Jill left the warm car and shivered. The temperature had dropped during the short drive. She took her keys from her pocket as she walked up the driveway – then dropped them when a shadow suddenly moved.

'Bloody hell, Don! What in God's name are you doing creeping around? You nearly gave me a heart attack.'

'Sorry, sorry.'

Don Cornwall, wearing a smart suit as always, stood beneath the security light looking very sheepish indeed.

'I was driving past and thought I saw someone lurking around. I left my car at the end of the lane and walked back to have a look.' He put his hand on her arm. 'Sorry.'

'And did you see anyone?' Jill's heart was pounding.

'No.'

She unlocked her door and pushed it open, pausing only to straighten the holly wreath. There was nothing lying on her doormat.

'Do you fancy a coffee now you're here?' she asked.

'Well, yes, that would be good if it's no trouble. And I'm really sorry I scared you.'

'Forget it. I'm a bit jumpy at the moment, that's all.'

A bit jumpy was putting it mildly.

'Hey, this looks good – very tasteful.' Cornwall admired the festive decorations. 'You've been busy.'

She had. Determined to make her first Christmas in Kelton Bridge a good one, she'd bought new decorations, all in a red and green theme, and decked the place in holly sprigs and fir cones . . .

Jill hadn't even had time to put the kettle on when there was a hammering on her door that set her heartbeat off even faster.

Cornwall looked at her, and must have seen how she'd jumped at the sound. 'Do you want me to get it?' he asked curiously.

'No.' She smiled at her own stupidity. 'I'm a little paranoid at the moment. You'll have to bear with me.'

When she opened the door, it was Bob Murphy who was bathed in the orange glow given off by her security light.

'I thought I'd drop these prices in for you,' he said.

'Gosh, that was quick. Thanks, Bob. Are you coming in?'

'Thanks, but I'm in a rush. Another time perhaps. Have a look through those.' He gestured at the large white envelope in her hand. 'Give me a ring sometime.'

'I will, and thanks again.'

He was halfway along her drive, heading back to his white van, when he suddenly turned. 'What do you think of Sundown's chances? He's running at Wolverhampton tomorrow.'

'I know he is. Not a hope in hell.'

'You're probably right,' he agreed with a laugh, giving her a wave as he carried on his way.

Feeling all kinds of an idiot, Jill returned to the kitchen to make coffee for herself and Don Cornwall.

Chapter Thirty-Four

He hit the button and the car's window purred open.

'How much?' he asked, when she leaned on the roof and peered inside.

'Depends what you want.'

This one looked uninterested, as if it were her choice and not his.

He took his wallet from his top shirt pocket, flicked it open so she'd see the wad of notes, then returned it to his pocket. 'I want the best.'

She was interested now. Bitches. They'd do anything for money. They would even die for it.

'I can give you an hour you'll never forget,' she promised.

Likewise, sweetheart, he thought, suppressing the urge to laugh.

'Get in then.'

She opened the door, threw a well-worn brown handbag in the passenger footwell and was about to get in when she suddenly changed her mind.

'I need a pee,' she gasped, pulling a face. 'Give me two minutes. I'll nip round the corner there. No one will see me.'

Before he could argue, she dashed off towards a block of flats where the walls were covered in graffiti and the doorways probably stank of urine.

'Don't drive off,' she yelled after her. 'You've got my handbag.'

Bitch. Stupid fucking bitch!

He couldn't hang around here like a sitting target.

The seconds ticked away. What was she doing?

'Fuck! Fuck! Fuck!' He wasn't taking this shit. He slammed the car into first gear and drove off fast.

'Don't panic,' he told himself as he drove. 'Don't panic.'

He slowed the car and drove at a steady thirty miles per hour.

There was nothing to worry about. The silly bitch would be standing on the pavement wondering where he – and her hand-bag – had gone. She'd be thinking about the cash she'd missed out on. The thought made him smile.

He was still smiling when he saw the police car in his rear-view mirror.

Chapter Thirty-Five

The incident room was like something from the forthcoming Burnley versus Blackburn Rovers cup-tie. Everyone was shouting at everyone else and Max swore that violence was only a breath away. He should have calmed things down, but he felt far from calm himself and was having to shout to stand even a slim chance of being heard.

'If Hutchinson so much as looks at a double yellow,' he shouted, 'I want him hauled in. OK?'

'But, boss, we've got enough to do without wasting our time on him,' someone argued.

'We've got nothing on him,' someone else complained.

'Stop arguing,' he yelled at them. 'I don't like the fucking creep, and that's reason enough. You want more reasons? His gun's been stolen, he's already lied to us – Jesus! How much more do you want? You're supposed to be detectives. Now get out there and fucking detect.'

The door opened and Jill stood there, reeling slightly at the din that met her.

'I'll be with you in a minute,' Max snapped at her.

She went out, closing the door quietly behind her.

'Right, you lot,' Max went on, 'we've got dead bodies turning up like Reader's Digest prize draws, we're getting bollocked left, right and centre from above, and the press are making us look like Miss Marple on Valium. We need a soddin' result.'

Before they could argue any more, Max marched out of

the room, gave the door a satisfactory slam, and left them to call him unspeakable things at their leisure.

He had a million things to do, including yet another bollocking from the powers that sat behind executive desks all day, but he went off to find Jill first.

When he eventually spotted her, she was outside in the car park, and he ran to catch up with her. 'Did you want me?'

She nodded at the second floor of the building. 'What was all that about?'

'Tempers are running high. We're getting nowhere with anything and frustration is beginning to show.'

'I only wanted a quick word, Max, and it's probably nothing.' She told him of her meeting with Ella, and Ella's description of Tony Hutchinson's behaviour on the train. 'The thing is,' she warned him, 'it's a bit tricky. He spotted Ella so if you go questioning him about it, he'll know where it's come from. She doesn't strike me as the type to be easily scared but she admitted it made her nervous.'

'Don't worry, we'll tread carefully.' She was right; it was probably nothing. All the same, it was still coming back to Hutchinson. 'Could the woman in question have been a prostitute?'

'That's what I wondered,' Jill said with a sigh. 'The way Ella described her, she could have been. She said she wore lots of make-up, had plenty of cleavage, and was showing off her assets. Yes, she might have been.'

God, he'd nail Hutchinson for something, even if it were only driving without due care and attention.

'I'm glad I caught you,' he said. 'I'm just off to see a working girl, and I wish you'd come along.'

'Oh?'

'She lives in Burnley with her husband and a couple of kids and, apparently, works the streets of Preston.'

'Uh? That's a long way to go.'

'It is. Her husband knows nothing about it. She's told him she's got an overnight job at one of the supermarkets. She reckons selling her body pays better than stacking shelves. Anyway, on Monday night, she was about to get in a bloke's car when she spotted what she thought was a silk scarf in his jacket pocket. His jacket was lying on the back seat. It gave her a funny feeling and she ran off.'

Jill's eyes widened. 'And you think it was Valentine?'

'I don't know. Probably not,' he admitted.

'But you're not –'

'I know, I know, but Cornwall reckons it's nothing. They've spoken to her and dismissed her. I want to talk to her – unofficial. I don't know, Jill, call it a hunch.'

She nodded. 'OK.'

'So what exactly spooked her?' Jill asked as Max drove them to Janie Fisher's address.

'Just a scarf she saw. If it was a scarf. She said it gave her a funny feeling. Oh, and she's as mad as hell at us apparently because she ran off and left her handbag in his car.'

'You what?'

'Our fault, she reckons. We should make the streets safer.'

'Ah, right.' Jill shook her head, bemused.

Janie Fisher lived on a sprawling estate that was mainly local authority housing. Jill had seen better places to live, but she'd also seen a lot worse. In fact, the houses were almost identical to the one Jill had been brought up in. Some of the cars parked outside the houses looked road-worthy. Most didn't.

They got out of the car and Max was about to open the gate to number 27 – even the house number was the same as the one from Jill's childhood – when an angry-looking German shepherd appeared from nowhere. It was barking and snapping with teeth bared.

'Shit!' Jill backed away in fright.

'OK, Lennox,' Max muttered, 'you win. We'll stand here and look like a pair of prats for a minute.'

After what seemed an age, with Jill convinced her eardrums would never recover, a woman appeared at the front door.

'Yes?' Her snap was as intimidating as the dog's.

'Janie Fisher?' Max had to yell to make himself heard over the dog's noise.

'Who's asking?'

'Detective Chief Inspector –'

'I've already seen you lot,' she cut him off, coming to the gate.

This wasn't going to be easy, Jill realized.

'Yes, I know, but we wanted to ask you a couple of questions.' He looked at the dog, then looked at her. 'Can we come in for a minute, please?' She hesitated. 'Look,' he said, 'if we piss you off, you can set the dog on us. Right?'

There was a moment's hesitation. 'Tyson, get in the back,' she said, resigned.

Tyson didn't budge. He did quieten down though, content now to make the odd deep-throated growl, and they managed to get to the front door and then inside the hall with their limbs intact.

'You'd better come in,' Janie Fisher muttered, pushing open the door to the sitting room.

She looked as if she'd just got out of bed. Perhaps she had. Long blonde hair was tied back in a blue band. She wore shapeless black leggings, a dark blue sweatshirt and worn suede slippers.

The room looked like Santa's grotto, but it was clean and tidy. Kids' toys had been put neatly in a corner. A huge television set dominated most of one wall. It must have cost more than the rest of the furniture put together. Paper chains criss-crossed the ceiling, a huge tree was covered in baubles and flashing lights, and Christmas cards had been stuck to the walls.

'What do you want to know?' Janie Fisher demanded impatiently.

Tyson had wandered off into the kitchen and Jill began to breathe more easily.

'I'm Jill Kennedy.' Well, Max hadn't bothered to introduce her. 'And we'd like to hear anything you can tell us. Anything at all – no matter how insignificant it sounds. The man you saw might have been responsible for a number of murders.' Janie Fisher shuddered at that. 'The truth is,' Jill went on, 'we haven't got a lot to go on. We want him caught and quick. So do you. If it was him, you're the first person to get away alive.'

Jill waited for that to sink in.

'If things had been different, we could have been calling here to tell your kids that their mum was dead,' she pointed out. 'Not the Christmas present you'd want for them, I'm sure.'

She waited for that to sink in, too, and watched her mull over it.

'We believe,' Max explained, 'that our man lures prostitutes into his car, drives them off to some deserted spot and strangles them. We know nothing else about him. So anything you can tell us will be a step forward.'

'If it *was* him,' Janie Fisher pointed out. 'I feel a bit daft about it now. It was probably nothing. The thing was, a couple of us had been talking about this killer, even having a laugh about it, and we'd spooked ourselves. Daft really. But when I saw that bleeding scarf –'

'What sort of scarf was it?' Jill asked.

Janie Fisher sat down and, without waiting to be invited, Max and Jill followed her example.

Jill could see she was shaken and doing her best to remember everything.

'It was a dark maroon scarf. Looked like silk to me. Of course, it might have been a flashy handkerchief or something.'

'Did he look the type to have silk handkerchiefs?' Jill asked.

Janie Fisher shook her head.

'And the scarf or handkerchief, whatever it was, was in his jacket pocket? Right?' Max asked.

'Yes, his jacket was lying on the back seat of the car. A brown corduroy casual jacket.' She thought for a moment. 'He was wearing a shirt, brushed cotton probably. It was a pale colour – yellow perhaps. And he was wearing a baseball cap that kept his face in shadow. I don't know, it was dark and I could only go by the car's interior light.'

'Tell us about the man himself. What did he look like?' Jill asked.

'I don't know because I couldn't see much. He was big, though. Big shoulders.'

Jill knew the description wouldn't be too reliable. If people were frightened, the person responsible was always described as being big, powerful and threatening.

'What about the car?' Max asked. 'You said it was a big car, either dark blue or black. Is that right?'

'Yes, but it was dark and, to be honest, with Christmas round the corner, I was more interested in the cash he showed me. Must have had at least a grand in his wallet. But as soon as I saw that scarf, I lost my nerve and scarpered. Lost my bleedin' handbag, too.'

'This car, though, was it a big saloon or an estate?'

'I don't know. It might have been the same as yours.'

Jill and Max both turned to look out at his car, reassuring themselves that it was still there. They didn't have a good view, though; the wheels could easily be missing.

'He had big hands,' Janie said vaguely.

'Big hands?' Jill queried. 'What sort of hands? Did they look soft and well cared for? Or were they work-roughened? Do you think he worked at a desk or something more manual?'

'I don't know.'

'What about the inside of the car?' Max asked. 'What was that like?'

'Dark upholstery. That coat lying on the back seat.' She sighed. 'I can't remember anything else.'

'Could he have had grey hair?' Max asked. 'Tall, early fifties, grey hair, fit-looking?'

Jill scowled at him. He'd just described Tony Hutchinson.

'I didn't see his hair. It was under that baseball cap,' she explained. 'He was younger than that, though. He sounded younger anyway.'

'Any sort of accent?' Jill put in.

'Nothing I noticed.'

'OK, humour me, will you?' Max asked, giving her one of his coaxing smiles. 'Tell us again exactly what happened, where you were, and where you went afterwards.'

'Are you lot fucking thick or what?'

Gritting her teeth, Janie told them exactly what had happened from start to finish. They'd hoped her story might have changed, or that something else might have come to mind, but she told them nothing they didn't already know.

'I found my mate quickly which was just as well because I had to borrow the taxi fare off her. She lives in Burnley, too. We both work out in Preston.'

'And your husband thinks you have a job in a supermarket?' Jill asked.

'Yes, and I don't want him knowing any different. OK?'

'Of course.' Max got to his feet. 'Thanks for that. We'll be off now. One more thing, though. Will you come out to my car and see if you can spot any differences?'

She frowned, puzzled.

'You reckon he might have been driving a blue Ford Mondeo like mine. If I sit in it, and we pretend I'm him, it might jog your memory.'

'Sure.' She wanted to be rid of them.

They got as far as the hall and then the dog was there, breathing on Jill's hand and growling menacingly.

'It's OK, Lennox,' Max said. 'We're leaving now.'

'What did you call him?' Janie asked.

'Ah, sorry, he's Tyson, isn't he? He looks more like a Lennox to me.'

Janie Fisher looked at him as if he were mad. Jill knew how she felt.

'You're sure you can't remember even one letter or number from the registration plate?' Jill asked as they walked outside.

'I didn't even look at it.'

Max flicked the remote to unlock the car. At least the wheels were still attached.

'OK, I'll sit inside,' he said. 'This chap wound the window down to talk to you, right?'

'Yeah.'

Max sat inside the car, started the engine and hit the button for the window.

Janie peered inside. 'His car was cleaner and tidier.'

Jill also peered in and saw the passenger footwell. There were at least four empty plastic cups. The rest of the car was no better. Pens and loose change were scattered around, CDs were waiting to be put back in cases, and there was more dog hair than Tyson could boast. Jill hadn't thought anything of it when he'd driven her out here, but it was a mess.

'Other than that,' Janie said, 'it might have been a car like this.'

'What about the man himself?' Max pushed on. 'What was the difference between him and me?'

'You're better looking.' For the first time, Jill saw a hint of a smile on her face.

'Why, thank you,' Max said, taken aback.

'Mind you, *he* was probably better looking in daylight. You do smell better, though.' She frowned. 'There was a funny smell to his car. It was a mixture of dampness, something musty, and orange air freshener. Yeah, his car smelt damp.'

'Damp?' Jill queried.

'Yeah.' Janie straightened up. 'Sorry, that's all I can tell you.'

'OK, Janie. Thanks for that. If we need to talk to you –'

'Don't come at the weekend or in the evenings,' she warned. 'I don't want my old man knowing about it.'

'Don't worry. But if you think of anything else, anything at all, give me a call, OK?' Max took a card from his pocket. 'That number will get straight through to me.'

She took the card from him.

'And be careful,' he warned as he pushed opened the car door for Jill.

Jill suspected Max was relieved to be driving out of the estate with a full set of wheels.

'I reckon you were well in there,' she quipped. 'With a bit of luck, you'd probably get a discount.'

'Oh, very droll. So what did you think?'

'I think,' Jill said carefully, 'that Janie Fisher's one lucky lady.'

He looked at her as he slowed for a corner.

'I think she's the first witness,' Jill said.

'You really think it was Valentine?'

'Yes, I do. Who else would carry around a grand in cash? With that sort of loose change, you don't have to waste your time kerb-crawling. Now, why in hell's name would his car smell damp?' she murmured, puzzled. 'Because it's not used often,' she answered her own question. 'It spends most of its time locked away in a garage – a damp garage. So he has two cars.'

'You'd better mention all this to your mate Cornwall,' Max told her.

'Oh, great. And how do I explain how I came to be out here with you?'

He laughed. 'You'll think of something.'

Chapter Thirty-Six

With Christmas and the New Year celebrations over, the office was returning to normal, and Max wasn't sorry about that. He preferred normal.

Christmas was great for the kids, but there was nothing else to recommend it. Max hated the waste. Instead of buying presents no one wanted, he wished people would donate the money to charity. It would be far simpler. It would cut down on the number of burglaries, too.

But Christmas was over, thank God.

'I sometimes think,' he said to no one in particular, 'that if people in this country stopped owning dogs, we'd never solve a crime.'

'You what, guv?' Grace looked up from the computer on her desk.

'We've had a call from a woman out walking her dog,' Max told her. 'The dog found a shotgun.'

'Great stuff.'

'Indeed. It was at the bottom of a bonfire that had been built for a New Year party they were having in Kelton. The party was cancelled because of the bad weather.' He looked at his watch. 'Alan and Fletch were near Kelton so they should have it by now.'

No sooner had he spoken than Atkinson put his head round the door. 'That gun, guv?'

'Yes?' Max knew from the smile that Atkinson was failing to hide that he didn't want to hear this. 'It's not a sodding toy one, is it?'

'The dog thinks so,' Atkinson said, grinning. 'They can't

get it off her. Thinks it's a stick, they reckon.' His grin grew broader. 'They've called in for back-up.'

'Bloody hell!'

'We've got a vet and the local dog warden on their way. And a couple of uniforms are out there.'

'Oh, for fuck's sake!' Max muttered.

'The dog's owner is getting hysterical. I suppose that's understandable if the gun's loaded. The dog could shoot itself. Or Fletch,' he added with a guffaw of laughter. 'Now that'd be a first. Has a copper ever been shot by a dog?'

'God knows. But if Fido's a good shot, he can come round here for some bloody target practice.'

'It's Tilly, guv. A Labrador cross puppy, by all accounts. I thought it might have been a Rottweiler at the very least, but no, it's an Andrex puppy.'

Unable to control his mirth any longer, Atkinson left the room.

Max was glad someone was finding something to smile about. He wasn't. As each day passed, any clues left by the killer or killers of Alice and Jonathan Trueman were being lost. They were getting nowhere.

This shotgun had been found at the bottom of a pile of wood less than a quarter of a mile from the church. Surely to God it had to be the one used to kill Jonathan Trueman, the same gun that had been stolen from Tony Hutchinson.

As soon as that damned Andrex puppy had finished playing with it and they could confirm it was Hutchinson's gun, he was going to lean on that man. Heavily.

It was almost two hours later when Alan and Fletch returned.

'Woof, woof,' someone growled.

'Fuck off!' Fletch snapped back, but this merely brought forth gales of laughter.

When they had Hutchinson in the interview room, Max wondered where to start. Hutchinson was already pissing him off, simply because he was delighted to be asked to help them. The cocky bastard enjoyed being the centre of attention.

'I suppose,' Hutchinson said as soon as they'd switched on the tape and identified themselves, 'that now you've found my gun, I'm chief suspect?'

'You are. So tell me again where you were on the evening of November twenty-ninth, the night Jonathan Trueman was murdered.'

'I arrived at the school at 7 p.m.,' he explained patiently.

'And your mistress?' Max asked. 'Where was she? Still in the hotel room in Manchester?'

'I dropped her off at her house,' he said, reddening slightly. 'We didn't think we should arrive at the school together. You know how tongues wag.'

They didn't wag as much as Max would have liked.

'So I dropped her off and drove straight to the school. That would have been seven o'clock. No, it was a few minutes before that actually. I remember wanting to hear the seven o'clock news on the radio and I was planning to sit in the car until it came on. However, a lad's mother, Mrs Tooney – I can give you her address – arrived and parked alongside me. I thought it would look rude to ignore her so I walked into the building with her.'

Mrs Tooney had already confirmed that.

'Have you ever slept with Mrs Tooney?'

'Have you seen her?'

Max hadn't, but Fletch had said that given the choice of a night with Mrs Tooney or a night with a dozen rats, he'd choose the latter. Not that there would have been much difference, Fletch reckoned.

'Perhaps she'd like you to,' Max said with a shrug. 'Perhaps she'd cover for you.'

'Perhaps she would,' Hutchinson answered, eyes narrowed, 'but even if she did, there were plenty of other people there who spoke to me. All those present were named in the minutes and I gave you a copy of the minutes.'

Yes, they'd seen the minutes.

'The minutes typed by your mistress,' Max pointed out.

'The minutes typed by my secretary,' Hutchinson corrected him.

'What time did the meeting finish?' Max asked.

'Eight thirty-two according to the minutes,' Hutchinson said crisply. 'As soon as it closed, we had tea and biscuits. A few left straight after the meeting, but I was there until the bitter end.'

'And you drove straight home?'

'No, I gave Pam Struthers a lift home. That only took me about ten minutes out of my way.'

'So you gave your mistress a lift –'

'She was with me in her secretarial role.'

'What time did you get home?'

'Just after nine thirty.'

Jonathan Trueman had been killed when Hutchinson was at his meeting conveniently surrounded by witnesses. Max had begged and nagged, insisted everything was double-checked, but the pathologist was adamant that death couldn't have occurred any later. Besides, Max had been there not long after nine thirty.

Whether Max liked it or not, and he didn't, Hutchinson had watertight alibis for the afternoon Alice Trueman's throat had been cut, and the night Jonathan Trueman had been shot in the legs before being killed at point blank range with a 12-bore shotgun.

'I had a chat with your wife,' Max remarked.

'So she told me. Fine. I have nothing to hide.'

'I came across a scrapbook you've been keeping,' Max said casually. 'You're very interested in murder, aren't you?'

'So are you. That doesn't make either of us killers.'

'All I want is a safer place for my kids to grow up. I'd be delighted if no more murders were committed.'

'I'm interested in anything that happens locally,' Hutchinson said, 'and this serial killer makes a good story.'

'What are your views?'

Hutchinson frowned. 'On what?'

'This killer. The victims. The police involvement. Anything.'

'Well, the killer's obviously a complete maniac. That's obvious, isn't it? The victims are prostitutes and that's always been a dangerous job. The police, I'm prepared to believe, know a lot more about it than Joe Public is being told.'

Max let his last comment go. If Joe Public believed that, at least they were getting something right.

'Is that it?' he asked, feigning disappointment. 'You're fascinated – your word, I believe – by forensic psychology. Don't you have any theories?'

'Ah, but I don't have the background info you have.'

'Do you like prostitutes?'

Hutchinson laughed. He was a cocky one. 'I neither like nor dislike them. I don't know any personally. I'm sure they're like every other group. Some good, and some bad.'

'I suppose you're right. Let's get back to this gun of yours. Have you any idea at all as to who might have stolen it?'

'None. There's been no sign of a break-in, as you know.'

'You don't seem too concerned about it,' Max commented. 'If my home had been broken into, I'd be extremely upset.'

'I'm sure you know how many burglaries – unsolved burglaries – take place these days, even in a place like Kelton,' Hutchinson replied smoothly. 'I consider myself lucky in that (a) neither my wife nor I were home at the time to come face to face with the culprit and (b) nothing else was taken.'

'You said that only you and your wife have keys?'

'Of course. Who else would have one?' He raised his eyebrows at the stupidity of the question.

'Who knows? My mother-in-law has a key to my house. So does a neighbour.'

'No one has a key to ours.'

'Except Molly Turnbull, your cleaner.'

Hutchinson looked surprised. 'Does she have one?'

'According to your wife, there's a key left under a tub on the patio for her.'

'There doesn't seem much point because Liz is always there when she arrives but – well, if Liz says there's a key left there, then obviously there is. Damn silly thing to do, though. I'll have words with Liz about that.'

'Good idea,' Max said. 'So does anyone else have access to your home?'

'Not that I know of.'

'Your mistress perhaps?'

Hutchinson smirked. 'Don't be ridiculous.'

Max rose, signalled to Fletch to keep at him in the hope that he'd get somewhere, and left the room.

He grabbed a coffee and sat down in front of the camera to see Fletch asking Hutchinson about Chloe Barratt, the woman Ella Gardner had seen him with on the train.

'Why did you arrange to meet her that particular day?' Fletch asked.

Hutchinson rolled his eyes, then laughed with feigned exasperation. 'How many times do I have to tell you? I didn't *arrange* to meet her. We both happened to be travelling on the same train.'

That's exactly what Chloe Barratt had said, and Max didn't believe either of them. Something was going on, and Max would love to know exactly what. Ella Gardner had said he hadn't been pleased to be spotted, and she swore he'd handed over an envelope.

'An ex-pupil of yours, I gather,' Fletch said.

'Until the age of eleven, yes. She left secondary school at sixteen to become a hairdresser. That's five years ago now.'

'Does your wife dress up in a school uniform for you?'

Fletch's question took Hutchinson completely by surprise. It had a similar effect on Max. 'Of course not. What do you think I am, for God's sake?'

Fletch, wisely Max thought, chose not to answer that.

'But you did have an affair with Chloe Barratt?'

'We had a fling a couple of years ago,' Hutchinson told

him. 'She was nineteen then and I imagine she'd outgrown her uniform.'

'A fling. An affair. It's the same thing, isn't it?'

'If you like.'

Max turned away from the screen and went back to his office.

Chapter Thirty-Seven

Jill didn't know why she had agreed to this day out with Max and the boys. Kate had been persuasive, no doubt about that.

'It'll do you good,' Kate had said, 'and it'll do Harry and Ben good.'

'Max said he wants to pick my brain,' Jill had pointed out, 'so we'll only be talking shop.'

'Even that might do Max good. He's struggling with this case.'

Jill knew that. Until he could forget Valentine for more than ten minutes at a stretch, he would struggle with every case they gave him. He couldn't accept that there were dozens of equally capable people working on Valentine's case and that he was senior investigating officer on the Truemans' case.

'Have a good walk on the beach,' Kate had said. 'Enjoy the fresh air and enjoy being with the boys for a day. Hang it all, Max will even buy you lunch . . .'

So here she was, walking along the beach near Southport, with Max at her side. Harry and Ben were racing around with the dog. Fly hadn't seen the sea before and was barking like something demented every time a wave appeared.

January was always a flat month, the weather usually too bad to venture far, and Jill had to admit that it was bliss to feel the sun on her face, and the wind whipping at her hair. It was cold, but exhilarating. Besides, she had never wanted to distance herself from Harry and Ben. She would see them at Christmas and around their birthdays, and keep up a contact in between.

'You're miles away,' Max remarked.

'I was just thinking what a refreshing change it made not to be staring at a VDU.' She looked at him. 'What will you do when this is all over? I don't mean the Truemans' case, I mean when Valentine is behind bars.'

'I'll persuade you to marry me, and retire,' he said immediately. 'I'll buy a beach bar in Spain. Shergar can fix the drinks, Lord Lucan can take care of the cellar, Elvis can cook the steaks.'

She smiled at the picture he painted. 'Yes, Max, but what will you *really* do?'

'I'll persuade you to marry me, retire, buy a beach bar in Spain –'

Her loud, impatient sigh cut him short.

'Why did Jonathan Trueman kill his wife?' he asked, changing the subject.

'You think he did?'

Max bent to pick up a pebble. He turned it over in his hand, then threw it at the sea, watching as it bounced and skimmed across the waves.

'I think that's the most likely explanation, yes.'

So did Jill. It was the only sensible explanation.

'He got there early,' Max said, 'they had a row, and he killed her. Assuming he found her in bed, or in the bath with someone else, do you think he might have lost it and killed her?'

'No. He was too calm and exact a character for losing control like that,' Jill replied. 'He loved her, though, no doubt about that. He worshipped the ground she walked on. If he did kill her, it was because she was leaving him for someone else.' She thought for a moment.

'No one believes she would have looked twice at anyone else.'

'Except Jim Brody,' Jill pointed out. 'Molly Turnbull thought she had a soft spot for him.'

'I think that might have been Molly's over-active imagination. Brody's adamant he was just the gardener. Along with everyone else in the world, he reckons Alice Trueman was one of the nicest people ever born, but he swears they only talked about gardening. Added to which, he's got a cast iron alibi for both occasions. When Alice Trueman was murdered, he was at the hospital having a couple of stitches and a tetanus jab. He was there for hours so he hadn't spent the morning in bed with Alice.'

'That's some alibi.'

'It is. He'd been sawing up logs for Ella Gardner. She drove him to the hospital and that all checks out.'

'What about the night Jonathan Trueman was killed?'

'He was visiting his brother in London. He even went to great lengths to get the used rail ticket out of the dustbin to show us.'

Jim Brody hadn't struck Jill as a criminal, and certainly not a killer. She didn't know him well, but they'd had a chat earlier in the week when they'd both been in The Weaver's Retreat talking to Andy Collins. He seemed a likeable, friendly chap. According to everyone she'd spoken to, he was an asset to Kelton Bridge. He'd lived in the village for several years, he mowed the grass in the churchyard for nothing, and arranged an annual collection for the RNLI.

'What about Tony Hutchinson's gun?' she murmured. 'That's odd, isn't it?'

'Very,' Max said grimly. 'I wouldn't trust that bloke as far as I could chuck an elephant. There was no sign of a break-in, and he hadn't even noticed it was missing. According to Molly Turnbull, and Liz Hutchinson has confirmed this, she left a key for Molly underneath a patio tub if she was going out. It's feasible that someone knew that.'

'Or found it. Where's the first place you'd look for a key?'

'Quite.'

Seagulls circled overhead, dipping and diving on the air currents.

Jill had always enjoyed this, walking with Max and bouncing ideas back and forth. When they'd been together, though, their ideas had seemed sharper, their minds quicker. Now, they both seemed dull and tired. Or was that her imagination?

'It's Alice's past that intrigues me,' Jill remarked. 'How does that check out? Any former lovers who might have come back into her life? Anyone she left? Someone she left for Jonathan? They'd been married for some time before Michael was born so it wasn't as if she felt she had to marry him. There has to have been some sort of regret there, though. No matter how much she loved Jonathan, and I'm prepared to believe she did love him, she must have longed for her former life.'

'We're checking it out, but she could have been as happy as Larry with Jonathan Trueman. Just because that life wouldn't appeal to us, it doesn't follow that Alice hated it.'

'I know, but I can't see it. If someone more romantic, fun and exciting came back into her life for any reason, I think she might have been tempted. Oh, she wouldn't have done anything drastic perhaps, but she might have met up with an old friend for coffee, maybe an evening out.'

'You think Jonathan was the jealous type?'

'Yes. He lived in fear of losing her to someone else,' Jill said. 'Living that way for almost twenty-five years would take its toll on anyone.'

They walked on. The boys, oblivious to their presence, were kicking a football for the dog to chase. Jill wondered if they would remember this day in years to come. There was nothing memorable about the day, yet they were happy and carefree . . .

'Everything takes so long,' Max complained. 'Imagine the time it's taking to try and track Alice's movements over the last year or so. And then imagine trying to contact everyone she's ever known.'

'It's always the same, Max. You know that. That's the

job. You plod away until something turns up. And something always does turn up.'

'Not always.'

'Yes, always. Even if it takes thirty years or more.'

Max groaned at the thought of that, and Jill had to smile.

It was true, though. Something always turned up. Always. The killer or killers of Jonathan and Alice Trueman would be found, and so would Valentine. She was confident of that.

Chapter Thirty-Eight

Max and Grace were back in the interview room. Grace switched on the tape and named those present.

Andy Collins looked nervous as Max took his seat opposite him. His face was pale and he kept licking his lips and swallowing as if he doubted his ability to talk. He was there of his own free will, however, and had said he was more than happy to answer their questions.

Here was another man Max didn't like. Hell, he didn't like any man who managed to take Jill out to lunch. Thanks to Kate and the kids, Max had bought her lunch on Sunday, but she wouldn't have dreamed of dining alone with him. Was that the only reason he disliked Andy Collins? Probably, he admitted to himself.

Collins' past was proving tricky to unearth and discovering he'd spent time alone with Alice Trueman was a breakthrough of sorts.

'Where were you on the afternoon of Monday, eighth of November?' Max asked him.

'The day Alice was murdered?'

'Yes.'

'I was working. I don't have my diary with me but, from memory, I was out in Haslingden all day. I'd had a couple of appointments, possible house sales. I was definitely in Haslingden during the afternoon. My last appointment was with a Mrs Smith – a four-bedroomed detached that we'd just had an offer on. I expect she'll vouch for that.'

She already had.

'And when you left Mrs Smith?'

'It wasn't worth going back to the office, so I drove home. I changed, then went down to The Weaver's Retreat for a drink. It was while I was there that I heard about poor Alice. I liked her.'

'Most people liked her.'

'Everyone liked her,' he said quietly.

'Not everyone,' Max pointed out. 'Someone murdered her.'

Andy Collins began swallowing rapidly. 'Yes,' he agreed, his voice hoarse.

'Any ideas? Can you think of anyone who might have borne a grudge, someone she'd upset, anyone who might have disliked her enough to kill her?'

'No. No one.'

'Do you know much about her past?' Grace put in.

'Not really. She was a dancer, I heard. She was on TV a few times.'

'She had the body of a dancer, didn't she?' Grace murmured. 'A very attractive lady, wasn't she? Sexy, I suppose. Did you find her sexy?'

'I never thought of her that way, no.' Collins ran a finger around the inside of his collar. It was warm in the interview room, Max thought. Probably too warm.

'Tell me about the time you were charged with rape,' Max demanded, and Collins cleared his throat.

'It was a long time ago –'

'1987,' Max supplied helpfully.

'I was a student at university,' Collins explained hesitantly. 'A girl there, Lucy Rickman, asked me out. She'd had a lot to drink and it was coming up to Christmas. I couldn't make it so I declined. She seemed upset. Days later, when she'd sobered up, she apologized for being so pushy, and I suppose I felt sorry for her. I also regretted being a bit rude when I declined. So I asked her out for a couple of drinks, the cinema and then more drinks. Afterwards, we went back to her place.'

'And?' Max prompted.

'We had a kiss or two. A bit of a fumble, I suppose. Look, is this relevant?'

'Who knows? Define fumble.'

'A bit of petting, you know. We kissed, and I fondled her breasts. That was all, I swear. She didn't turn me on.'

'Why not?' Grace asked.

'She just didn't. Apart from the fact that she wasn't anything special to look at, she talked non-stop. I found her tedious.'

'Then what happened? After your, er, fumble?' Grace asked.

'I went home,' he said. 'The next day, I was informed I'd been accused of rape.'

'Why do you think that was?' Max asked.

'I couldn't say,' Collins replied thoughtfully. 'Either she was mad at me for turning her down the first time, or she felt bad when I didn't take things further. I got the impression I could have spent the night with her if I'd so desired.'

'Why did she drop the charges?' Max asked.

'I imagine that all she wanted to do was scare me. And if I'm honest, she did. No bloke wants to be on a rape charge. But I doubt if she wanted to go to court any more than I did.'

'Have you seen her since?' Max asked.

'What do you think?' Collins demanded scathingly. 'And I really can't see what any of this has to do with Alice and Jonathan.'

'Probably nothing,' Max agreed. 'You're not married, are you?'

'No.'

'Why's that?' Grace asked. 'A good-looking bloke like you, I would have thought they'd be forming a queue.'

He didn't smile. Was he used to such flattery?

'I haven't met the right person,' he answered. 'I'm not anti-women, if that's what you're driving at. I simply haven't found the right one. I was with a girl for six years – we came close to marriage, but neither of us wanted to spoil things.' He looked Max straight in the eye. 'I'm not gay, either.'

'It hadn't crossed my mind,' Max said mildly.

'Do people think you might be gay?' Grace asked.

'I neither know nor care what people think,' Collins retorted.

'A lot of blokes wouldn't like people thinking they were gay,' Grace persisted.

'Well, I don't care.'

'What about Monday, the twenty-ninth of November, the evening Jonathan Trueman was murdered?' Max asked. 'Where were you?'

'I was at home.' Once again, he ran a finger inside the collar of his shirt. 'And no, there's no one who can vouch for that. I left the office at five thirty, and drove straight home. I was alone.'

'The weapon used to kill Reverend Trueman was stolen from Mr Hutchinson. Did you know that?'

'Everyone in Kelton knows that,' Collins muttered.

'Could you have stolen it?' Max asked.

'Anyone could have stolen it, I imagine. I knew Tony had guns, and I knew where they were kept. Four, he has – three now presumably – in a cabinet in the dining room. I sometimes think he only invited people to dinner so he could show off his trophies.'

'A bit of a show-off, is he?'

'He's OK.'

'So if anyone wanted to steal a gun, you reckon it would be easy enough?' Max asked.

'I didn't say that. I said I knew they were there, and I knew where they were kept. The cabinet was locked, so whoever did it would have to get in that. And presumably, they'd have to break into the house in the first place.'

'Unless they had a key,' Max pointed out.

'Unless they had a key,' Collins agreed, somewhat sarcastically.

So Collins hadn't stolen that gun. If he had, he'd have

known there was only one there. He presumably didn't know that Hutchinson had sold his collection.

The rape charge could be as innocent as he made out. Even if it wasn't, it hardly mattered.

'How often did you see Alice Trueman?' Max asked.

Collins frowned, not sure where this was leading. 'Once a week or so, I suppose. If I went to church, which wasn't often, I'd see her there. If there were gatherings, concerts, fêtes, dinner parties, I might see her there.'

'Any other times? Days out? Anything like that?'

'No. Of course not.' Collins still looked scared half to death. 'Oh, there was once,' he remembered. 'I had to go to an auction in London on behalf of a client last summer. Without looking at my diary, I couldn't tell you the date, but it was either June or July.'

It was June the seventeenth. And probably as innocent as Collins was about to describe it. Sod it!

'We were buying a few pieces on behalf of a client. Alice saw the catalogue, fell in love with some of the pieces, and wanted to go. Of course, I immediately invited her to join me. Jonathan wasn't happy about it,' he remembered. 'He joked about it, said he was worried Alice would spend too much, but I think . . .' He hesitated.

'Yes?' Max prompted impatiently.

'I gained the impression Jonathan didn't like to let her out of his sight. I'm not sure why that was. Jealousy perhaps. I don't know.'

'But she went?'

'Oh, yes. And thoroughly enjoyed herself.'

Max thought over the conversation he'd had with Jill that morning.

'It's supposed to be a powerful aphrodisiac,' he remarked.

'What is?'

'Good versus evil,' Max explained pleasantly. 'On the one hand, you've got the devoted vicar's wife – godliness, goodness and purity. On the other hand, there's the chance of bringing out her evil side – making her forget the sanctity of marriage, the Word of God, the fact that respectable girls don't do oral or anal.'

'That's disgusting!'

'Who knows,' Max continued, ignoring his outburst, 'perhaps she had fantasies of rape?'

'Oh, no!'

'Lots of women do, I gather.'

'No!'

Max turned to Grace. 'What about you? Have you ever fantasized about being raped? About being powerless?'

Grace didn't even blink. 'I might have.'

'There you go,' Max said, addressing Collins with satisfaction. 'Women *do* fantasize about it. Perhaps Alice did. Perhaps you fulfilled those fantasies for her.'

'No!'

'Perhaps you had an affair with her and perhaps she planned to leave her husband for you.'

'That's ridiculous!'

'Perhaps it was her idea,' Max ploughed on, 'and perhaps you didn't want the commitment – or the scandal. So perhaps you had her killed. Or perhaps her husband killed her and you killed him out of revenge.'

'No, no, no!' Collins was on his feet. 'I'm answering no more questions without my lawyer present!'

Chapter Thirty-Nine

Max was sitting in his office when Fletch burst in waving a piece a paper.

'This had better be good news,' Max warned him.

'It is, guv,' Fletch said breathlessly, hitching up his trousers. 'It's about that train Jim Brody caught back from London.'

'And?'

On the night Jonathan Trueman was murdered, Brody had caught the last train back from London to Manchester. He'd even shown them his ticket.

'It was cancelled,' Fletch said triumphantly.

'So what alternative arrangements were made?' Max refused to build up his hopes. 'They can't leave dozens of passengers stranded in London, Fletch.'

'The passengers eventually got a train to Stoke, and then a bus was laid on for those going on to Manchester.'

So much for caution. Max's hopes were already sky high.

'And there's no way Brody could have caught a train all the way from London to Manchester? Even if he'd done a different route?'

'It's possible,' Fletch allowed, 'but he would have known it was cancelled and he would have had to do one hell of a detour. If that were the case, he would have mentioned it.'

'Let's go and have a chat with him.' Max was already putting on his jacket. He had an appointment with his superior but, as he knew the script by heart, that particular bollocking could wait. 'And why the bloody hell wasn't this checked out sooner?'

'Dunno, guv. Because he found that ticket, I suppose, and we were –'

'Gullible enough to believe him,' Max finished, striding out of his office.

They went in Fletch's car and that was even more untidy than Max's. As Fletch drove, Max gathered up half a dozen empty coffee cups.

'The wife's pregnant,' Fletch said, as if that explained everything.

'You what?'

'Sandra's pregnant again. Instead of cleaning out the car, she's been getting the spare bedroom ready.'

'Yeah? Hey, congratulations.'

'Thanks.' Fletch grinned sheepishly and Max knew there was no point reminding him of the sleepless nights spent walking the floorboards that would soon be upon him.

'But why can't you clean the car yourself?'

'Good question.'

One to which there clearly wasn't an answer.

'Do you know what you're having? Boy or girl?'

'Yes, I expect it'll be one of those.' That was Fletch's idea of a joke. 'Sandra doesn't want to know. Says it will spoil the surprise. A boy would be great,' he said, somewhat wistfully, 'but we'll probably have another girl. She's doing the spare bedroom out in yellow which is sort of neutral, I suppose.'

'You'll be better off with a girl. Boys are hell. They're too energetic, too wily, and too conniving by half. I still can't believe I got talked into having that damn dog.' He gave Fletch a sideways glance and grinned. 'Sorry, Fletch. Dogs are still a sore point, I imagine.'

'Bloody thing. And it wasn't an Andrex puppy, far from it. It wasn't even a puppy, it was almost a year old. When the vet thought he might have to dart it, he estimated its weight as between twenty and twenty-five kilos. A pity that shotgun hadn't been loaded . . .'

They were soon driving into Kelton Bridge.

There were some odd characters living in the village, Max thought, but there must be hundreds of normal people, too. It was just the ones he came into contact with that seemed odd.

Fletch took a wrong turning and they ended up going past Jill's cottage. A bearded chap was working on the roof, and Max assumed it was Len. According to Jill, he'd arrived early yesterday morning, worked till late, and hadn't stopped singing traditional folk songs all day. Jill reckoned she'd never known a man so happy in his work.

'Of course, Brody might not be at home,' Max mused. 'It was his day for working on the vicarage garden so he might have taken on another job to replace that.'

'We'll soon find out,' Fletch said as he pulled the car on to Brody's drive. 'Let's hope we can nail him for Trueman's murder,' he added grimly.

As they got out of the car, Brody came out of his front door, his car keys dangling from his fingers, but he stopped when he saw them. The ever-present collie was at his heels.

'We'll only take a minute of your time,' Max told him.

'You'd better come in then.' Brody went back inside and held the front door open for them.

Max and Fletch followed him into the lounge. No one sat down. The dog lay by Brody's feet, watching Max and Fletch.

'We thought you might have found a replacement job for the vicarage,' Max remarked.

'No.' He didn't elaborate. Nor did he seem unduly bothered about the lack of income.

'Plenty of work around, is there?'

'Seems to be.'

'The evening Jonathan Trueman was killed,' Fletch said, getting straight to the point, 'would you describe your movements for us again, please?'

'I drove to Manchester Piccadilly, parked the car and

caught the 11.15 train to Euston. I got there at around half past one, had a coffee at the station, then took a cab out to my brother's place just off the King's Road.'

'Was the train on time?' Fletch asked.

'Give or take.'

He looked uncomfortable, as well he might. Max guessed he had no idea if the train was on time or not.

'And then what?' Fletch asked.

'I spent the rest of the day with my brother. He'll vouch for that. I took a cab from his place back to Euston to catch the 9.05 p.m. train and then drove straight home from Manchester.'

'How about that train?' Fletch said, notebook at the ready. 'Was that on time? Give or take?'

'I don't rightly remember. I imagine so.'

'You imagine so,' Max repeated. 'Now, the thing is, we've checked with your brother and he confirms that you were with him until you left to catch that train. The problem, however, is that the 9.05 train to Manchester Piccadilly was cancelled.'

'Has that jogged your memory?' Fletch asked casually.

'No, but I must have caught a later train, mustn't I?'

Credit where it was due, he didn't even flinch. He stared Fletch straight in the eye.

'No trains went into Manchester that night,' Fletch informed him. 'Surely you remember taking a different route.'

'Ah, now you mention it, yes I do. I had to catch a train to Stoke and then a bus up from there.'

Fletch looked at Max, and Max could see his own thoughts mirrored there. Shit!

Did Brody catch that train and then the bus from Stoke, or was he taking a guess? The Manchester train had terminated at Stoke for a week, while track repairs were carried out. Brody could easily have heard about it.

'Did you have an affair with Alice Trueman?' Max asked.

The question should have taken him by surprise, but it didn't.

'What would she see in me?'

'Was that a yes or no?' Fletch asked impatiently.

Brody gave his dog a quick glance before looking straight at Fletch. 'No, I didn't have an affair with Mrs Trueman.'

'I don't know how a woman's mind works,' Max said, walking over to the window and looking out at immaculate borders, 'they're far too complex for me. However, I can imagine a woman like Mrs Trueman, a woman married to a vicar and feeling stifled by life at the vicarage, finding a gardener, a man with a passion for warmth and colour, and especially a man who made her laugh, quite appealing.' He spun round. 'I've been told she used to look forward to your visits.'

'I couldn't speak for Mrs Trueman.'

'So what time did you get to Manchester on the night Reverend Trueman was murdered?' Fletch asked.

'I really can't remember.'

'Do you know anything about shotguns?' Max asked.

'Yes, I've done some shooting in my time. Clays mainly, but pheasant too. I know Tony Hutchinson's shotgun was stolen and I assume it was the same one used to kill Jonathan Trueman.'

'A good shot, are you?' Max asked.

'Good enough.'

I bet you are, Max thought. Not that one would need to be a good shot to make such a mess of a body.

Brody was a very cool, calm individual. Perhaps he could afford to be with his brother providing an alibi, but Max was convinced he'd killed Jonathan Trueman.

'Do you think Mrs Trueman was murdered by her husband?' Max asked him.

'If he and young Michael are the only suspects, then yes, it's possible.' Something resembling a smile touched his lips and left his eyes cold. 'I didn't kill Mrs Trueman if that's what you're thinking. If you check with the hospital, you'll find I was there at the time. In fact, I was there for about five hours.'

'Yes, we've checked,' Fletch told him.

'Right,' Max said briskly. 'Thanks for your time, Mr Brody. We'll be in touch. Oh, and if you hear anything, give us a call, will you?'

'I will.'

As they were walking out, the collie moved forward and touched a cold wet nose against Max's hand.

'Funny how she's taken to you,' Brody murmured.

Max bent to stroke the dog's head. 'I've got a dog so I expect she can smell that one. Goodbye then, Mr Brody.'

Max and Fletch stepped out into the sunshine, and then got back in Fletch's car.

'Well?' Fletch asked.

'He's our man,' Max said confidently.

'That's what I thought,' Fletch replied. 'God, he's bloody cocky, though. You really reckon he was having an affair with Alice Trueman?'

'Yes, I do. Given all we've been told about the squeaky clean Alice, it's hard to believe, but yes, I reckon he was. And how the hell did they manage that in a place like Kelton? I want his every movement checked and double-checked. We'll have another chat with his brother, too. He has to be lying. And I want Brody's van checked out. We need to know where it was when he was supposed to be on that London train. I'll issue details to the press . . .'

Max dared to believe they were finally getting somewhere.

Chapter Forty

He loved this. He was so close to her, almost close enough to smell her, yet she was oblivious to his presence.

It was risky, too risky, but he hadn't been able to resist. The challenge appealed to him.

He was lying on his back in her dark attic, his hands clasped behind his head as he listened to her moving around beneath him. He'd already heard the shower running and now he could hear the radio. Impossible to make out what was being said, or which record was being played, but he reckoned she was listening to the late night country music show. He often listened to that himself.

Her phone rang, and the radio was silenced as she spoke to the caller. He heard her laughing.

Make the most of it, sweetheart. You won't be laughing for much longer . . .

She was going to be his next victim. That was a pity in some ways, but she wasn't much fun. He could have greater pleasure pitting his wits against Detective Chief Inspector Trentham, a man he'd taken a great dislike to. Some days, you couldn't switch on the television without seeing his face on the screen. Except Trentham had forgotten all about Valentine. He was busy seeking the glory from the murder of the vicar and his wife.

Valentine would have to jog his memory. Oh, yes. He could hardly wait.

It was cold in her attic, but he didn't feel it. He'd brought a sleeping bag up here and that was keeping him snug. His exciting thoughts were keeping him warm, too.

He would have to strangle her, of course. To make sure

Trentham got the message, he would remove those heart-shaped pieces of skin from her body, too. A dozen hearts.

Next week perhaps . . .

First, he wanted her to panic. She was cool, one of those individuals who refused to acknowledge that death could be round the corner. Perhaps she believed she was too clever for death.

As soon as she left in the morning, he would arrange the thirteen red roses in one of her vases and leave them on her kitchen table. The small, accompanying card was already written: From Valentine.

He hated having to sleep with the roses in the loft, but there was no alternative. It was exhilarating to share her home for the night, so he must concentrate on that. No need to think of competing for air with those blood red buds . . .

He closed his eyes and concentrated on killing her. The brief moment of panic on her face, using his scalpel to turn her body into an object of beauty, imagining Trentham finding her . . .

Of course, there were still the details to work out. Where would he kill her? How would he get her there? He was tempted to kill her here, in her own house. Perhaps he would. He could do it now. All he had to do was jump down from this loft, walk out through the spare room and into her bedroom. Easy!

Chapter Forty-One

Jill's eyes were tired. It had been a long day, spent poring over statements, and it was good to get away.

The Green Man was almost opposite headquarters so it was inevitable she'd recognize a lot of people in the bar.

'What are you having?' Cornwall asked her.

'A long, cold lager, please. I'd have something more exciting but I've got to drive.'

'Me too.'

She found a table while he queued for the drinks and she was amused to see him, a minute later, bringing a glass of lager and an orange juice to their table.

'You're allowed one drink, Don.'

'It's not worth the risk.'

Cornwall wasn't a risk taker. She wasn't either, but she did know she could have one drink without being found drunk in charge of a motor vehicle.

She'd like to think she was getting along better with Cornwall, but she wasn't. He might be able to tolerate her more easily these days, but they weren't getting along. His views on psychologists were well known, and she felt he didn't give her all relevant information. It made for a tricky relationship.

'Look who's here,' he said, nodding at the door.

Max and Grace spent a large part of their working day together so it wasn't unusual to see them having a drink occasionally. Jill wondered if their relationship went beyond work these days. She didn't think it did, but who knew?

Max often needed a female officer with him to offer support to people he might be questioning or to protect himself from accusations of impropriety. They made an attractive couple, Max and Grace. Grace was much younger, but she was striking, intelligent and as hard as nails. She was laughing at something Max had said.

Jill dismissed all jealous thoughts from her mind and put a smile on her face as they joined them.

'Anything new?' Cornwall asked Max.

'Nothing. What about you two?'

'Nothing I consider significant,' Cornwall said, and again, Jill was irritated. Either he'd learned something new or he hadn't.

He looked across at the quiz machine. 'Anyone fancy trying to win a tenner?'

'No, thanks,' Jill said.

'I'm quite good at these,' Grace said, rising to the challenge. 'Best of ten, Cornwall? Loser buys the next round?'

'Sure,' Cornwall replied.

Jill watched them go, but she had more important matters on her mind. 'Anything more from Janie Fisher?'

'No, not a whisper.' Max nodded towards the quiz machine. 'How did Cornwall take it when you told him you'd seen her?'

'How do you think? He's convinced there's nothing in it and, even if there were, she can't tell us anything. But if it was Valentine she saw,' Jill said, voice low but confident, 'he'll kill again and probably soon. Escaping like that, she will have robbed him of control. He won't like that. He'll probably be angry. This next one might be more vicious.'

'There's not much I can do about it. I have to concentrate on the Truemans' murders.' He took a swig from his half-pint of beer. 'What's Cornwall doing about it?'

Jill tapped the side of her nose, just as Cornwall often did. 'He has his methods.'

Max smiled at that. 'And you still reckon Valentine lives in the Rossendale area?' he asked.

'Yes.' Jill hated the thought of that, but it was what the computer believed.

'What about Hutchinson, Jill? Could he have anything at all to do with sending you photos and Valentine cards?'

'I don't know,' she admitted. 'He's not killing prostitutes, though. Tony's been married for years, and seems to be used to the odd affair. Valentine isn't in a long-term relationship, I'm sure of that.'

'Yes, but these photos and cards. The more I think about it – firstly, it only started when you moved to Kelton.'

'I don't know,' she said again. 'He likes the idea of my work – not that he has a clue what it entails – and I'm sure he believes it's far more fascinating than his own job. And he does like to impress people with his knowledge. He might, but it's a big might, be keen to remind me that I'm not as great as I like to think I am.'

'Mm.' Max nodded. 'And how about Andrew Collins? He isn't in a long-term relationship, he's been accused of rape in the past, and he has to keep reminding people that he's not gay.'

'Does he?'

'Yes. He reckons he had a long-term relationship in the past, but it could be a figment of his imagination.'

'He's told me about that. They were together for about six years, I gather.'

'Not usual, is it?'

'What? To have a long-term relationship?'

'To keep reminding people of your heterosexuality.'

'It doesn't make him a killer.' At least, Jill hoped not. She'd been invited to the manor for drinks tomorrow night and he was sure to be there. 'These days, lots of people choose to stay single. Marriage isn't what it used to be. People choose careers over marriage and kids.'

'Yes, but –'

'Cornwall's around the same age as Andy and he isn't married,' she pointed out, gazing across at the quiz machine where he and Grace were frantically jabbing buttons. 'No one gives it a second thought. You certainly wouldn't suspect him of being gay.'

'I suppose not,' Max murmured, thoughtfully. 'No, you're right, I hadn't given it a thought. Until you just told me, I wouldn't have known if he was married or not.'

'I only found out because I asked.' Jill took a swallow of lager. 'He doesn't talk about himself – something of a loner. He's not the easiest bloke to get along with, either. He's ambitious, but I don't think he considers himself part of a team.'

'Yes, I've heard a couple of people say that. Anyway, do you want another drink?' Max asked.

She did, but she couldn't. 'I'm driving.'

'Me too, and I have to collect the kids from a party.' He picked up her empty glass. 'You can have another. Leave your car here and I'll give you a lift home.'

'Hey, great. In that case, I'll have a gin and tonic. Oh, and don't let them put the tonic in the glass. They'll drown it.'

He smiled, and wandered off to ask Cornwall and Grace if they wanted more drinks.

Jill watched him chatting to them. He was laughing. She guessed he answered a question correctly for Grace before leaving them to it.

'Cornwall is an oddball, isn't he?' he remarked, when he returned with her drink.

'I think so, yes. But what makes you say that?'

'He's ambitious, no doubt about that, and doing well for himself, but you have the feeling that he keeps his ideas and his methods to himself. I'm not sure what he wants more – Valentine arrested or the glory for being the hero of the day by catching him.'

Jill knew exactly what he meant. 'He's very critical, too,' she mused. 'He spends a lot of time telling you how much better life was in Newcastle – the place, the people he worked with. I've been tempted several times to ask him why, if it was so great, he doesn't piss off back there.'

Max chuckled at that.

As he was in no rush to leave the pub, probably because he had time to kill before he needed to collect Harry and Ben from their party, Jill had another gin and tonic.

It didn't take Cornwall and Grace long to lose their tenner on the quiz machine, and they soon joined them.

'My round,' Grace said with a grimace. 'Don had some lucky questions.'

Cornwall shrugged modestly, but he was clearly delighted with his win. He was petty.

Jill watched him closely and decided that it wasn't only a case of not liking him. There was more to it than that. There was something about Don Cornwall that raised too many questions in her mind. She didn't trust him.

'You ready then, Jill?' Max asked eventually.

She was. All she had planned for the evening was a long, leisurely bath with lots of foam, stretching out on the sofa with a good book, and then an early night. Bliss.

They said their goodbyes to Cornwall and Grace who were about to have another game on the quiz machine, and walked back for Max's car.

Jill could easily have fallen asleep as Max drove. The glare of oncoming headlights had her eyes closing on several occasions. Perhaps she did doze off. It came as a surprise when Max stopped the car outside her cottage.

He followed her inside, just as she'd known he would.

Jill saw them immediately – glaring triumphantly at her through the open door.

'Oh, God!' She grabbed Max's arm.

'What is it?'

Still with her hand on his arm, she extended a finger in the direction of her kitchen table.

'Fuck!' His voice was very low, barely audible.

She didn't let him go. Together, they walked into the kitchen.

One of her vases had been filled with roses. Thirteen dark red roses. On each side of the arrangement was a tall white candle. Lit.

Thirteen? Why thirteen? And why, she wondered, had she counted the bloody things?

'The candles,' Max said, voice still low. 'How long have they been lit? Ten minutes? Half an hour?'

Not expecting a reply, he lifted the small card that was with the roses and she read it at the same time he did.

From Valentine. Not your Valentine . . .

'Don't move,' Max whispered, but Jill wasn't staying on her own.

She was right by his side and together they checked every room in her cottage – the sitting room, the bedrooms and the bathroom. Max even had a look in the attic. Everything was as it should be.

'Right,' Max said, 'get on the phone. Ring Tony Hutchinson and thank him for the flowers.'

'What? Are you mad? What if Liz answers? I can't –'

'Just do it, Jill.'

She hesitated, but only briefly. Perhaps Max was right. If Tony Hutchinson was playing a sick joke on her, it was time she put a stop to it. But if he wasn't – and she honestly didn't think he was – she'd be making a fool of herself. Still, better a fool than a nervous wreck.

She had to look him up in the phone book and, after hesitating again, tapped in his number. He must have been right by the phone because he answered it on the first ring.

'Tony? Tony, it's Jill Kennedy.'

'Hello there, this is a nice surprise,' he said jovially. 'What can I do for you?'

'To tell the truth it's a little delicate. Is Liz there?'

'She's isn't, no.' He laughed softly. 'Now you've got me intrigued. What is it, Jill?'

'The flowers,' she said. 'I wanted to say thank you, but really, I'd rather you didn't. Liz is –'

'Hang on a minute,' he cut her off. 'What flowers? I don't know what you're talking about.'

'Oh, erm . . .' She gave a light-hearted laugh. 'You mean it wasn't you?'

'Unless you tell me what you're talking about, I can't say, can I?'

'You didn't send me flowers?'

'I didn't, no.' He sounded uncomfortable with the idea. 'Jill, I don't know what gave you that idea, but if you have a secret admirer – well, I admire you – but if someone is sending you flowers, I'm afraid it isn't me. Were they sent through Interflora? If so, I believe you can contact them and –'

'No, it wasn't Interflora. Sorry, Tony, I've got completely the wrong end of the stick. Something on the card made me think of you and I thought – well, it doesn't matter what I thought. Forget it, will you? Please? I've made enough of a fool of myself.'

'Not at all. Really, Jill, if I weren't a happily married –'

'Please, no more about it. Thanks, Tony. Goodnight.' Jill cut the connection.

She looked at Max and shook her head. 'He didn't know anything about it. I believe him, too.'

'OK, but you're not spending the night here,' Max told her. 'Shove the cats in their cages and put them in the back of my car. Then pack a bag. Tomorrow, we'll get all the locks changed, but tonight you'll have to stay –' He broke off. 'Somewhere else,' he finished.

Dear God. Did he really think someone was listening to their conversation?

For Jill, that was the final straw. She went to her bedroom, and packed an overnight case. Then she put three protesting cats in boxes.

That maniac, whoever he was, had been in her cottage. He had touched her things, and walked through her rooms. The knowledge made her feel sick, and she didn't start feeling better until she was sitting in Max's car again.

'Who has a key to your cottage?' Max demanded as he drove.

'No one. Not a soul.' She was struggling to talk, and she knew her teeth were about to start chattering. 'Unless someone has one from the time Mrs Blackman lived there.

She was elderly and neighbours might have kept spare keys in case she needed anything. Helpful neighbours don't make killers, though.' She tried to think. 'I asked Bob Murphy, you know, the builder, if he wanted one, but he didn't. He said he didn't like having people's keys.'

'What about Andrew Collins?' Max asked. 'He sold the house to you so who's to say he didn't keep a spare?'

'No one,' Jill admitted. 'He said he gave me all the keys he had but – I don't know. I suppose anyone could have one.'

Chapter Forty-Two

Max was idly shuffling papers on his desk, but his mind wasn't on his work.

The locks had been changed at Jill's cottage and she was adamant that, tomorrow, she would go back home. Getting into Fort Knox without being seen would have been easier, but he still didn't like it.

Who the hell would put sodding roses and candles in her cottage? Apart from Valentine?

Grace knocked on his door and pushed it open.

'Guv, there's a lady outside, a Mrs Margaret Green, who wants to speak to you. She says she has important information about Alice Trueman, and won't speak to anyone but that nice Detective Trentham she's seen on the television.'

'You'd better show her in then,' Max said, adding a grim, 'Another crank is just what I need this morning.'

Grace grinned and went away again.

The woman she showed into his office didn't look like a crank. She did, however, look very nervous. Nervous enough to get Max intrigued. He introduced himself, and shook her hand.

'I've seen you on the television,' she said.

'Yes. Please, sit down.'

She took a deep breath, fiddled with her black handbag, and looked straight at him. Margaret Green would be in her late fifties, Max supposed. A slim woman, fairly tall, with her hair styled neatly and a very erect carriage.

She was wearing a dark blue skirt and jacket. A teacher perhaps.

'I hope I'm not wasting your time, Chief Inspector, but ever since I saw the story on television about Alice Trueman, I thought I ought to say something. It's been preying on my mind.'

'Did you know Mrs Trueman?' Max didn't want to rush her, but he felt the stirrings of excitement. She was no crank, he was sure of it.

'Sort of. Well, only by reputation,' Margaret Green said, 'and it was a long time ago. A very long time ago. I always wanted to be a dancer, you see, and I saw her in a few shows. She was good. A lot of it was her bubbly character and her natural sensuality coming through. There was never anything forced about her performances.'

So how the devil had Alice Trueman, with her bubbly character and natural sensuality, married Jonathan Trueman and settled for what Max was convinced had been a stifling life at the vicarage?

Come to that, if Margaret Green only knew her by reputation, what was she doing in his office?

She fiddled with the straps on her handbag again.

'I didn't have what it took to be a dancer,' she continued, 'and my parents wouldn't have allowed it anyway. So, instead, I trained as a nurse and got a job at a private clinic in Middlesex. The clinic offered vasectomies, fertility treatment, terminations . . .' Her voice trailed away.

'Can I get you a drink?' Max asked, but she shook her head.

'One day, a young girl was brought in for a termination. She was just eighteen, I learned. It was Alice Trueman – except in those days, of course, it was Alice Walshingham.'

'Are you sure it was her?'

'Oh, yes.' She thought for a moment. 'I knew it was her immediately, even though she was booked in under a different name. It was her age that surprised me but, apparently, she'd been dancing with Mainly Legs since she was fifteen. She was the youngest member the group had ever had.'

'And she had an abortion?' Max asked.

'Yes. Sadly, there were complications and she was quite poorly. She was with us for over a week, I remember.'

'Why did she book in under a false name? She wasn't that well known, was she?'

'No, but her father thought *he* was,' she said grimly. 'He was a lawyer and he disapproved of her boyfriend. I gather the termination was at his insistence. He was something of a bully.'

Adrian Walshingham was dead now, as was Alice's mother, but from what Max knew of the man, the fact that he was a bully didn't come as any great surprise.

'One day when I was on duty,' Margaret Green continued, 'poor Alice cried and cried for her lost baby. She was distraught. I talked to her. Tried to console her. I thought that if I spoke of her dancing, it might remind her that she had plenty to live for. I told her I'd seen her on the television and knew who she was. She didn't care about people knowing who she was, about dancing, about anything. All she wanted was the child she'd lost. And her boyfriend, of course.'

'Do you know who that man was?'

'I don't,' Margaret admitted. 'He wasn't allowed anywhere near her. Alice's father made sure of that. Let me think – she did talk of him. She cried for him. Jim, that was his name. He was a student.' She frowned. 'He was studying something a bit different – ah, yes, I remember. He was at horticultural college.'

A gardener called Jim!

'He was at horticultural college in Middlesex?' Max asked.

'Yes.' Margaret Green tugged nervously on her handbag's straps. 'I doubt if the poor girl ever saw him again. I imagine, however, that the murder of that child, as she saw it, haunted her until her death. I was pleased to read she'd had a son, though. I remember at the time that there were doubts about her ability to have more children. She must have gained a lot of pleasure from her son.'

'Yes. Yes, I believe she did.'

'Do you have children?' she asked softly.

'Yes, two boys.'

'Then perhaps you'll be halfway to understanding how that poor girl felt.'

'Yes.'

Max couldn't understand, though. His own father was a gentle, loving man. He'd been a strict father, but fair. All he had ever wanted for Max was his happiness. How could anyone understand how it felt to lose your own child, simply because your father disapproved of the child's father?

'That's all I can tell you, I'm afraid,' Margaret Green said, getting to her feet.

Max also rose. 'You've been very helpful. Thank you for coming to see me.'

'Have I?' She sounded surprised.

'You have.'

So helpful that Max now had to go and arrest Jim Brody for the murder of Reverend Jonathan Trueman.

The thought filled him with no satisfaction whatsoever.

Chapter Forty-Three

Max and Fletch arrived at Brody's house just as Brody was pulling up outside.

He got out of his van slowly, his dog running ahead slightly to see who the visitors were. Holly licked Max's hand, but Max couldn't look into those huge, trusting brown eyes. He was about to take her master from her.

This was wrong. It should have been Alice's father they were putting away.

'He's a murderer, guv,' Fletch pointed out grimly, as if he could read Max's thoughts.

'He is, Fletch, and in his position, I'd probably be one, too.'

Brody walked over to them. He waited for them to speak, but no one did. Fletch must have been waiting for Max, and Max couldn't find the words.

'How did you find out?' Brody asked at last.

'A nurse came to see me,' Max explained. 'She looked after Alice when she had her termination.'

Brody's eyes filled with pain, but all he said was, 'Right.'

Max left the formalities to Fletch.

Fletch was already leading Brody to the car when Brody stopped and looked at Max.

'Holly,' he said simply. 'She's eight, and I doubt I'll see her again before she's gone. She don't take to people as a rule and might be difficult to – well, will you see to her, please?'

See to her? Put her out of her misery?

Max looked from Brody to the dog and back again. It was far easier to look at Brody than the dog.

'Yes, I'll see to her,' he promised.

'Thank you.' Those two words were spoken with a quiet dignity that had Max wondering, not for the first time, what had happened to justice.

'We'll put her in the car with us,' he decided. Brody had known enough grief in his life. Max was damned if he'd grieve for his dog, too. 'Front seat.'

'You what, guv?'

'You heard.'

Fletch had heard; he simply didn't believe it. He didn't like it either.

Holly sat in the passenger seat, facing the back of the car and panting as she stared at her master. Fletch drove and Max sat in the back with Brody.

They were almost at the station before Brody spoke. 'We were so happy when we knew Alice was going to have our child, you know.'

Max looked at him. 'Did you follow her here?'

'I would have followed her to the ends of the earth.'

'And her husband killed her because she was finally going to leave him for you?'

'Yes. Her father, her husband – they were both the same. They had to own her. She wasn't even allowed to think for herself.' He shook his head in disgust.

'Why did she marry Jonathan Trueman?' Max asked curiously.

'Her father liked him so Alice was persuaded to marry him. Alice liked him in her own way, too. He was a good enough husband to her – so long as she stayed with him.'

He fell silent again, and they were soon back at the station.

It was late that night when Max finally drove home. He was tired, and in no mood to have a dog whining on his back seat.

'I don't like this any more than you do, Holly, but the choice is yours. You can either have a trip to the vet's, a quick shot and end up being cremated, or you can come with me and make friends with Fly – always assuming Fly doesn't swallow you whole. So what's it to be, eh?'

Holly threw her head back and howled.

'Bloody hell!'

Max grabbed a CD, one of Harry's, put it in the player, increased the volume by several decibels, and allowed Eminem to drown her out.

'Yes, I know it's shite,' he told her, 'but it's a bloody sight more tuneful than you.'

Eminem had the power to silence the dog, but Max could feel her accusing eyes boring into the back of his head . . .

Harry and Ben were still up when he walked into the house with a reluctant Holly following. Jill was in the process of picking up several model cars off the floor. There was no sign of Kate.

It was good to be home, despite the mayhem that followed. Predictably, Fly raced around the newcomer and then jumped all over her. Holly stood still, trembling slightly, and trying her best to ignore the fuss. Meanwhile, Max attempted to answer his sons' many questions.

'Her owner's had to go away, and she doesn't take to strangers. I thought we'd see if she'd settle here with us. If not . . .' If not, what? It would be no use trying to rehome her, and Max didn't relish taking her to the vet's. He certainly couldn't mention such a fate to Harry. 'If not, we'll have to think of something else.'

Jill stroked the dog, her eyes as sad as the collie's. She would have recognized Holly as Brody's; she must have guessed what had happened.

The boys had been ready for bed when he'd arrived, but another hour passed while they tried to coax Holly to have some food. The dog merely lay down, her head on her paws, not interested in food or anything else.

'She'll feel better tomorrow,' Jill told Harry and Ben,

'which is more than you two will if you don't get off to bed. The sooner you go, the sooner you'll be awake to see Holly.'

They argued, but they went. Eventually. Fly followed; the dog usually slept at the foot of Ben's bed.

'Do you fancy a drink, Jill?' Max asked when they were alone.

'Please. A small Scotch with lots of water.'

He was pleasantly surprised; usually, she went straight upstairs to Kate's flat. During the short time she'd been staying there, Max had hardly seen her.

She sat on the floor with her drink in her hand. 'What's happened then?' she asked. 'I assume Jim Brody's been arrested for Jonathan Trueman's murder?'

He told her of the conversation he'd had with Margaret Green, and the subsequent conversation he'd had with Jim Brody.

'It seems that Alice's father was a bully,' he remarked grimly. 'Funnily enough, he didn't mind her dancing.'

'No, it'll be a Daddy's little girl thing,' Jill said. 'He'll have imagined her dancing for him alone.'

'He didn't want her falling in love with another man, though. He ended her relationship with Brody as soon as he found out about it. Then, when he discovered she was having Brody's child, he whipped her off to a clinic for an abortion.'

'Poor Alice. And had they been seeing each other ever since?'

'No. Her father decided she ought to marry Jonathan Trueman and she went along with it. He must have been one hell of a forceful bloke. Or she was very weak. Anyway, she was happy enough, or at least content with her lot, I gather. Trueman was a good husband, and she tried to be content with that. And of course, Michael was her life. Brody says he pursued her. He spent all his time trying to track her down. He did – just before the Truemans moved here. When that happened, he followed. No one in the village knew about their early relationship, not even Jonathan Trueman.'

'And they fell in love all over again?'

'I don't think they ever fell out of love,' Max murmured. 'They both decided enough was enough, and they wanted to live together. Brody wanted her to disappear without telling Trueman where she was going, but even he knew that wouldn't work. There was Michael for one thing. Alice insisted on telling Trueman the truth. She was frightened of his reaction. Terrified, according to Brody. He wanted to be with her when she told him, but she wouldn't hear of it. She wanted to do the right thing.'

'And Jonathan killed her?'

'Yes. She'd told him she was leaving the night before, and she rang Brody the following day, saying that his reaction had been much as expected – a cold anger. His anger had frightened her. Anyway, it seems that Jonathan Trueman came home early the next afternoon, when Alice was in the bath, and went for her with a knife. She managed to get down the stairs and –'

'The poor woman.'

'If Trueman couldn't have her, no one else was going to. Brody had heard Molly say that Liz Hutchinson left a key outside for her. Brody knew Hutchinson had guns, and getting into that cabinet was easy enough. The key was on a hook in the kitchen.' Max let out his breath on a long sigh. 'He killed him quite calmly by all accounts. There's no remorse whatsoever. I think,' he added, 'that if it hadn't been for Holly, he'd have handed himself in at the start.'

'God, poor Alice. What a sad life. And poor Michael.'

Yes, it was Michael Max felt sorry for. Divorce was common enough these days and Michael would have coped with being part of a blended family, or whatever fancy term they used these days. He would have been happy with Alice and Jim, or with Jonathan. Instead, the poor kid had lost both parents.

'Do you think Holly will settle?' Jill asked. 'And if she does, will you keep her?'

'I hope she settles, but I don't know. Brody's been a bit of a loner, and the dog has spent almost every minute of her life with the man. I'll keep her if she'll stay. I just hope she doesn't starve herself to death in the meantime.'

'What a damn fool, Jim Brody I mean. Killing Jonathan Trueman wouldn't bring back his Alice. All it's done is deprive Michael, the boy who'd meant so much to Alice, of his father.'

'I know,' Max replied, 'but I can understand it – his anger and perhaps his need for revenge, too.'

Jill sighed. 'Yes. So can I.'

They fell silent, both watching Holly. The dog was lying with her head on her paws – waiting. Waiting for a command from her master, waiting to feel his gentle hand on her head, waiting to please him, waiting for normality to resume. It was a depressing sight.

Yet such unconditional love from a dumb animal was moving.

'You and Grace?' Jill asked suddenly.

Max waited for more, but nothing was forthcoming. 'What about me and Grace?'

'Are you friends outside work?'

'We're friends, yes.' Max considered the question. 'If you're asking if we've slept together, or are likely to sleep together, then the answer's no. God, Jill, you're the psychologist.'

'Meaning?'

'Meaning Grace is years younger than me, goes clubbing at every opportunity and insists on listening to Radio One. We're miles apart.'

'Oh.'

'Added to which, she got engaged to the man of her dreams last month.'

'I didn't know that.'

'She's been shouting it from the rooftops for a month.'

Grace was a good officer, and Max liked having her on

his team, but anything else had never crossed his mind. What a strange question.

A disheartening question, too. Why couldn't she see how much he loved her?

But he knew the answer to that. He'd spent the night with another woman.

Looking back, he found that hard to believe himself. Sharon had meant nothing to him. He'd barely known the damn woman. She'd been ten years younger than him, she'd had a great body with legs up to her armpits – and that had been it. He'd been flattered when she'd made it clear she was interested in him. He'd imagined a night with her would make him forget his problems. All it had done was make him long for Jill, the Jill he'd had before Valentine had screwed them up, before Rodney Hill committed suicide, before the fighting and the nightmares . . .

'Do you want another?' he asked. He was tempted to drink himself to oblivion.

'I don't. And you'll be out of a job if you don't stop drinking, Max.'

'I don't drink much. Really, I don't,' he insisted at her raised eyebrows. 'I have a Scotch, maybe two, when I get home at night. That's nothing.'

'When's your next assessment due?'

'In about nine months' time,' he replied, 'and before you ask, the last one was fine. I'm perfectly fit and, despite living in this madhouse, mentally stable. An ideal man for the job.'

'That's good then,' she said in her 'I can't be bothered to argue' voice.

She walked over to Holly, who was still lying with her head on her paws. A car drove past and she pricked up her ears, but she soon flattened them again.

'In the morning,' Jill whispered, stroking those flattened ears, 'I'll cook sausages and bacon. We'll see if that tempts you, eh? If not, I'll go out at lunchtime and buy you a good, thick steak.'

Max had thought she was determined to return to her cottage tomorrow. He wouldn't raise the issue, though. The longer she stayed here, the better he liked it – for a variety of reasons.

Chapter Forty-Four

Jill had walked down to The Weaver's Retreat, but now, faced with the prospect of going back to the cottage alone, she was wishing she hadn't.

A group of them had been sitting at a large table by the fire for an hour. Tony and Liz Hutchinson were managing to be pleasant to everyone else and to one another, although Liz was knocking back the vodka and Jill guessed that would cause problems before too long. Andy Collins was there; he'd had a fair amount to drink, too. Bob Murphy was nursing the same pint he'd bought shortly after Jill arrived. While Andy was talking a lot, Bob seemed happier to listen.

They were a genial bunch, and there was a lot of laughter around the table.

Perhaps Tony and Liz would get a taxi. Liz wouldn't be able to walk far in her heels, and her coat was more fashionable than windproof. If that were the case, perhaps Jill could share a taxi and invite them inside for a drink. Tony was sure to be easily persuaded. The prospect relaxed her slightly.

The cottage was under surveillance, yet she knew it couldn't be watched every second of every hour.

Talk, unsurprisingly, soon returned to Jim Brody.

'You couldn't meet a nicer chap,' Andy said for at least the tenth time.

'For a thief and a murderer,' Tony said, grinning. He sobered immediately. 'Sorry, bad taste. I'm a bit annoyed with him because he stole my gun and got me into all sorts of trouble with the police. But yes, Jim always seemed a good enough sort.' He looked at Bob. 'You built that extension of his, didn't you?'

'Yes, and he was a pleasure to work for. He didn't mess you about like some do. They'll tell you what they want doing, and then change their mind fifty times mid-job. Jim left me alone to get on with it. He knew his own mind, did Jim. And he was a good payer.'

'Molly Turnbull says she always suspected him and Alice of having an affair,' Liz put in, 'but I think she's talking with the benefit of hindsight. I can't imagine Molly keeping something like that to herself. And why did none of us know about it?'

'Even Olive Prendergast didn't know,' Tony said, chuckling.

'What gets me,' Bob said, 'is that we all sat and listened to Jon's sermons. I can't believe he could stand in his pulpit one day and kill his wife the next.'

'That's what I can't believe,' Liz agreed. 'Vicars, doctors – they simply aren't killers.'

'It just proves that anyone can kill if provoked,' Bob said.

'Do you think so?' Jill asked curiously.

'Well, yes, I reckon.' He didn't seem so sure now.

An icy draught hit them as the door opened, and Jill was amazed to see Don Cornwall walk up to the bar and order a glass of orange juice.

'Don!' She got to her feet, albeit reluctantly. What the devil was he doing here? 'Come and join us.'

He put up his hand in acknowledgement.

'You don't mind, do you?' she said to the others. 'Don's a policeman. I've been doing some work with him lately.'

'The more the merrier,' Liz said. 'Besides,' she added to Jill in a stage whisper, 'he's got a really cute bum.'

Jill spluttered with laughter. 'I can't say I've noticed.'

Yet she had noticed how Cornwall cared about his appearance, and she'd noticed a few females give him admiring glances. And yes, the suits he wore did show off a good body.

'The very chap,' Tony told Don Cornwall as soon as everyone had been introduced. 'We're a bit divided here. Doctors, vicars, and the like – we don't believe they're killers. Bob, here, thinks anyone could kill if provoked. What do you think?'

'Are you a detective?' Liz asked before he had a chance to reply.

'I am, yes.'

'So do you think anyone could be a killer?' Tony persisted.

'I suppose so, yes,' Cornwall said, having considered the matter. 'Any idiot could poison someone. It's easy enough to fix the brakes on a person's car, too. And so long as you're not squeamish, you could shoot someone. Any fool can pull a trigger.'

'That's just the mechanics, though,' Tony pointed out. 'What about mentally? Do you think anyone is capable of taking someone else's life?'

'Probably. Yes,' Cornwall said. 'Most wouldn't have the brains to get away with it, though.'

'Getting away with it is a different matter altogether,' Bob said. 'Few get away with it. Jim Brody didn't.'

'It's not just reading a police procedural and learning about forensics,' Cornwall went on, 'it's having the intelligence to think things through carefully, to act methodically, and put that knowledge into practice.'

'God, what creepy talk,' Liz said, pulling a face. 'Let's talk about something more cheerful or we'll all be having nightmares. Let's have another drink, Tony.'

Jill couldn't have agreed more.

'What are you doing out here anyway, Don?' she asked curiously.

'I was passing through,' he replied, cagily Jill thought, 'and thought I'd stop for a drink.'

What did that mean? There was no need for him to be in Kelton Bridge at all.

She knew she was bordering on paranoia now but, in the morning, she was going to have a good look at Cornwall's police assessment record. He couldn't – No, she'd had too much to drink and her imagination had gone into overdrive. Don Cornwall was a lot of things, but he couldn't be a killer.

She knew very little about him. He wasn't married, he'd lived in Newcastle-upon-Tyne for years but had applied for a transfer. When Jill had asked how he knew the area, he'd said, 'I used to have family round here.' She hadn't pressed the matter, and he hadn't elucidated. He had a strange admiration for murderers who could get the better of the police. And, of course, he also had inside knowledge of forensic procedures.

But, no. Cornwall couldn't have killed Anne Levington and the others. He couldn't have put those red roses on her kitchen table.

'So what's the perfect murder weapon, Don?' Tony mused. 'Poison? A bath of acid?'

'You'll have to leave me out of this debate,' Bob said, laughing. 'Some of us have an early start in the morning.'

'Me, too,' Jill said with undue haste. 'I don't suppose I can beg a lift, can I, Bob?'

'Of course,' he replied immediately, 'so long as you don't mind the van. It's filthy.'

Jill didn't mind at all, and it wasn't as dirty as she'd feared. It also meant she could ask Bob to hang around while she went inside her cottage for the set of drawings she wanted to give him.

'I reckon Sherlock Holmes and Dr Watson will be there till throwing-out time,' Bob remarked with amusement as he drove them along Pennine View.

'Not the most cheerful of subjects, was it?'

'I hope Liz isn't paying too much attention. If Tony comes up with the perfect murder, she might just put it into practice.' He gave her a sideways glance. 'Sorry, that wasn't funny. Not with poor old Jim locked up in a cell.'

'Dreadful thought that, isn't it?'

'It is,' he agreed, slowing the van to a stop by Jill's drive.

'Will you come in for a minute, Bob? A coffee or something? I'd like to give you those plans.'

'OK. Yes, thanks.' He killed the engine. 'A quick coffee would be good, although I really do have an early start in the morning.'

'Oh? Busy?' she asked, as she took her keys from her bag and let them into the cottage.

'I'm having a couple of days in Dublin. A chap who used to work for me lives over there now and I've been promising to visit for a couple of years.'

'Very nice.'

'Had any winners lately?' he asked, following her into the kitchen.

'Nothing spectacular,' she told him with a laugh, 'although I did have a couple of quid on Son of Sailor and that raced well. Not a very good price, though.'

She put the kettle on while he looked through the drawings.

'Nothing too difficult here,' he said, folding them and putting them back in the envelope, 'and it should make a difference to this place. It's a nice cottage – lovely spot.'

'People always tell me it's too remote,' Jill said, handing him a cup of coffee, 'but I like it. It's good for the cats, too. I wouldn't want to be too near a main road.'

There was no sign of her cats at the moment. It had rained earlier so it was good mousing weather.

'If you don't mind me asking,' he said curiously, smiling, 'how come the celebrated psychologist spends half her time in the bookies?'

She laughed at that. 'Ah, it's terrible for my image, isn't it? All my father's fault. As a kid, I hung around while he was choosing horses to back, and then I'd be as excited as can be waiting for the results to come through. My mother, of course, was horrified. Let's take our coffee into the sitting room,' she suggested, changing the subject. 'It's warmer in there . . .'

She didn't want to think about her mum right now. The surgeon had found a tumour, a benign tumour, thank God, and had removed it. Mum still wasn't well, though. Jill was convinced she was keeping something from them.

Chapter Forty-Five

Jill had only been in the office for an hour, and twice Cornwall had asked if she was OK.

'You seem a bit tense and jumpy,' he said.

'Really?' She gave him a smile. 'No, just tired probably. I sat up reading until late last night.' In truth, she'd spent the night wondering about him. She was determined to get hold of his career details.

'I'll be back in a minute,' she added. 'I need to go and see Max about something.'

She was surprised to find Max sitting at a clear desk, and then she saw the leaning towers of paperwork on the floor.

'Filing?' she asked, and he smiled.

'I wish I could file the lot in the bin. So what brings you here?'

'I'd like a word with you sometime. Not here, though.'

He frowned. 'What's up?'

'I don't know, but I don't want to discuss it in the building.'

He was surprised, but he didn't comment. 'I can grab an early lunch. Say an hour?'

'Thanks.'

'Meet me in the car park in an hour then.'

Feeling better, and guessing she was getting everything out of proportion, she went back to her office.

'Are you sure you're all right?' Cornwall asked again. 'You're not going down with something, are you? Several people have been off with this flu thing.'

'I'm fine, thanks. Really.' She knew she had to tell him something. 'It's personal. I've agreed to have lunch with Max and I'm not sure I've done the right thing. I don't like mixing business and pleasure.'

'Ah.' That was all he needed to know. 'You and Max used to have a thing going, didn't you? Lived together, didn't you?'

'Yes, we did.'

'It always ends in tears,' he said briskly. 'Business and pleasure never mix well.'

'Do you speak from experience?' Jill asked.

'Only other people's.'

Max already had the engine running when Jill arrived in the car park, and she climbed in, grateful for the car's warmth.

He drove them a mile or so away, parked the car and then turned in his seat to look at her. 'So what's the problem?'

There were so many problems, she didn't know where to start. 'God, how long have you got?' she asked with a smile. 'I've lost all confidence I ever had, haven't I?' she murmured. 'I used to be good at offender profiling, but not any more.'

'You're still good,' he said thoughtfully, 'but yes, you've lost confidence. You know how you feel, but you're too scared to say so because of what happened to Hill. There are dozens of blokes out there who fitted your profile, Jill, and we would have arrested any one of them who'd been with the murdered girl.'

'I know that.'

'What's really bugging you?'

'Don Cornwall,' she said softly.

She told him how he'd come into the pub last night, and how he and Tony had talked of the perfect murder. 'And what the devil was he doing in Kelton anyway?' she asked. 'He said he was just passing, but that was crap.

I don't trust him, Max. I want to know something of his background.'

Max thought for a moment. 'I don't know much about him,' he admitted. 'I do know that he applied to come here about five, maybe six years ago.'

Her eyes widened at that.

'Jill, he might be a lot of things, but he's no killer. He's bright, he's doing well. He'll be Chief Constable one of these days.'

'He's not popular,' she pointed out.

'I know.'

'Mind you, that might be just his way. He's very anti-me because he thinks I go running to you with any information I might have. He still hasn't forgiven me for going to see Janie Fisher with you. It's a clash of wills, I suppose. He thinks I'm holding out on him and I'm convinced he's holding out on me.'

'I'll see what I can dig out,' Max promised.

'Thanks.'

He gazed at her for several moments. 'So are you all right back at your cottage?' he asked at last.

'Fine.' The reply was automatic. 'Well, it's OK,' she said carefully. 'Last night, I was going to get a taxi home with Tony Hutchinson –'

Max's eyebrows shot up at that.

'And his wife,' she added. 'Tony's a show-off and a general pain, but he's not a killer. And yes,' she added with a rueful smile, 'I am sure of that.'

'Killer or not, Jill, don't spend any time alone with him. OK?'

'I didn't,' she explained. 'As it turned out, I cadged a lift with Bob Murphy.'

'Good. Keep away from Hutchinson. I mean it.'

Max fired the engine, but didn't drive off. 'Hey, try to relax,' he said. 'Your place is as safe as anything now.' He gestured to a building across the road. 'Do you fancy a coffee?'

'Please.'

He was right; she must try and relax. It wasn't only Don Cornwall, though, and the delivery of those roses. What worried her more than that was that she'd lost the ability to do her job. OK, so she hadn't wanted to return to the job, but she had been good at it. Now, a kid of five could make as much progress as she had. Before Hill was arrested, she'd felt as if she actually knew Valentine. She had truly believed that if they'd met in the street, she would have recognized him. Now, she couldn't get into his mind at all . . .

On the way home that afternoon, Jill stopped at Ella's bungalow.

As soon as Ella opened the door, Jill was treated to a broad smile, but there was no mistaking that Ella had been crying.

'I heard Tom had gone into hospital,' Jill explained, 'and I thought I'd call round to see if there was anything I could do.'

'Bless you. Come in, Jill, come in.'

'How is he?' she asked. 'And what exactly is wrong?'

Ella automatically headed for the kitchen, but Jill's words stopped her in the doorway.

'He's sworn me to secrecy,' Ella said with a sad smile. 'He doesn't want any fuss so –' She swallowed hard. 'So if you hear he has terminal cancer, you didn't hear it from me.'

'Oh, Ella, no.' Jill could have sat and wept with her.

She'd only met Tom once, but even if she hadn't, she would have known just how much he meant to Ella. He was responsible for Ella's happiness, for her acceptance of life's knocks, for her sense of fun.

'Ella,' she said again. 'I'm so sorry. So very, very sorry.'

After the scare with her mum, and Jill still wasn't sure all was well there, she knew just how terrifying the c-word was.

'Don't you start,' Ella warned, 'or we'll both be in tears. Seriously,' she added, 'I haven't told a soul except you.'

Jill felt honoured, and touched. It was funny how she'd hit it off with Ella.

'And all I've been doing,' Ella said, 'is going through our old wedding photos. Do you want to look?'

Jill hadn't planned on stopping, but she couldn't refuse now. Her own plans for the evening were very trivial compared to poor Ella's worries.

'I'd love to.'

They went and sat in the sitting room where a couple of photograph albums lay on the table.

'Everyone has their own problems,' Ella said briskly as she opened one of the large albums, 'so I shouldn't complain. I've had a good life with Tom.'

'That doesn't make it any easier, does it?'

'Not really, no.' Ella smiled. 'I'm just trying to concentrate on other people's worries at the moment. There's young Michael without his parents, Jim Brody – well, I still can't believe that. He's such a good, honest, decent chap. The salt of the earth. Still, I suppose we'd all be surprised what lengths we'd go to if pushed. To think of him locked up in a cell, though. That's awful. He needs the wind on his face, does Jim.'

She turned and looked at Jill. 'And what about you, young Jill? What problems are you wrestling with?'

'Me? None. Touch wood,' she added lightly, putting a hand on Ella's coffee table.

'No men trouble?'

'No. What makes you ask?'

Ella laughed, a pleasant sound. 'While everyone at the bonfire party was making eyes at Bob Murphy, you barely gave him a second glance. I thought you must have someone special in your life to make you blind to our Bob.'

'Bob's an attractive man,' Jill agreed. 'I did notice that much.'

'He is. I keep telling Tom that if I was forty years younger, I'd be after that body of Bob's.'

'He'd make a fortune in TV advertising,' Jill agreed with a laugh. 'He'd have to do long cold drinks. You can just imagine him topless, sweat running down that impressive chest of his as he knocks back a can of something cold.'

'Actually I've been meaning to catch him,' Ella said, 'and tell him about a girl I met. Like me, Gemma has been digging into her family history, which is why I met up with her. Anyway, her aunt is the same woman Bob refers to as Aunt Jenny. Apparently, she's his foster mother. Isn't it a small world?'

'Isn't it,' Jill agreed, 'and isn't it strange how we all jump to conclusions? I'd assumed David and Lindsay Murphy were his parents. Is it David and Lindsay? Live up by the church?'

'It is, but no, they're no relation. I don't know about Bob's father, never heard mention of the man, but I know his mother died in a house fire when he was only ten years old. A terrible business it was. They never did find out who started that fire.' She broke off. 'Hark at me. I'm turning into a worse gossip than Olive Prendergast.' She opened the photograph album. 'It's just that it takes my mind off – you know.'

Jill did know. 'Talk all you like,' she told Ella. 'I'm a good listener, and an awful talker. I won't repeat anything, you know that.' She tried to get Ella's mind back to Tom. 'Is there anything I can do, Ella? Anything I can get for you? Do you need ferrying to the hospital?'

Smiling, Ella shook her head. 'There's nothing, love, but thanks for asking. If I need anything, I'll let you know. Promise. With any luck, he'll be home again in a few days.'

Jill hoped so.

'Meanwhile,' Ella went on briskly, 'I refuse to even think about the day he won't be home.' A teasing light crept into her eyes. 'So this mysterious man of yours, and I know there is a man – it's not that policeman who followed you into the pub last night, is it?'

'Don Cornwall?' Jill smiled, but she didn't like the way

Ella said 'followed you into the pub'. Had he followed her? 'Honestly, you can't move in this place without everyone knowing about it. How did you know about that?'

'Liz told me,' Ella explained. 'She reckoned he spent the entire time mentally undressing you. A cute bum she said he had.'

Mentally undressing her?

'He does,' Jill told her, 'but he's just someone I work with. Nothing more than that.' She knew Ella wouldn't rest until she'd got the truth from her. 'I had a fling with someone, a detective, but we split up a year ago. The trouble is, I'm seeing quite a bit of him at the moment because of work.'

'Ah, so he's the one who makes you immune to our Bob?'

'Probably.' Max was the man all men had to measure up to. Few managed it.

'And does he have a cute bum?'

'I haven't inspected it closely for some time, Ella,' Jill confided with amusement, 'but, yes, it's not bad.'

'Don – Cornwall, did Liz say his name was? That name rings a bell.'

'Oh?' Jill was immediately alert. 'In what context?'

'I don't know.' Ella looked impatient with herself. 'That's the trouble with getting old.' She flicked through the album's pages with a heavy sigh. 'I can remember every detail of our wedding day, but I struggle to remember what I did this morning. Don Cornwall . . .' She shook her head. 'It'll come to me.'

'Will you let me know if it does?' Jill asked. 'I don't know much about him, and I like to know who I'm working with.'

'Of course I will. Mind you, I'm sure it's nothing important.'

They looked through the albums and laughed at the fashions of the day. Ella and Tom's happiness was there for all the world to see . . .

Jill hated going home in the dark but there was nothing

else for it. With the knowledge that her cottage was as secure as it could be, and a couple of police officers were keeping a watchful eye on it, she had to assume she was safe.

As she was slowing down for her driveway, she saw Tony Hutchinson out running. She was out of the car when he jogged over to her.

'I saw your car parked at Ella's,' he told her. 'How's Tom?'

'He's doing OK. I gather they're still doing tests.'

'I'll call on Ella later, and see if there's anything I can do.'

'I told her the same thing, but there's nothing at the moment. She's very independent, is Ella.'

'Yes, she's a capable old bird.'

'Indeed,' Jill agreed, wondering what Ella would make of that description.

'Did she tell you? Yes, I suppose she did. I saw her on the Manchester train one day,' he explained, and he looked decidedly shifty.

'Really?' Probably best to play dumb, Jill decided.

'Thinking back, I'm not surprised she was suspicious enough to rush straight to the police. They said they didn't hear it from her, but it can't have come from anyone else. And God knows, I'm not their favourite person at the moment. Not that they've got anything on me,' he added quickly. He glossed over that in a man of the world, couldn't care less sort of way. 'Anyway, a young girl was trying to blackmail me. We'd had a brief, meaningless affair and she'd got herself pregnant. She claimed I was the father. In the end, it was either get a DNA test done, remortgage the house or go bankrupt. Or, of course,' he added sarcastically, 'I suppose I could have killed her.'

Jill was trying to keep her face bland and composed, but it wasn't easy. 'What did you do?'

'The DNA test,' he said. 'And I'm pleased to say, not that I had any doubt, that it cleared me of all responsibility.'

'I'm glad,' she said.

'I told Liz all about it, and she was very good. She's not a bad stick – apart from her drinking.'

'A lot of women would drink,' Jill couldn't help pointing out, 'if their men were having affairs.'

'I know, and I've promised her it will stop.'

Jill remembered how well he and Liz had been getting on in the pub last night. There had been none of the usual animosity flying between them.

'I'm glad, Tony, really glad.' She would like to see Tony and Liz, Liz especially, in a happier relationship. 'Are you coming in?'

Max would have been horrified, but Jill knew she was safe enough with Tony. She just knew it.

'Thanks, but no. I need to get in training. Another time, Jill.' He was about to move on, but stopped again. 'Those flowers . . .'

'Oh, that.' She pulled a face. 'Sorry about that, I thought it might have been you playing a joke. Your initials on the card, you see. Anyway, the case has been solved.'

'That's good then. Be seeing you.' And he jogged off into the darkness.

Chapter Forty-Six

The work on the Truemans' murders was just beginning for Max. He now had to prepare the case for court.

Brody's dog was giving him as many headaches as Brody himself had. The confounded animal refused to eat properly. It was possibly eating enough to stay alive. Possibly. When the dog had first taken a few morsels out of the bowl, Max had thought that was it. No. He'd offered her steak, chips, sausages and anything else he thought might tempt her. She simply looked at him in that accusing way she had and wandered off to another room . . .

Max forced his mind back to work. He'd done a little unofficial digging into Cornwall's past, but nothing had come to light. Jill might be interested to know that he'd been adopted after his real mother had abandoned him outside a hospital, but although sad, there was nothing particularly telling about that. His adoptive father had worked on the force, as a detective with the West Midlands CID, so perhaps that had something to do with Cornwall's determination to be the best. Other than that, there was nothing of note. He'd done OK at school, no better than that. He'd been accepted by the army, then changed his mind for some reason. More importantly, to Max at any rate, was that he'd been on duty each time Valentine had struck.

Fletch knocked at the door and came inside.

'I thought you'd gone home for the day,' Max said.

'I was on my way when something caught my eye. One of the traffic cops stopped a dark blue Mondeo in

Preston,' he said quickly, 'the night that prostitute, Janie Fisher, escaped from the weirdo. It had a defective rear light. The funny thing was, the owner had filed an off-road notification.'

'Oh?'

For a reason Max couldn't explain, his interest was caught. The night was right, and the car fitted Janie's vague description. Claiming a car was off the road wasn't unusual, though. Max would like a quid for everyone who did that to avoid paying road tax.

'It belongs to a Robert Murphy.'

The name meant nothing to Max.

'He has his own building firm and lives in Kelton Bridge,' Fletch explained.

'Ah!' Bob Murphy. He was working on Jill's cottage. 'You saw him when Alice Trueman was killed, didn't you, Fletch?'

'Yes. He seemed an OK sort of chap. Kept apologizing, saying he couldn't help. He'd done some work at the vicarage, last summer I think it was. He said he liked the Truemans. His business is doing well so he's sitting pretty financially, I imagine.'

'Then why would he say his car was off the road? And what was he doing in Preston that night? Do we know?'

'No one's spoken to him about that.'

Max was ready to go home, and so was Fletch.

'Have you passed this on to Cornwall, Fletch?'

'Dunno where he is, guv,' Fletch said innocently.

'Right, how about we call on Murphy on our way home?' Max suggested.

'It won't do any harm,' Fletch agreed. 'I expect it's a waste of time, but it did strike me as coincidental.'

Yes, it was coincidental, and Max knew how important coincidences were in this job.

Max would have made an offer on Murphy's house if it had been on the market. A barn conversion, it sat right on the edge of Kelton Bridge, overlooking the village and guarded by the Pennines. The upper floor was one huge picture window. The gardens were large and informal, the driveway was block paved, and low walls enclosed the building.

His white van was parked outside on the drive and the man himself came out of what looked to be a storeroom.

Max made the introductions. 'Nice place you've got here,' he added.

'Thanks.' Murphy looked around him. 'It's taken years to get it in shape, but yes, I like it. It suits me.' He wiped his hands on his jeans. 'Sorry, you'll freeze out here. Come inside.'

He led the way into a farmhouse-style kitchen. It looked as if he more or less lived in that room. A desk took up one corner, and on that sat a computer and a pile of brochures and mail.

'My office,' he explained ruefully, pointing at the computer. 'I use an accountant but I like to keep an eye on things myself. And, of course, there are always quotes to go out, accounts to be settled.'

'Is business good?' Fletch asked.

'It is, yes. I've had to turn quite a few jobs away. I don't like doing that, especially when it's local people who've used me before, but neither do I like to keep them waiting too long. I'm thinking of taking on another labourer or two but it's difficult finding anyone interested. I've just taken on an apprentice, and that's more trouble than it's worth. The paperwork is unbelievable. And of course, as soon as I've trained him, he'll set up in competition, I expect.' He stopped. 'Sorry, you won't want to be bored with my problems. How can I help you?'

'You probably can't,' Max told him, 'but our job is a bit like yours. It would be OK without the paperwork, and it's the paperwork that brings us here. On the evening of the twentieth of December, a Monday, your car was stopped in Preston. Is that right?'

'It is, and I still can't believe I was so stupid. It was the

Mondeo. I was planning to sell it, but I didn't get much interest when I advertised it, so I thought I'd leave it a while and then put it in *Auto Trader* or something like that. Meanwhile, as I wasn't using it, it seemed daft to tax it. I filled in the form to say it wasn't being used, and forgot all about it. I climbed in the thing, forgetting it wasn't taxed and – bingo. Your blokes got me for a duff light.'

That seemed feasible.

'What were you doing in Preston, Mr Murphy, if you don't mind me asking?' Fletch said.

'I don't mind at all. About six months ago, I was invited to tender for a hotel refurbishment in Preston. It was too big a job for me, so I didn't bother. Here . . .' He walked over to his desk and shuffled through the papers. 'Ha, can't find it now. I must have filed it somewhere. Anyway, I was just being nosy. I thought I'd drive out there, see how the work was coming along, and find out who'd got the contract. It was a spur of the moment thing.'

'Who did get the contract?' Fletch asked.

'Mmm? P and R Projects.' He was still hunting through papers on his desk. 'Ah, here it is.'

Max glanced at the letter asking Murphy to tender, but he wasn't interested.

'What time were you in Preston?' he asked, handing it back.

'I got there about ten o'clock that night, and would have been out of the place by ten thirty at the latest. I was on my way out of the town when your lot stopped me.' He picked up a handful of paperwork. 'I'm sure I've got the letter here somewhere. I expect there will be a time on that. Here it is.' He shook his head at the letter in his hand. 'Nope. That's the parking ticket I got in Rawtenstall. I got done for parking on double yellow lines in Rawtenstall back in November. It was throwing it down when I parked, and I thought I was clear of them. Typical. Still, never mind. I'd gone to watch United play – on the big screen, you know? Anyway, United won 2–1 so I suppose it was worth it.'

'I remember that,' Max said, struck by the coincidence.

'It was a cracking game, wasn't it?' It was played on the thirteenth of November, the night Anne Levington was murdered.

'It was,' Murphy agreed. 'I've resisted getting Sky so far, but that game tempted me. The trouble is, though, I'd never get a thing done if I had the sports channels. Far better to drive into Rawtenstall and watch it on the pub's big screen.'

'It means you can't have a drink, though,' Max pointed out.

'Ah, yes, that's the disadvantage. I don't drink a lot, so I'm OK. If I do have more than a pint – usually if it's a dull game – I get a taxi home and fetch the van in the morning. It depends on what work I've got on the following day. The van's safe enough. There's a street camera there so if the yobs of Rawtenstall decide to nick the wheels, at least they'll be caught on camera. That's the theory, anyway.'

He returned the letter to his desk. 'Sorry, I can't find the letter about the defective rear light. At a guess, I'd say it was around twenty past ten that night. What's this about anyway?'

'Probably nothing,' Max said briskly, 'but something happened in Preston that night and we don't have a lot to go on. At the moment, we're trying to eliminate as many people as possible.'

'Oh, right. Well, there's nothing more I can tell you really. I drove in, looked at the hotel from the outside – it was too dark to see a lot – and drove home again.'

'That's enough, thanks.' Max turned towards the door, then stopped. 'You're doing some work for a friend of mine, Jill Kennedy.'

'Ah, Lilac Cottage,' he said. 'Well, don't tell her business is booming,' he added with a smile, 'or she'll think I'm overcharging her.'

'I think that chap – oh, the estate agent – what's his name?'

'Andy Collins?'

'That's the one. I gather he gave her a rough estimate of what it should cost.'

'Did he? A good job I didn't overcharge her then. Mind, she's lucky I could fit it in. Fortunately, Len, my roofer, is pretty quiet at the moment. Ah, I should have guessed you knew her. We were both at a bonfire party at the manor, and I remember Tony Hutchinson talking about her work with the police. She looked quite embarrassed by the attention. Tony was calling her our celebrity, and I felt a bit of a fool because I'd never heard of her. But there, Tony likes to impress people with his vast knowledge.'

'So I gather,' Max said, amused. 'OK, thanks for your time, Mr Murphy.'

Max and Fletch walked back to their cars. They stopped by Max's.

'We might have known it was a waste of time,' Fletch muttered.

'Indeed. A duff rear light lands him in Preston at more or less the right time, and a parking ticket gives him an iron-clad alibi. We'll just check on the times, and make sure he got the date right, but it looks as if he was safely in Rawtenstall getting nicked when Valentine was killing Anne Levington.'

'You can't win 'em all, guv. It was worth checking. Right, I'm off home. Hey, how's that dog of Brody's doing?'

'Don't ask. I take the damn thing in out of the kindness of my heart and the sodding animal refuses point blank to eat. I've got Kate and the kids buying very expensive titbits to tempt it with, but nothing. Fly, on the other hand, will eat anything. It was one of my shoes yesterday.'

Fletch laughed. 'I bet the boys love it, though.'

'Yeah.'

They did, and on that thought, Max got in his car and drove home.

Chapter Forty-Seven

Whenever Jill came to the Trafford Centre, which was only three or four times a year, she always spent nigh on a year's income. It was just as well she didn't visit the shops very often. Today, she was laden down with two pairs of shoes, a dress, a jacket, small presents for Prue's kids, a picture for her sitting room and some new cutlery.

It was a relief to find a café, drop her bags on a chair, take off her coat, and wait for a cappuccino to be brought to her table. She'd have a sandwich or something more substantial as soon as her coffee had revived her.

She was enjoying her coffee when she saw Liz Hutchinson, also laden with carrier bags, walk into the café and look for a free table.

'Liz, over here!' Jill got to her feet and waved her over.

'Hey, Jill, if I'd known, we could have come together.'

Strangely, Jill would have liked that. Liz had her problems – Tony mostly – but Jill liked her.

'Next time,' Jill said, 'which will be in about three months, I'll give you a call.'

'Exhausting, isn't it?' Liz laughed happily, not looking in the least bit tired. She put her bags on the floor, and ordered them both coffees. 'You look as if you need another,' she told Jill, and she was probably right.

They chatted about the shops, the way other shoppers looked as if they'd entered hell, and how lucky they were not to have children to supervise while they shopped.

'So how are things?' Jill asked her.

'Not bad,' Liz said, eyes twinkling. 'Tony's had a bit of a fright lately, so he's behaving himself for a change.'

'Oh?'

'He wouldn't admit to it, of course,' Liz chuckled, 'but he was nearly having kittens when the police were questioning him about that missing gun. And he felt such a prat. I mean, what kind of an idiot has something stolen and doesn't notice for months?'

'At least that's one mystery solved.'

'Yes. It saddens me to think of Jim though,' Liz said. 'I always thought he was a lovely chap. The sort you could trust – well, with your life.'

'I liked him, too,' Jill agreed. 'I didn't know him well, but I liked him.'

Jill still did like him. He'd obviously been deeply in love with Alice for most of his life. Her death, or her murder at the hands of her husband, was too much for him to bear. It would have been too much for many men to bear. Really, Alice's father or Jonathan Trueman were to blame for the tragedy. It was their anger, their jealousy and their possessiveness.

'But the fright Tony had,' Liz said, lowering her voice to a whisper, 'was far more personal than that. It's no secret that he's had affairs, is it? Everyone in Kelton must know that.'

Jill gave a vague shrug, which Liz pulled a face at. 'Even you know about them and you've only lived here two minutes. Anyway, he had a fling with a young girl, and I mean really young. Only about twenty, she was. She thought she was on to a good thing, got herself pregnant and was trying to get money out of him by claiming he was the father. He had to get one of those paternity tests done.' She dropped her voice even lower. 'No one was more relieved than Tony to find himself in the clear.'

'Oh, dear.' Jill didn't know what to say. She couldn't tell Liz that Tony had already confided in her. But what if Tony told her? Talk about a tangled web . . .

'I'm not sure if it will have frightened him enough to

keep him close to home for long,' Liz said, 'but I'm enjoying it while it lasts.'

'That's good. I'm pleased for you.'

'Thanks.' Liz smiled a little shyly. 'They say you shouldn't marry the man you can live with, you should marry the man you can't live without. For all our problems, and all the grief we give each other, we do belong together, you know.'

'That must be a good feeling.' It was a feeling Jill had known herself. She'd always thought she and Max belonged together. 'It's not easy living with someone who's been unfaithful,' she murmured, 'and yes, I do speak from personal experience. The sense of anger and betrayal is overwhelming. I admire you, Liz.'

'Because I'm daft enough to have him back?' Liz scoffed.

'No, because you can forgive and forget.'

She pulled a face and Jill guessed she did neither. Or if she forgave, she never forgot.

'The first time it happened,' Liz said, 'I chucked him out. That was years ago now. Probably fifteen years. But then, you have to ask yourself what it is you're gaining. Was my life better without him? No. It's the same with forgiveness. Would I gain anything by not forgiving him? No.'

Jill knew exactly what she meant. She also knew how hard it was to make such a wise decision.

'Not that I give him an easy life,' Liz went on. 'I'm spending his money for all I'm worth and I check every penny he spends now. The other week, I gave him hell. There was an invoice from some florist's on the credit card bill and I assumed he was up to his old tricks again. But no – one of the dinner ladies at the school was leaving and Tony wanted to give her something personal. The school had bought her gifts, of course, but Tony thought she should have roses from him and me.'

'Roses?' Jill queried, a sick feeling in her stomach. 'How nice.'

'Not for Tony,' Liz said with a grin. 'I gave him real

grief for it. That'll teach him not to tell me when he's buying flowers.'

They chatted over sandwiches and one more coffee.

'Are you game for more shopping?' Liz asked. 'I'm planning to treat myself to a sexy new dress. Do you fancy helping? It should be fun.'

Jill's mind was still on those roses. 'Why not? Come on then.'

Chapter Forty-Eight

When Max walked into her office, Jill leaned back in her chair and rubbed her aching neck muscles.

'I thought I'd come and see if there was life down here,' Max said, sitting on the edge of her desk. 'On your own?'

'Yes. Cornwall's about somewhere but, for the moment at least, he's keeping out of my way, thank God.' She tapped her pen on the desk. 'I'm still not convinced about him,' she admitted, 'and I don't like working here with him. There's something odd about him.'

'There might be something odd about him,' Max agreed with a wry smile, 'but he's not killing prostitutes. On every occasion, he's been on duty.'

'Doesn't that strike you as coincidental?'

'Not really, no. He's made entries on the computer, and he's got witnesses. Even without the witnesses, he can't change dates on the computer.'

'He tried to get a transfer here at just about the time Valentine started his killing spree,' Jill pointed out.

'True,' Max agreed, 'but he's not our man. There's nothing in any of his assessments to suggest anything untoward. He's got a good record. And on the night of the very first murder, he was on TV helping with a live reconstruction. You can't get a much better alibi than that, Jill.'

'I suppose so.'

He nodded at her computer. 'What are you working on?'

'I was looking at the Rodney Hill papers,' she admitted, 'and trying to see if I can find anything from that.' But it was hopeless. 'He'll strike again soon, Max,' she said with conviction. 'And my bet is Valentine's Day.'

'That's next week.'

'I know.' The shops were awash with red heart-shaped balloons, red roses were in every supermarket and filling station, and it was a waste of time trying to find a birthday card. 'He thinks he's clever,' she explained, 'and he wants everyone else to know he's clever. Killing on Valentine's Day will appeal to him. His ego will be massive. He'll believe it's his day. His special day.' The thought sickened her.

'But where?' she asked, speaking more to herself than Max. Where was he going to choose his victim? 'I've been trying to find a pattern to the geography, but I can't. My best bet is Preston, simply because he may – if he was indeed the man Janie Fisher saw, and I think he was – return to the place he was thwarted. That way, he'll regain his control over the situation.'

'Have you told Cornwall?'

'Of course, but he didn't seem particularly interested. Either uninterested or planning to patrol the streets of Preston single-handed.'

The man himself walked in at that point, and Jill didn't feel inclined to say more. Not that there was more to say.

'Well?' Cornwall asked, looking from one to the other.

'I'm on my way back to the office,' Max told him. 'This evening then, Jill, eight o'clock? I'll call for you.'

Jill had no time to ask what he was talking about; he'd gone, closing the door quietly behind him. What the devil was that about?

At eight o'clock sharp, Max pulled up outside Jill's cottage.

'What,' she asked, holding the door open for him, 'is this about?'

'I thought we'd have dinner out,' he said. 'I didn't want to say too much in front of Cornwall. We don't want the office grapevine working overtime, do we?' He looked at her shocked face. 'Come on, then, get your coat. I'm starving.'

It was only when Jill had checked on the cats, grabbed her coat, locked up the cottage and was sitting in Max's car, that she seriously began to doubt her own sanity. It was always the same with Max. She'd never been able to resist him. He said jump, and she didn't even bother to ask how high.

The worst thing was that she was absurdly pleased to be going out with him. Would she never learn?

Was it as Liz had said, that her life was better with Max around? It was better, but if it went too far, he could so easily hurt her again. Of course, one should love as if one had never been hurt, but that was nigh on impossible.

'What do you fancy?' Max was asking. 'Indian? Chinese? Italian?'

'English. I fancy roast beef, Yorkshire pudding and all the trimmings.'

'Can you still get English food in Lancashire?'

'With difficulty, yes.'

After a couple of miles, he turned the car around and headed out towards Burnley. 'The Ram?' he suggested.

'Sounds great. And why are you in such a good mood?' she asked curiously.

'I've escaped two kids and two dogs to be with the woman of my dreams.' He grinned as she pulled a face. 'And you know the old saying, all work and no play makes Max a miserable bastard.'

'How are the kids?' she asked.

'Fine,' he said softly. 'They're good kids.'

'They are. A lot better than you deserve.'

'That's what everyone says,' he replied, exasperated. 'What sort of kids *do* I deserve?'

Jill laughed. 'I don't know, but you don't deserve those two.' Yet, if Max wasn't the man he was, Harry and Ben wouldn't be the boys they were. 'Although I suppose you deserve a bit of credit,' she allowed grudgingly.

He was a good father, she couldn't deny that. Sometimes work kept him too busy, but when he was home those boys enjoyed real quality time. They adored him, worshipped him.

'How are the dogs?' she asked, unused to putting Max in too good a light.

'Fly's manic. If he were human, he'd be your typical petty criminal, in and out of prison, dreaming of the crime to end all crimes. Holly is different. She's eating just enough to stay alive, although she's getting painfully thin. Occasionally, if you're stroking her or encouraging her to play, the light will come back into her eyes for a moment, but most of the time, she lies by the front door waiting for Brody. She wags her tail when I get home, and I think we've got a bit of a breakthrough, but then she goes back to the door and waits.'

'You love her to death, don't you?'

He turned off the road and into the car park. 'I've got a soft spot for her, I suppose, yes. Come on then – food.'

They chatted amicably during their meal, and Jill still didn't know why he was doing this. She was pleased he was, but she kept waiting for him to get to the point of it all.

He had a mineral water with his meal, and then they lingered over two coffees – chatting all the while. Still he didn't get to the point.

It was late when they left, and Max seemed relaxed enough as he drove her home. He stopped long enough to drink a coffee – and to satisfy himself that no one had been inside – and then went to leave.

'Max, this evening – what's it all about?'

'No reason.' Seeing she wasn't satisfied with that, he thought for a moment. 'I don't know. It just seemed the right thing to do.'

'Yes, but why?'

'I honestly don't know. I thought we both deserved an

evening out. It's been too long, Jill.' He kissed her, a light touch of lips on lips, and then walked away down her drive.

'And keep that bloody door locked!' he called out.

As if she needed reminding.

Chapter Forty-Nine

The net was closing and he had to move quickly now.

The mighty detective had left half an hour ago. 'Keep that bloody door locked,' he'd instructed her on his way out.

Did he truly believe a locked door would save her?

The man was stupid. All the time Trentham had been with her, he'd been watching them both from the dark shadows of her garden.

Where had they been? He hoped they had enjoyed a pleasant evening as time was running out. They only had two more evenings left . . .

He'd wondered where he might take her to kill her, but what could be better than killing her in her own cottage? A couple of policemen drove past a few times during the night, but other than that, she was vulnerable. They'd put all their faith in the new locks, bolts and chains and a highly sophisticated alarm system.

Not that it mattered. He would be welcomed. The door would be opened wide.

The thought made him want to laugh out loud.

Idiots, idiots, idiots!

They thought she was safe enough at Lilac Cottage. That's exactly where they would find her body.

She was more special than the others, more highly prized by the great detective, so he would make her death more special. As it would be Valentine's Day, he would buy red roses. Dozens of them. He'd cover her body in hundreds of rose petals. It would make a striking photograph for the great detective to hang on his wall . . .

One of her cats wandered through the garden. Even that, a creature of the night, didn't spot him. He heard the click-clack of the cat flap opening and closing.

The excitement was becoming almost unbearable but he had to wait. Just two more days. But oh, it was so tempting to kill her now.

He longed to see her face on the front pages of the newspapers and on the television. People would say good things about her, turn her into a saint, a martyr.

What would they say about the mighty detectives? How many of them were trying to catch Valentine? And how many had even come close? None.

The public was right; the police force was only good for catching speeding motorists . . .

On Valentine's Day, he would make them look even more stupid.

Chapter Fifty

Jill almost jumped out of her chair at the knock on the door. She laughed at herself. That would teach her to watch horror films on her own.

She'd been edgy all day as she waited for something to happen. Yet nothing had. No Valentine's cards had arrived. There had been no floral deliveries. As far as she knew, no girls had been reported missing. Valentine's Day was almost over and, as yet, nothing untoward had happened.

Her smile quickly died. It was a few minutes before ten, late for visitors, and she hoped it wasn't Ella with bad news about Tom.

She slipped on her shoes and hurried to the door.

It was a relief to see Bob standing there.

'Hello, Bob, you gave me a fright. I was watching a horror film and the noise made me jump. Then I wondered if it might be Ella with bad news. Come in.' She closed the door after him, shutting out the cold, wet night. 'I don't suppose you've heard how Tom is?'

'No.'

The abrupt answer and his lack of interest took her by surprise.

She was about to comment on it when he turned around, locked her front door – and slipped the keys in his pocket.

It was Valentine's Day. Valentine was a strong man; Bob was strong. Hadn't she laughed with Ella about his stunning physique? *They never did find out who started that fire.*

No! Oh, no!

The bile was already rising in Jill's throat. Paranoia, she told herself . . .

'What –?' Her throat was suddenly too dry to get the words out. *They never did find out who started that fire.*

'One day you'll be mine,' he said, and there was a light of triumph in his eyes as a gurgle of almost childish laughter escaped him.

She turned in panic, but he was too fast – and strong. His leg flew out to trip her, and her wrist was caught in a vice-like grip as she fell.

'You think you're so clever, don't you?' He took a knife from his pocket, and the blade glinted in the glow of the lamps. Then, with that in one hand, he quickly tied her wrists tight behind her back. He tied her feet together at the ankles.

Think, Jill's mind was screaming at her. Think!

Yet she couldn't think. Not a single coherent thought came to her. All she seemed capable of was making terrified, babbling noises. *Think, think, think!*

'You're so dim,' he said scathingly. 'You, those stupid police officers who were watching this place – they couldn't watch grass grow – and that jumped-up detective Trentham.'

Play to his ego, Jill told herself. Flatter him. Let him bask in his small glory.

He'd locked the front door but she was fairly sure the back door was still open. She'd been in and out a couple of times, messing around with the cats, and, unless she was having a major panic, she often forgot to lock it until she went to bed. *Keep that bloody door locked*. Sorry, Max, but I'm fairly sure the back door is still unlocked and it might, just might, save my life. Dear God, she hoped it was open. If it was locked, the key was on the ring in his pocket . . .

Yet how the hell could she get to the door? Her arms and legs were tied.

Think, think, think!

She could scream, but no one would hear. Her mobile phone was in the kitchen so she couldn't even send a text message. Someone might phone her, but he wouldn't let her answer it. It was getting late for phone calls anyway.

If someone did phone, and if she could persuade him to let her answer it, she could pretend it was Ella with news of Tom and, somehow, let that caller know she was being held.

'It's not that we're stupid,' she said, amazed by two things – one that her voice was audible and two that she sounded reasonably calm – 'it's more that you're so clever. We've always known that. No one working on your case has agreed on much – other than the fact that you're the cleverest killer they've ever come across.'

They never did find out who started that fire.

Of all the people in the world, Bob Murphy was probably the man she would have suspected least. Everyone liked him. Everyone in Kelton Bridge thought he was marvellous. He did a good job, they said, and he was reliable. The women worshipped him. Even Ella had noticed how good his body was.

'You with your fancy profiling,' he scoffed. 'All the locals think you're a miracle worker, that you can read minds –'

'No.'

'The local celebrity.' His voice was sneering.

'You're the local celebrity,' she said. 'People will talk of you for years to come. For as long as people live, they'll talk about you.'

He dragged her to her feet – God, he was strong – and pushed her down into the chair in front of her desk. Then he leaned back against her desk, facing her. The frighteningly sharp-looking knife was only inches from her throat.

Play for time. Flatter him. So long as there was time, there was hope.

'Why me?' she asked. 'You've always killed women who –'

'Whores!' He spat out the word. 'Dirty, filthy, cheap little whores.'

His anger was tangible.

'Yes,' she agreed, too terrified to argue with him, or point out that Anne Levington had been a young girl whose life had gone so sadly wrong. 'So why me?'

'It's time Trentham had something to think about. I'm sick of seeing that smug face of his on my television.'

'That was because of Jonathan and Alice Trueman,' she said.

'And what did he care? Huh? So long as it's his face on the screen, his name in the papers, he doesn't care who lives or who dies.'

Bob wanted the fame for himself. What he wouldn't know was that Max hated the press conferences. Given the choice, Max would let someone else do them, and he certainly wouldn't agree to one unless he thought it would help an investigation.

Yet Bob wanted his picture on the small screen.

'What does he care if the odd whore gets killed?' Bob went on. 'He doesn't. Who does?'

Max cared.

'You think he'll care if I'm killed?' she asked. 'He won't, you know. I'm just someone he works with, that's all.'

'Don't try and be clever with me. I've seen how much time he spends with you. I've seen his kids with you.'

'We used to be friends, but that was a long time ago.'

Her phone rang out, pushing her nerves to breaking point, and she gave him an appealing look.

'It might be Ella with news of Tom. She said she might call. It's late and she'll think it odd if I don't answer. She might come and investigate.'

He rammed his hand down on her shoulder, just in case she thought of moving. The knife was icy cold against her neck.

'Don't try and be clever with me.'

Jill only wished she could.

'You've reached Jill Kennedy . . .' Her recorded message sounded so carefree. Another world.

'It's only me, Jill,' Ella said. 'Sorry, it's a bit late. You've probably gone to bed. Just thought I'd let you know that Tom should be home tomorrow. He's much better, thank God. Oh, and Don Cornwall? It came to me, and it's nothing to do with your Don. The Don Cornwall I was thinking of was a pal of Tom's. If he hadn't died last year, he'd be eighty-three now. Anyway, I'll catch you tomorrow.'

The machine clicked off just as a burst of canned laughter came from the television.

Jill felt an almost overwhelming urge to burst into tears, and the knowledge infuriated her. Hard facts: he'd killed several times; he killed with a casual ease; he was good at it. She recalled the photographs of all the girls he'd killed. If she didn't outwit him, she would end up just like them, strangled, and with heart-shaped pieces of skin removed from her lifeless body.

'Why me?' she asked again.

'Told you.'

He was short, snappy, disinclined to talk. She had to make him talk.

'I've sat for hours at this desk working on your profile.' Her only hope was to keep him talking. Until what? She didn't know. She only knew that she had to keep him talking. 'Not that it did me much good. That computer –' she pointed at it – 'is full of stuff about you.' She paused, letting him mull that over. 'Pages and pages and pages of reports on you. There are notes about the people who have claimed to be you. Oh, yes, they've all wanted to be you. We've been able to suss them out straightaway, though. We've known they aren't as clever as you. My report says . . .' She paused again. 'Still, it doesn't matter what my report says, does it? I like to think it was a fairly good profile of you but – well, we'll never know.'

He was breathing hard.

Then, just as Jill had hoped, his ego got the better of him. He hit the button, and switched on her laptop.

'We've got all night,' he said.

Chapter Fifty-One

Max was uneasy. Every time his car phone rang, he expected the worst.

Valentine's Day had started bright and sunny, completely at odds with his mood, but the weather had soon deteriorated.

Perhaps Jill was wrong; perhaps Valentine wouldn't strike today. She'd been fairly confident of that, though. More confident, in fact, than she'd been of anything for a long time.

Was Cornwall taking her seriously? Max wasn't sure. Having said that, there were more patrol cars on the streets than usual.

His phone rang and he saw from the display that it was Fletch.

'Where are you, guv?'

'Preston,' Max said vaguely.

Jill had thought Cornwall might patrol the streets of Preston single-handed, and that's exactly what Max was doing. Unlike Cornwall, though, he had no choice. His neck would be on the line if they thought he was even thinking about Valentine.

'You?' he asked.

'At home. Where you should be.'

Max should. What did he expect to see in Preston? Nothing really. What was the point of driving round and round the blasted town?

'You're probably right,' Max agreed. He was definitely

right. 'I just thought I'd have a look round. There's not much happening. I'll be heading home myself in a minute.'

Jill had thought Valentine might strike today, and she'd thought he might strike in Preston. She could be wrong. He might strike tomorrow. Worse, he could have got his victim last night. There had been no reports of missing working girls, but that meant nothing. And he might fancy Blackpool or Burnley. Who knew? Certainly not Max.

'So if there's not much happening,' Fletch pointed out, 'you may as well go home now. Unless you're enjoying driving round the fleshpots of Preston.'

Max wasn't. It was pissing down with rain yet, despite the weather, there were a few louts on the streets, young kids kicking tin cans around.

'There aren't many girls around,' he told Fletch. 'If I had cash burning a hole in my wallet, I'd be hard pushed to find one.'

'That's a good thing. I reckon they're more twitchy than usual.'

'They damn well ought to be. They've been warned.'

'Yeah.' There was a pause. 'Go home, guv,' Fletch said with a sigh. 'You were pulled off the case, remember?'

'Yes, and you're right. I'll be going home in a minute.'

Max spent another hour driving round the wet, dark streets of Preston. What did he expect to see? A prostitute getting into a black or dark blue Mondeo?

The shop windows were still decked out with red roses and hearts. The pubs were doing a good trade by the look of things, and a lot of them had special offers – cheap drinks for Valentine's Day. Couples, the blokes in shirts, and the girls dressed in nothing worth wearing, walked the streets, going from one pub to the next. It was just a normal night.

He should go home. He'd already had warnings from above about his lack of ability to delegate, interviewing people when less senior officers should be doing it, forgetting he was part of a team and all the rest of it.

He was driving out of town, eyes still boring into every person on the street, checking every car –

Looming out of the darkness, he saw it. The Newland Hotel. There was scaffolding around it, signs keeping people out of what was, at the moment, a construction site. There, on a huge yellow board in bright red lettering, was the name of the company doing the refurbishment. Not P and R Projects, as Bob Murphy had said, but Drake Construction Ltd.

Max pulled over, switched off the engine and stared at the sign. So Bob Murphy had got the name wrong. Or he hadn't been anywhere near this site on the night he'd been nicked for that defective light.

I get a taxi home and fetch the van in the morning.

Max hit the button on his phone.

'Robert Murphy got a parking ticket on the thirteenth of November,' he explained, his mind working fast. 'Apparently, he parks in front of a street camera. I want the camera checked for that night, and I need to know if his white van was parked there all night. You can't miss it. It's got R. Murphy Building Contractor scrawled all over it.'

Who's to say Bob Murphy even watched the United game? He could have read all about it in the morning's papers.

While United's finest were playing their socks off, Bob Murphy could have been killing Anne Levington.

If the yobs of Rawtenstall decide to nick the wheels, at least they'll be caught on camera . . .

Did Murphy park in front of that camera to ward off Rawtenstall's yobs? Or did he park there to give himself an alibi?

'You fucking idiot, Trentham!'

He was on the phone again, his words falling over themselves in his attempt to get them out quickly.

'That camera in Rawtenstall,' he said, 'I want it checked for the twentieth of December – the night Janie Fisher called us. I want to know if Murphy's white van was parked outside that pub.'

He drove fast, shouting instructions down his phone as he did so.

Then he phoned Fletch and gave him his possibly half-baked theory.

'I'll meet you at Murphy's place,' Fletch said doubtfully. 'You could be reading something into nothing, though, guv. Perhaps he just got the name of the contractor wrong.'

'Yeah, and a fucking pink farmyard animal just flew over my bonnet. There are too many coincidences for my liking. I'm convinced the bastard's using that fucking van as a decoy. He leaves it in full view of a camera, then goes out in his bloody Mondeo.'

Murphy, if he was going to strike tonight, would be out. His van would be parked in front of a street camera somewhere, and his dark blue Mondeo, the car seen by Janie Fisher, would be gone.

He could be anywhere.

When Max arrived at Murphy's place, Fletch was already there.

'There's no sign of him, guv,' Fletch greeted him. 'I've had a quick look round. The van's nowhere to be seen, but the Mondeo's in the garage.'

Max breathed a sigh of relief. If he was out in his van, with his name emblazoned on the side for all to see, he was unlikely to be killing anyone. He might be leaving his van in front of that camera, and he might be sitting in a taxi coming back for his Mondeo but, for the moment at least, all was well.

'You might have got it all wrong, guv,' Fletch said, clearly not amused at being dragged from a warm house and a pregnant wife.

'I might,' Max agreed. 'I just wish they'd hurry up and get the CCTV checked out.'

Feeling slightly easier, thanks to the presence of the Mondeo, Max decided they'd have a drive round and see if they could spot Murphy's van.

Soon afterwards, the call came through and Max was informed that it was in Rawtenstall.

'Parked in front of that camera?'

'It is, guv, yes. It's parked in the same place that he got the parking ticket in November. Tonight, Murphy got out of the van and walked through the doors of the pub opposite. That was almost two hours ago.'

'Let's check it out,' Max said to Fletch.

As he drove, with Fletch behind him, a huge red heart in a shop window caught Max's eye.

One day you'll be mine.

His heart seemed to stop beating for a second. That fucking card, those roses – how many more clues did they need?

The bastard had lined Jill up as his Valentine's Day victim months ago!

Chapter Fifty-Two

Jill stared at the computer's screen. There were several folders pertaining to Valentine. She tried to think fast. What did the folders contain? Where were the notes that claimed he was sexually dysfunctional? Which set of notes would best flatter his ego?

Someone would see his van outside. If his van was there for hours, someone was sure to spot it and think it suspicious. Or would they? They would think it odd perhaps, but not unusual enough to do anything about it. By morning, Olive Prendergast would probably be telling everyone in the post office that Bob Murphy was having an affair with that fancy psychiatrist . . .

They heard her mobile phone ring out in the kitchen. She looked at him; his face was expressionless.

It was late for a call on her mobile. Few people used it.

She opened a folder. If her memory served her well, it contained little other than her notes on the geography involved and the basis for her assumption that Valentine lived in the Rossendale area, and possibly Kelton Bridge.

A game show was on the television, bringing the contestants' laughter and shouting into the room.

Bob Murphy wasn't interested in the television; he was looking for items of interest on her computer. He clicked on a file named 'parent'. There it was, with a few notes underlined in red, her conviction that his mother had been a prostitute and that his father hadn't figured in his life.

'Clever, aren't you?' he sneered.

'Was your mother a prostitute?' Jill asked.

'A dirty, filthy, disgusting whore.' He spat out each word.

'She died when the house burnt, didn't she? They never did find out who started the fire, did they? No one would suspect a child of ten.'

He said nothing.

'So even as a child you were clever,' she mused. 'Even as a child you were determined to make the world a better place. That's what you're doing, isn't it? Your mother was a bad person, so you got rid of her. You set fire to the house. You started the fire that killed your mother.'

'She shut me in a cupboard. Every night, as soon as the men were due to call, she locked me in the cupboard out of the way.'

'Was it dark?'

'Yes.'

'And you were frightened?'

'No! Wasn't frightened! Wasn't a baby!' His saliva landed on her face, but she daren't brush it off. 'I spent hours in that cupboard, and I wasn't frightened. I took a biscuit she'd made and she hit me, then put me in the cupboard. After that, whenever she made the biscuits, I had to go to the cupboard. Hated those biscuits. They were all the same shape. All she had was a heart-shaped cutter and the biscuits were all the same.'

Biscuits? Jill had to keep swallowing to stop herself vomiting. The heart-shaped pieces of skin he removed from his victims . . . surely to God he didn't cook them.

'It was only going to be her,' he said, scowling, getting agitated, 'but there was another whore in Blackpool. She thought I'd pay to have sex with her. Filthy bitch.'

'No!' Jill managed to sound scandalized.

'Bitch. Stupid, dirty, filthy, disgusting bitch.'

Jill's mobile phone rang out again. Who was trying to call her at this time of night? Her family and friends would try her at home first. Hardly anyone used her mobile.

'And that was what?' she asked. 'About five years ago?'

'Yes. And you lot had to arrest Hill,' he scoffed. 'He was nothing. A nobody.'

'He was,' Jill agreed, 'but we didn't know that until we'd arrested him.'

'You *never* knew it. Until he killed himself, you thought he was me. I had to kill again, just to show you.'

'We were stupid,' she agreed. 'You were the clever one.'

'Don't humour me, bitch.'

'I wasn't. Sorry.'

He suddenly picked up a heavy glass paperweight from her desk and hurled it at the television screen. Glass went everywhere and the noise seemed as if it would never end.

When all was silent, he was listening.

'What was that?' he demanded.

'I didn't hear anything.'

'I did.'

'These stone walls are two feet thick in places,' she reminded him. 'It's impossible to hear anything. I didn't hear your van pull up.'

'I didn't come in my van. I walked.' He was distracted, listening for sounds. All was silent, except for the thud of Jill's heartbeat.

He took a dark red, silk scarf from his pocket and wound it around his wrist a few times. He was still listening.

The phone in the sitting room rang out. Jill wondered if she could hurl herself at it, knock it off the hook and yell for help. No. He might be distracted, but he still had a knife and a scarf in his hands. And he was strong. Ridiculously strong.

Again, her recorded voice on the machine shocked her with its light-hearted frivolity.

'Hi, Jill, it's Max. We've caught Valentine so I reckon I'll soon be Chief Constable Trentham. You were right; he struck in Preston. We caught him in the act – just as he was removing his trademark hearts from the dead girl's skin –'

'What the –?' Bob Murphy was furious. His breathing was fast and hard.

'And he's confessed to everything,' Max continued. 'Thought you'd like to hear the good news. All we have to do now is wait for the cranks to come out of the woodwork. I guess all of Kelton Bridge will claim they're Valentine – Andy Collins, Tony Hutchinson, Robert Murphy. They'll all reckon they're Valentine, but we know the truth. I expect I'll be stuck in Preston all night so I'll catch you tomorrow.'

The machine clicked off.

'Stupid fucking bastards!' Bob Murphy screamed.

He looked at Jill, as if he expected her to do something about this terrible error.

Hi, Jill, it's Max. Max never said that. He always said, Hi, it's me. All that nonsense about Chief Constable Trentham? Max hadn't been talking to her at all. He'd been talking to Valentine.

'What the fuck's going on?' Screaming with rage, Bob Murphy strode towards the answer machine. He was yanking it from the wall when a single shot rang out.

Jill watched, a sudden numbness claiming her, as Bob Murphy collapsed to the floor.

Blood was seeping into her carpet as he clutched his injured leg. An officer was standing over him, his gun pointing at Murphy's head.

She looked at Max, but he wasn't looking her way. He was giving Murphy a vicious kick in the ribs as Fletch and two uniformed officers handcuffed him.

'If you had any fucking idea,' Max roared, 'of the hassle involved every time an officer uses his gun – but you would, wouldn't you? You're well read on police procedure. But remember this, there's so much fucking hassle involved, that it would be no worse if we blew your fucking brains out.' He kicked him again. 'If I thought anyone would so much as mention diminished responsibility, I *would* blow your fucking brains out!'

Max was breathing heavily; fury in every inhalation. Murphy was writhing in pain.

Two more uniformed officers came inside and one of them untied Jill.

She was shaking. Every part of her body was shaking, and her teeth had started to chatter.

Max hadn't glanced at her; that piercing stare of his still hadn't left Bob Murphy. The gun – and she knew Max was itching to take it from the other officer and pull the trigger – was still aimed at Murphy's head.

'Are you all right?'

Jill focused on the officer. She didn't recognize him.

'Yes. Yes, I'm fine.'

She had never been less fine. The numbness was quickly wearing off and reaction was setting in. She was suffering from shock.

But she would be all right. Soon.

The wail of a siren announced the arrival of an ambulance. When Murphy was lifted on to the stretcher, he smiled at Max. It was a smile that chilled Jill.

'A ten-year-old boy has to watch his beloved mother burn to death?' he gurgled. 'That would do terrible damage to a boy's mind . . . send him mad, I shouldn't wonder. A young boy so damaged, so lacking in love, that he turns his victims into objects of beauty – that's a damaged mind . . .' As they carried him away, he was laughing.

Jill knew she would hear the sound of that laughter for the rest of her days. She guessed Max would, too.

Chapter Fifty-Three

An almost full moon lit the path to Jill's cottage. Max stopped the car, switched off the engine and sat for a moment to watch the shadows dancing around as the moon slid behind small clouds before emerging again.

Three weeks had passed since Murphy had been taken in – Max still wished he'd blown the fucker's brains out – and he hadn't seen Jill since.

He knew she'd spent a week in Liverpool with her parents before returning to her cottage. Max, guessing she needed time, had left her alone. Perhaps he'd needed time, too.

He'd asked Kate to keep an eye on her. She and the boys had been regular visitors to the cottage over the last fortnight.

'She's fine, Max,' Kate had insisted. 'Busy. But fine.'

Jill, he knew, was an expert at keeping her feelings well hidden. He wanted to see for himself.

He got out of the car, flicked the button to lock it, and walked up to her front door. He knocked loudly, realized belatedly that he'd probably frightened her half to death, and quickly called out, 'Jill, it's me!'

He was expecting to hear the locks being unfastened and the chain being released. What he hadn't been expecting was for her to call out, 'It's open!'

'For fuck's sake!' He barged through the door and she was standing two feet from him. 'Is it really so difficult to lock a bloody door?'

'No. Sorry, Max.' She laughed, and Max had to admit it

sounded carefree and relaxed. Perhaps, after all, she was doing OK.

'I don't suppose you're expecting a takeaway?' he asked hopefully.

'Nope. Are you hungry?'

'Only when I thought of a takeaway.' He spotted a bottle and a glass of red wine on the coffee table. 'I'll have a glass of wine though, if you're offering.'

She fetched a glass from the kitchen and filled it from the bottle. 'So is this a professional or a social call?'

'Purely social.' He took off his jacket, threw it over the back of a chair, and sat on the sofa. 'Thanks.' He took the glass from her and tasted the wine. 'That's not bad at all.'

She sat beside him, looking very relaxed.

Two suitcases sat in the corner of the room, he noticed. 'Are you going somewhere?'

'Spain,' she replied. 'Just for a week. It was a spur of the moment thing. I booked it on the internet yesterday.'

'Very nice. You can buy me a beach bar while you're there. So how have you been?'

'I'm good, Max. You?'

He wouldn't say he was good, although he was improving by the minute.

'Not bad. No nightmares?' he asked.

She looked at him then. Straight at him. 'A couple,' she admitted, 'but they've been different. In these, you've been coming towards me, I've turned to run and come face to face with Bob Murphy swinging from a rope.'

'There's an easy answer to that.' He ran his finger round the rim of his glass.

'Oh?'

'Stop running from me.'

'Perhaps you're right.' She laughed again. 'But no, I'm good. Although I'm still pissed off at myself for being so stupid.' She shook her head. 'He was everything my damn profile said he was – including sexually dysfunctional, no doubt. Creep! He lived alone, right on the very edge of

Kelton Bridge, he's as strong as a bloody ox, and the worst thing is that Ella had told me about the fire that killed his mother. Why the bloody hell didn't I take note? God, no wonder he thinks we're all idiots. He's right. Cheeky bastard – coming to my cottage to work for me, putting envelopes through my letterbox, leaving bloody roses and candles on my kitchen table . . .'

'Hindsight is a wonderful gift, kiddo.' Max sprawled back on her sofa. He was relieved to hear her able to talk about it.

'Sometimes,' she said slowly, 'I wonder what would have happened if you hadn't driven out to Preston, if you hadn't seen the name of that construction company, if you hadn't put two and two together.'

They both knew the answer to that one: she would have been in the morgue.

'When he threw that paperweight at the television –' She shuddered. 'He was really losing it then, Max.'

'I know. That's why I had to get him away from you – leave that message on the machine and hope it both angered him enough and distracted him enough for us to manage a shot at him.'

Jill fetched the bottle and refilled her glass. She was about to fill his.

'I'm driving,' he told her, 'so unless I can persuade some lovely young lady to give me the use of her sofa for the night . . .'

'Just don't wake me when you go. My plane doesn't leave until the afternoon and I've promised myself a lie-in.' Smiling, she refilled his glass.

Something had changed, and Max didn't know what. He liked it, liked it a lot, but he felt as if he was on stage with the wrong script.

'Don't suppose you fancy a quick shag, do you?' he murmured.

She gave a burst of laughter, as she always had. It was a sound from long ago, a sound that brought a lump to his throat.

'Don't push your luck, Trentham. You might have saved my life, but if you were a half-decent detective, my life wouldn't have needed saving in the first place.'

'Given the help of a psychologist – one without a penchant for inviting maniacs into her home for late night coffee and chat – I might make a half-decent detective one day.'

'Ha!' She punched him in the ribs before giving another sigh of contentment.

'So how are the boys?' she asked. 'And the dogs? Is Holly settling in? Oh, and did I tell you I'm coming back to work next month?'

'No. Really?'

'Yup. I'm getting this book of mine finished, then I'm back on the job.'

'That's great.'

'Yeah. So how are the boys?'

As he drank his wine, he told her about Harry and Ben. He talked of Fly and Holly.

'Holly's doing great,' he said. 'I think, thanks to her, that Fly is finally learning what fetch means.'

Jill hadn't heard. She was fast asleep.

Max wasn't sleepy. He was busy thinking how good life was. His sons were happy and healthy, he had a job he enjoyed for the most part, Valentine was gone from their lives, and the woman he loved was sleeping nearby. Life couldn't be better.

Well, it would have been better if the wine bottle hadn't been empty but, hey, a man couldn't have everything.